THE NIGHTS ARE QUIET IN TEHRAN

Shida Bazyar, born in 1988, studied writing in Hildesheim, Germany, and worked in youth education for many years. She is the author of *The Nights Are Quiet in Tehran* — which has won the Blogger Literary Award, Ulla Hahn Prize, and Uwe Johnson Prize, among others, and has been translated into Dutch, Farsi, French, and Turkish — and *Sisters in Arms*.

Ruth Martin studied English literature before gaining a PhD in German. She has been translating fiction and nonfiction books since 2010, by authors ranging from Joseph Roth and Hannah Arendt to Volker Weidermann and Nino Haratischvili.

THE NIGHTS ARE QUIET IN TEHRAN

Shida Bazyar

translated by Ruth Martin

SCRIBE

Melbourne | London | Minneapolis

Scribe Publications
18–20 Edward St, Brunswick, Victoria 3056, Australia
2 John St, Clerkenwell, London, WC1N 2ES, United Kingdom
3754 Pleasant Ave, Suite 223w, Minneapolis, Minnesota 55409, USA

First published in German as *Nachts ist es leise in Teheran* by
Kiepenheuer & Witsch in 2016
Published in English by Scribe 2025

Typeset in Portrait by the publishers

Printed and bound in UK by CPI Group (UK) Ltd, Croydon CR0 4YY

Scribe is committed to the sustainable use of natural
resources and the use of paper products made responsibly
from those resources.

978 1 761381 41 6 (Australian edition)
978 1 917189 09 5 (UK edition)
978 1 964992 10 5 (US edition)
978 1 761386 00 8 (ebook)

Catalogue records for this book are available from the
National Library of Australia and the British Library.

The translation of this book was supported by
a grant from the Goethe-Institut

scribepublications.com.au
scribepublications.co.uk
scribepublications.com

For my parents

1979
Behzad

King of kings they called him, and they said, We rejoice in him, we rejoice in his wife and her beauty; they said, We love this country, and then we said, *We* love this country. We had to rejoice in his newborn son, for longer than we ever would a birth in our own family, his newborn son, in the far-off Palace of Flowers.

Our parents had been told that the oil, the Americans, the English, were part and parcel of the same thing, with the Shah, against us. Our parents stopped working, took to the streets, and then went home again; they were afraid of the secret service and they said nothing more, said nothing against the Shah ever again. Sent us to school and said, We love this country; now you love its schools.

His haughty gaze above the teacher's desk. We learned what we had to learn, got older, and decided that whatever was written in our schoolbooks, we wanted the opposite. We read *Long live the Shah* and thought, Death to the Shah. We heard *All work is owed to the king* and said, The work belongs to the workers. And when we read *He leads us to prosperity*, we spit on his palaces and on the English and the Americans. We smuggle books, copy them, learn them by heart, pass them on to the next person and the next. We have read and read and read, kept quiet at home and made a noise on the streets, cursed our parents and died for our children. The Shah has gone because he was sick, and the statues have fallen because the people didn't believe in them.

The Revolution is getting older every week, and we love this country more than ever. The schoolbooks have been changed, in no time at all; we ripped out the pages about the Shah, and took his photo down off the wall. Here's to no photo of any individual being put up in a classroom again, says Peyman. Here's to the Ayatollah being put up there soon, back from exile, says his mother. Here's to Marx and Engels, Che Guevara and Castro, Mao and Lenin being put up in these rooms soon, Sohrab and I say to each other at break time; we even say it in the staffroom now, louder than we ever could before. We're just waiting for the moment when we'll decide who fills the empty walls.

The Revolution is getting older every week, but it hasn't even begun yet. The Shah has gone, and we're at the beginning of a new age, a new system, a new freedom for which we are now preparing ourselves.

What remains is the turmoil on the streets, still euphoric, but a little less so with each passing week. What remains are the meetings of our movement, the plans, the pamphlets, the teaching units, the guerrilla exercises. They may once have been secret, but now they are ever more public, and we are ever more certain of victory — though sometimes our mood is more reflective, and sometimes more radical, and always with one eye on those people who also call themselves revolutionaries, but are religious with it. The real revolution, however, is still to come: the people's revolution in the institutions. All that has happened so far is just the first step.

Long live socialism, long live our homeland, our pearl, our Iran!

The Revolution is a month old, and Dayeh is making stuffed vine leaves. They're all sitting on the floor, my mother, my sisters, my cousins, my aunts. The wives of my older brothers. They have laid the sofrehs out on the living-room floor and are sitting around them with bowls full of rice and minced meat, herbs, lentils, and they are folding vine leaves, one after another, and laying them in a pot and talking and laughing and talking and laughing.

There were just as many women when we were little, though they were different women. Our dayeh would send my sisters and me outside; we weren't supposed to hear the women's conversation, to interrupt the neighbourhood gossip. You mustn't bother people while they're cooking, we were told, or the food will take longer to make, and we went outside, where we played marbles or pretended to shoot down the murderer of the great and oh-so-honourable Imam Hossein. That was Sohrab's favourite game. Sohrab didn't have any siblings of his own yet, and he would always hang around outside the house so that we and the other children would come and release him from his boredom. He'll be waiting for me again in a few hours. Not bored, not any longer, but driven by a restlessness that we have carried within us since the first stirrings of the Revolution and since it broke out and for the whole of the past month — and which we know we must hide. Restlessness is uncertainty, and future leaders must not show any uncertainty. Only someone who has known Sohrab since he was a child can see it in him.

Dayeh doesn't send me out these days, though she would like me to leave. Everything about her eyes, her posture says that I shouldn't be here, that I should only come into contact with the vine leaves once they land hot and cooked and round and gleaming on the sofreh, and I shouldn't talk about them before that, either, because before that they have no business being in my world. Dayeh has a look that is just for me. For me, sitting in the corner and smoking, a man who needs to leave already so that the women can have the interesting conversations they've been looking forward to all morning. Even as a child, I quite quickly realised that it was more interesting with the women. The men either talked about the politics of ages past or played cards, and I wasn't allowed to join the game. But the women talked about real people and real problems. Which neighbour had argued with her mother-in-law; whose daughter was engaged to whose son but had shown herself to be immoral; which families had drifted into an American lifestyle; which market vendor sold the best-tasting eggplant.

My nieces and nephews run and play between the

women, knowing that the moment is approaching when first I and then they will be sent out and they will have to find a new game. There isn't much to snack on when vine leaves are being stuffed; the rice mixture isn't very interesting, and the leaves don't taste good without their filling. When there's nothing to snack on, you can make a nuisance of yourself. My niece is the smallest, and she wants the smallest dolmeh. My brother Mehrdad is the fattest, and he wants the fattest dolmeh. The women give in with a laugh, planting kisses on the children's cheeks.

If I were a mother, a sister, an aunt, I would be sitting there doing the same; I would take every opportunity to kiss these little souls, because they're so joyful, and no matter what is happening outside, no matter what they're learning at school, no matter that their schoolbooks are suddenly endorsing the opposite of what they did a few weeks previously, no matter if a while ago their parents were still spending their nights on the roof and their days on the streets, returning with bloodied clothes — the children still spend their days laughing, questioning, eating, interrupting, sleeping. They deserve all the kisses in the world, I think, but maybe the life that is just around the corner, still wavering a little — maybe that is the much greater gift.

I could collar my brother Mehrdad, the fat one, could kiss him and tell him the new life isn't wavering, we aren't wavering, it just needs a bit more time, that's all. But Mehrdad is currently pulling his sister's plaits and being scolded loudly by our mother. He won't understand what he has to thank us for until later, a few years, a few decades from now, when he's leading the free and fair life that is his due. When it won't be the modest house he grew up in, but his own actions and learning that pave the way to his place in society; when he'll enjoy an education far removed from any propaganda and will exercise his freedom of thought; when he'll work and take our country forward without lining a dictator's pockets; when no one will be above or below him.

Dayeh's look has changed since I stopped being Behzad the snacking thief. I was quicker at swiping food than my nieces and nephews are now, and I interrupted sooner, always interrupted. He's a nuisance, but what can I do. He's so clever, you can't be cross with him, they said. Dayeh used to have a special look for us children, a severe look that went with her upright posture. Her head was always slightly raised, majestic, and her lips pressed purposefully together. There was a small, tender, almost imperceptible smile in her large, warm eyes. She is looking at me now, too, now that I have lit my second cigarette, the one that signals I have no intention of leaving yet, and her look is that of a woman who wants to do everything right for her guests, and I am the speck of dust she has overlooked while cleaning, the smell of food from the day before yesterday that just can't be disguised, the rumour about us hanging in the air that no one dares speak aloud. But rumours about the movement aren't things to be discussed in daylight with the neighbours; they aren't things to be examined for how much truth is in them. They are whispered behind your hand to people you trust, because no one knows what is yet to come.

Behzadjan, go and help your father in the shop, my

mother calls out to me. The women look over, and I laugh, shake my head, and flick ash into the glass ashtray by my feet. And take the little ones with you, my aunt says, with a long-suffering look that makes the others laugh. And since when do we smoke while food is being prepared? my eldest aunt says — but not to amuse the others, just to show once more what she thinks of me, this woman who didn't remove her hijab even after they were banned by Reza Shah. The women go on smiling into their vine leaves as their hands wrap dextrously, daintily. How many hands wrap just like this, day after day in this country, I wonder, how many knead, how many knot, how many dig, how many shoot, how many lose their fingernails in the battle for names? The women's hands are small and quick and wrinkled.

My eldest aunt carefully smooths her hair back under her hijab, a pointedly bored look travels in my direction, and she says to the group, Behzadjan, you still haven't told us how you liked my friend's daughter! Twice I brought her with me, such a nice, polite girl, and I'm sure she's waiting for you to propose. My aunts and cousins smile into their vine leaves. Khalejan, I say, I have no idea who you're talking about — the most honourable and upright women are sitting here right now around this sofreh, how am I supposed to notice any other girl? My aunt grouses. I smile and say, Maybe you need to invite her again, and Dayeh clicks her tongue. Don't take him seriously, she says, He has nothing in his head but his books and his friends, no woman will want him. The other women laugh. I stub out my cigarette, stand up, straighten my shirt, nod to them all, and say, If you'll excuse me, and they hiss me out of the room. Appealing to romantic feelings in these times only takes away from the struggle, but if they want to start inviting women to meet me, then why not the one with the serious eyes and the loud laugh, the one I've seen more often recently, whose name I am still trying to find out?

In the yard I put on my shoes — they are old and worn and Dayeh scolds me every time she sees them. What do you want from me? I say then, They're the same shoes my pupils wear. And then she gives me that new look, every time. Though she still holds herself very straight, she suddenly looks so much smaller than me, and she has suddenly stopped trying to conceal the fact that she is, now. I'm twenty-seven years old, the only one of her four grown-up sons who still lives at home, bringing in money, looking after the girls, giving the boys a clip round the ear. Her head is proudly raised, as it always has been, only now she has to do it in order to look up at me. As if she's trying to memorise my face, as if she wishes I would just go into another room and not out into the city streets, as if she can see the blood, all the blood we don't mention to her, but which she knows about all the same. Khoda negahdar, she says then, just a phrase you use to bid someone farewell, God protect you, except she doesn't say it like everyone else. She says it like a fresh realisation, making an effort to look not at my worn-out shoes but into my eyes.

Sohrab and I meet outside the university. Our meeting points have changed, and places we never used to frequent have become increasingly important to us in the past month. I spot him from a distance. Short, thin, his hands in his trouser pockets, the back of his military shirt drenched in sweat, his hair rather longer than his mother would like. He turns and doesn't smile. We don't let on that we are comrades, that we are together, that we fight side by side, that we each used to be reprimanded by the other's mother, and taken to the barber by the other's father.

The pavement is covered in plastic jerry cans. You queue for petrol, and you meet up with friends and neighbours while the jerry cans keep your place, serried ranks of brightly coloured plastic. It's Peyman's turn to go for petrol today — he, too, was always in and out of our parents' houses, but was somehow always slower than Sohrab and me. Slower taking off his shoes, slower to greet my mother, slower stumbling into the room. Peyman doesn't meet up with anyone when he goes for petrol; he just stands there, eavesdropping on what other people say.

Nowhere are you closer to them, he'll say afterwards, We can't keep sitting in our living rooms talking about the people if we don't *know* the people. I always just give him a little nod and think, if you need that, Peyman, if you want to listen to all the stuff that's doing the rounds and is believed by all those who were denied an education from the very start, then go ahead, queue for petrol and walk among the people and listen to the gossip. They're saying that Mossadegh was a member of the Tudeh Party, that the communists want to share everything, first and foremost their wives, that the assassination attempt against Ayatollah Khomeini failed because all his bodyguards suddenly morphed into him — you go ahead and listen to that, Peyman.

Though I don't actually think it's so wrong, what he says; we should know what people are saying about our movement. But there are more important things to be doing right now. And anyway, how could we not know the people? We *are* the people. Peyman's parents can't read, my grandparents still live in the countryside with no running water, and my pupils have lice, no matter how often I shave their heads — who are the people, if not us?

Peyman, like so many, wasn't at all political before the Revolution. When Sohrab and I made new friends after we finished school, he wasn't interested in their ideas, and when we read Gorky and Rousseau in secret, he wasn't interested in their books. When we were writing our flyers, not long before the Revolution, he wasn't interested in their demands. He always just smiled and said, We need to make sure there is food, there is water, and that the children are going to school, and *then* a people can stage a revolution. We need to make sure there are books, I replied, books from which we can learn how others did it before us, and we need to make sure the weapons don't remain in the soldiers' hands. Peyman's smile is the smile of a man who has understood something, but isn't managing to convince everyone else.

And because he is silently, conscientiously queuing for petrol, today Sohrab and I are the only ones going to the rallies at Tehran University, and when the two of us meet, it's different from when the three of us do, because even if the Revolution has somehow politicised everyone, even Peyman, Sohrab and I joined the movement first and will remain members until our deaths. I move closer to Sohrab and he gives me a sideways glance, then looks away again, at his feet perhaps, his shoes the same as mine. His leg is now fully healed.

You walk quickly at the demonstrations; we walked quickly that day, too, the day before the day when the Shah left and the Revolution celebrated its victory. A day we said we'd tell our children about: where we were and what we were doing when we heard that the Shah was leaving the country; we left our houses like we did every day then, with the momentum that drew us out, that still draws us out. It was no longer a conscious decision; in a revolution, the crowd takes over your thinking, the crowd replaces your judgement. There were Sohrab and I, outside the house — I can't even remember if we'd arranged to meet. We looked like we always did, and the streets looked like they always did, but everything was overlaid with a kind of enchantment, with a song, as at Eid Nowruz maybe — only, I have thought for a long time what a shame it is that Eid Nowruz is now just a memory of what it was like when I was a child, the smell of the hyacinths, the magic of new clothes, the first days of spring and the beginning of a new year. Everything in me was crying out that a revolution is different, it isn't just children who are moved by a revolution. Sohrab and I, keeping pace with one another — we always walk fast, we're always in a hurry — met the others on the streets of our beloved city, men and women from the neighbourhood whom we didn't know before, and who all became our brothers and sisters in the days and weeks when things were getting easier, less covert. Sweets and kisses on the streets, and you didn't even notice the transition: one minute we were sitting side by side and silent at home, and the next we were part of the crowd, part of the roiling, bellowing crowd, part of the movement, part of the struggle, and we flung our fists up at the sky. As if to reward us for all the times before, like a sprint you are running for the hundredth time when you suddenly break the record; like flooring the same man in a koshti bout for the hundredth time, but today he hasn't deliberately made it easy for you because he's your father or your uncle — you have won because you are finally old enough and strong enough to be a real wrestler. Sohrab's voice and mine flung the slogans into the cold winter sky, our smoky voices, no longer the voices of children, and so accustomed to mingling with one another. I raised my arm, and my arm was his arm, arms everywhere around us, black heads in front of us, behind us, military shirts and sweat, full beards and moustaches, hijabs and dyed hair, cigarette smoke and perfume, marching in step towards freedom, no questions anymore, no questions anywhere, all around us nothing but the answer we had prophesied for so long. *I* prophesied it, yelled a voice in my head, I said it after the first page of Marx, I said it after the first page of Lenin, and I'll say it until I die, until they burn me in hell or until they realise there is no path other than the one history prescribes, that it is pointless to oppose us, that we are mightier — my fist shot into the air, Long live international solidarity. But then suddenly Sohrab's fist was no longer my fist, suddenly his fist was no longer raised, and it was only then that I heard the echo of the shot that had felled him, and how small a person is when they fall to the ground in a crowd. He wasn't looking at me, just at his leg, his eyes filled with pain, and he was crying, Khoda! I never asked him about it later, and maybe he's forgotten it himself — but in a moment of terrible pain, he cried out to a god we don't believe in. And if there is one thing we learned in all those days on the streets of Tehran, then it is that someone is always a doctor. The shot to Sohrab's leg like a shot to my heart, and around me people with beards that had a touch of frost on them, and Sohrab's leg wouldn't stop bleeding, and for a second I thought, maybe this is the moment when someone dies right beside me, the moment when the photo of the martyr we raise aloft isn't some unknown hero, but just Sohrab. Sohrab was not to become a martyr, though; Sohrab got up, helped by strangers who took him into a doorway. Comrade, Sohrab shouted, keep marching, we need more of us among the people. And he said it even though the men helping him could hear, men carrying pictures of Khomeini. I nodded to them, resolutely, nodded to Sohrab, and hurried away. We are brothers, we are comrades, I thought, but the battle will not be fought in doorways down side streets, and I looked for the others, who two days before had cleared out the barracks and were defending their barricades, and I thought, if I throw a grenade today, hurl a Molotov cocktail, if I get a gun today, then I'll throw, then I'll shoot, at everyone's feet.

Since the Revolution, we have been venturing into buildings we didn't know before. Before, we were in living rooms, sometimes in secret offices, sometimes on buses, visiting the movement in other cities. Since the Revolution, all doors seem to have opened, to let everyone in everywhere. Evin Prison, open to visitors. The place to which we lost our brothers and sisters in all those years of struggle against the monarchy — a place that was actually never a place, but a parallel world, a parallel hell. The people who came out didn't talk about what had gone on inside; the people who came out had done their talking inside, and perhaps that was the most sinister thing about it. Evin Prison, a place that consumes people, a place almost too much discussed to be true. Suddenly the doors were open. Suddenly we were going in. Suddenly it was no longer a place of torture, but of the greatest derision. This Shah isn't coming back, every wall, every door screamed out.

Today, then, the university. Sohrab's leg has completely healed. He moves with pride and ease along the campus paths, and so do I.

We never studied here; we did our military service, because that's what the state wanted from us, and it gave our parents money. We learned how to use weapons, and we remembered those lessons. We used all the resources the military had, enlightened the other soldiers, rebelled against our commanders, and rejoiced when we heard: the military is no longer on the Shah's side — from now on, the military is neutral. Because the military had changed from within, and that was something we had helped to achieve. We used the military to become teachers, to learn all the things we wanted to learn, to receive permission to go out to the villages and teach the children what we wanted to teach them — for as long as the SAVAK permitted each time.

We didn't need university for any of this, but we need it now, when the doors are open, so that we can walk these paths with pride and ease. I don't know if Sohrab is walking like this because I am, if we are both walking like this because the other people in our movement do, and if the members of other movements walk like our own comrades. In fact, I believe I'd begun walking like this even before the others came into my life. Before the car, the gleaming white Paykan, stopped outside my school and a future comrade asked me to get in and I wasn't suspicious, because I felt, I sensed that this wasn't the SAVAK driving me out into the mountains, this man who looked at the forests with me and said, Think about it, comrade. And in fact, I would have been amazed if they'd never asked me.

The university campus is large and confusing; we follow the walls, looking at the posters and pamphlets. All these groups suddenly emerged a few weeks ago as if from nowhere. To proclaim what our country's future could be now and what their aims are, their ideals, and what kind of state they want to see, now that anything seems possible. As we walk and observe, Sohrab and I don't show any emotion. The days of the underground are over, but as yet no one has fired the starter's pistol, no one has said to our movement, Let yourselves be known, no one has given us permission.

The texts on the flyers are so different in what they say, and so similar in how they sound. And I don't have to read them; I think it's roughly the same waste of time as queuing for petrol in order to listen to the rumours about us. We don't need to read the things we're pointing out to each other; we just have to keep fighting, to create a new Cuba, a new Soviet Union.

Sohrab leads and I follow; Sohrab chooses the groups we listen to, the followers of the Ayatollah, the Tudeh, the Mojahedin. In the struggle and on the streets, they were our brothers and sisters, united against the monarchy, against oppression and American imperialism. We were many, and we were strong, and we still are. Even if some believe in a divine power and armed struggle, and others in *The Communist Party Manifesto* and pacifism. Cooperation was the first step, but after this, *we* will lead the way. Sohrab listens to the speakers for a while, not showing any emotion, then walks on. I follow, and we leave the university.

Outside, we smoke a cigarette. How's your leg? I could ask, but we don't ask these things. How did you find it in there? he could ask me, but we don't ask these things. Which group did you find most convincing? I could ask, but we really don't ask these things. We don't ask questions anymore. Since the Revolution, it feels as though everyone used to ask us questions, and the Revolution was our answer. Does your mother scold you about your shoes? I hear myself asking. Sohrab looks at his feet. It's bourgeois to talk about clothes, he says, stubbing his cigarette out on the grey wall of the building.

What actually happens after a revolution? I could ask, though we've answered that too many times already for the question still to be asked: class struggle, radical change in the institutions, a dictatorship of the proletariat. But actually, Sohrab and I have just spent the last few days walking around prisons and universities, and actually, for the last few weeks, my comrades and I have been holding the same meetings we did before. Actually, there were only a few days when our songs and chants were aired publicly, and actually every program is now full of Ayatollah Khomeini. Sending the religious leader into exile all those years ago was probably the Shah's gravest error; the Ayatollah led his and our people from abroad, and now he's back and calling himself the leader of the Revolution.

One day my children can ask me how a revolution happens, and I'll serve them up the answer on a silver platter engraved with a gun and a sickle. What actually, really happens after a revolution is something I've never heard anyone ask out loud.

Dayeh made dolmeh today, I say. Sohrab nods. My mother loves him like her own son. Peyman is certain to have delivered the petrol to her by now. I'm hungry.

Peyman takes photos. His camera is large and makes him look even smaller than he is. We act like it bothers us that he's taking photos of our meetings, like it's just kitsch and vanity. And yet no one stops him; I don't know where the prints end up. All I know is that Che Guevara and Castro wouldn't be up on our walls if one of their comrades hadn't had a camera to hand as well.

Today's meeting is over; it was about the clerics' current activities, and Sohrab and I gave a brief report on the rallies at the university. As so often, the conclusion of the meeting is far from being the end of the evening. There are no sleeping family members to consider, no one to suggest we get a good night's sleep for the sake of the Revolution. It's just us, with our cigarettes, our talk — which for a few moments is permitted to grow less serious — laughter and black tea.

Sometimes the women sit in a corner by themselves, whispering and giggling. Peyman, the shy one, gives them a wide berth with his flash, though they keep casting glances at him. The same women who until recently had perms and wore high heels and went to see American movies. Is it good that they've embraced the spirit of the Revolution and started dressing like we do, or is it a sign of weakness, I sometimes ask myself, because what use have we for people who act like sheep; how can we build a new state and a new system with people who could change their allegiance at any moment?

Beside me, Sohrab is chatting to a fat man, one of the movement's leaders, who keeps us — the base — up to date with what's going on. Next time, he told me, I will be the one they send to Ilam as group spokesman, to keep up the exchange between the local groups, and for a minute I wondered if that wasn't something the group should vote on — who their spokesman was — and I registered Sohrab's clenched jaw, his proud eyes staring into the distance. Sohrab never looks at the women, never greets them, doesn't like talking about them. In the Revolution, everyone is important, he says, But anything that goes beyond political action distracts from the revolutionary spirit.

Sohrab and the fat comrade are talking about the planned agreement that will put the clerics in government, and I can hear in Sohrab's voice that he doesn't quite believe what he's saying, but would like to believe it, though inside he is filled with fear, filled with a choking, gnawing, panicky fear that everything we want could disappear faster than we think. At least a government of clerics is an anti-imperialist government, he says for the hundredth time.

I listen to him and the fat comrade, still feeling proud at having been made spokesman for the group, making an effort to pay Sohrab the attention he claims as his due, but distracted by the woman who laughs louder than the others, who has the gentlest voice and the most listeners. Who doesn't toss her shoulder-length, henna-red hair, who doesn't make eyes at people, who just laughs heartily when she feels moved to. *Ashraf*, they call her, and I would give so much to know her real name, but people who are acquainted through the movement only know each other by aliases. She looks demure and careful, with her neatly combed hair and ironed military shirt, but when she laughs, she is full of energy. Unfortunately, she usually leaves these evenings early, because she has to study, to read, because she is doing a literature degree, because she loves the Persian language, because she loves the poetry of Hafez, because she talks so often about everything she loves without noticing that I'm listening, and then she will pack her bag, bid everyone a proud and calm farewell, and leave, with her flushed cheeks and her serious, clever eyes.

That's going to be a nice photo of you, says Peyman as he sits down beside me on the rug, having first slid the ashtray aside, knocking a few cigarette butts out of it in the process, and hastily picked them up again before the host saw. Of me? I ask, and Peyman laughs mischievously; maybe he learned that from always being the smallest in our neighbourhood, always the smallest but far from the stupidest, and he laughs and says, I'm going to call the photo I just took of you *Revolutionary, head over heels in love*. I don't laugh, and Peyman can only make jokes of this kind because we've known each other since we were children and because he is a support to me, someone I value. Better if you call it *Revolutionary, about to go home*, I say, and Peyman smiles his quiet, sly smile and nods. I get my things together. Let's go, I say.

Peyman has got thinner, and he looks tired. Peyman, you look tired, I say, and he waves it off as he's getting up. He has become contemplative in recent days and weeks, and even if I regard what he calls his political views as far too cautious and un-radical, they might be making it easier for him to deal with the change that his brother has undergone since the Revolution. Peyman loves his brother, loves Amin, who is currently growing a full beard. I've never thought about this little rascal, who we never allowed to join our games, being able to grow any kind of beard. Then I noticed Amin again at the protest marches, not with us, but with the others, the women who cover their hair with a headscarf and the bearded men. I picture Amin's beaming face as we cheered Khomeini on his return from exile. Peyman, Sohrab, and I cheering because he's a prominent figure in the Revolution. Amin because he thinks of him as the father of the Revolution.

Amin would probably agree with us when it comes to the use of weapons and violence, but only in the service of a god he never believed in before; only for his new friends, who with every passing day are causing us to speak more softly again on the streets. His new friends, whom our mothers listen to more than they listen to us, because believing in a god is so much easier than believing in new ideas. These clerics think they have the people and we have the intellect; we could profit from one another, they say increasingly often, and I don't know if I want to collaborate with a group that accepts people like Peyman's brother, no questions asked, and gives them weapons. Seventeen-year-olds who until recently were wandering Tehran's dusty streets, wondering what to do with all their energy.

Is Amin at home? I ask, and Peyman shakes his head. Probably not, why?

I don't say anything more, but I think, probably because I want to know what they're up to, the others. Lining themselves up on the streets more and more, stopping my younger brothers last week — because, I suspect, they all know me and they all know who my brothers are. In the middle of the street, near the bazaar, they started questioning people as if someone had authorised them to do it. Was it true that I'd made fun of the Prophet in public; had the joke come from me? I don't even know this joke about the prophet, and still they're laying it at my door. Being an atheist and being disrespectful are two completely different things, but the rumour alone was enough to get me banned from the mosque. Not that I care whether I'm allowed into the mosque. And maybe someone else made this joke, or the joke never even existed, it doesn't matter; they want to keep an eye on me and my family. I can live with that. We're strong, stronger than the others who have won Peyman's brother over with their propaganda.

But Peyman's brother is still a child, and we have to look after the children — I mean, everything we do is for the children, only for the children. We don't need to worry about Amin, Peyman says now, seeming to guess what I'm thinking. It's just a phase; he's made some new friends and he feels good about it.

We say goodbye to everyone but Sohrab, who we'll see later, leave the house, and head back towards our neighbourhood. It goes without saying that this is just a phase, I say. This whole religious movement is just a phase. Peyman turns his head to me, nods, his face brightens, and he quickens his pace a little. Amin is just trying things out, he says, We did that at seventeen, too, you know. I light a cigarette, thinking that it was only Sohrab and me who tried things out at seventeen. Peyman was always too cautious, even as a little boy — he was always there, but only to stand guard, give advice, try to mitigate the risk, clap us on the shoulder afterwards in admiration. The first time we put a cat's paws into walnut shells and then chased it through the streets; the first marble tournaments we held behind the school building despite the strict ban, to relieve the younger

pupils of their pocket money; the first cigarettes we bought
with the profits and smoked in secret.

Sohrab, Peyman, and I watch the days fade out from the roof.
The city looked different when I was a child. Fewer lights,
more space between the buildings. You heard more human
voices and fewer cars. There were more vendors on the street
selling lentil stew, chestnuts, and cooked beetroot, later
replaced by the American cafes, the cinemas and dance bars,
the limousines and convertibles. Until the streets belonged
to us. Destroy the banks, I thought, but threw stones at the
lewd cinemas instead. Perhaps that's the right first step;
first we have to halt the Americanisation of society, and
then imperialism. We threw the bar stools out through the
windows, and the tiled walls gleamed despite our vandalism.
People sat here once and were happy, I thought — how must
it have felt to be happy in here? How does it feel to ignore half
the country starving, to ignore our country giving its oil away
so that one man can revel in luxury, to ignore the prisons
filling up with people who were once your neighbours?

Sohrab is cutting his fingernails. He snips away in the
dark, a cigarette in the corner of his mouth. Peyman hums
a song. He can't sing but does it constantly. Actually, none
of us can sing, but we do it anyway. So, what's wrong with
your face? he asks suddenly, interrupting his song to jut his
chin in Sohrab's direction. What about my face? says Sohrab
without looking up. He has finished his tea and is dropping
the nail clippings into the glass, where they swim among

the tea-leaves. Is this another shaving boycott? What's that stubble in aid of? Peyman asks.

It's a long time since anyone has used the words *shaving boycott*. Peyman always clings so tightly to old things, mentions them out of the blue, and throws us all back into a time capsule of memories we really have no use for. In the military, the shaving boycott was our first collective rebellion against authority. Now, after the Revolution, we don't comb our hair, or wash it; the last thing we want is to look like the young Americans the Shah wanted us to be. We shave as badly as possible, but we still shave, so that we won't look like the bearded believers either.

Peyman is right. Sohrab doesn't look like he's making a conscious effort to maintain a stage between smooth and bearded; you can barely see the skin of his face, and it must be several weeks since he last stood in front of the mirror with a razor. And yet ten years ago, Sohrab declared shaving to be his number one favourite activity. He was the first of us who needed to shave, and he was so proud to stand in front of his parents' bathroom mirror, imitating what his father and brothers did as we looked on.

I'm reminded of my own father in front of the mirror, with a small, thick-bristled brush in one hand and a sharp razor blade in the other. As a child, I thought it must be yoghurt he was pressing onto his cheeks, the fine cream that floated on the white mass in Dayeh's pot when she'd let it stand in the sun for three days. If you mixed the cream with water and left it out in the sun again, it would ferment into fresh, fizzy dugh, and the children would pounce on it. I imagined my father skimming off the cream to use for shaving, because a good shave is more important than a chilled drink.

Father standing every morning in front of the piece of mirror that he clipped to the little shelf. He never lets anyone else shave his beard, and he says: Behzad, take note. No one is obliged to do something like that for you, even if you pay him for it, and you should never trust a person so much that you put a blade in his hand and let him lean over you with it.

My father in front of the mirror, singing songs from his youth. Fathers are never young, I think; fathers all have stubble that slowly gets whiter, thicker. My father shaved every morning except in Ramadan, and then his face would prickle us children with every kiss he gave, and his breath smelled of abstinence when he'd had no food or water, and his eyes were smaller and his singing quieter.

He still stands in front of the mirror every morning. But he doesn't sing as much, or talk about the blade and the money. Behzad, he said a while ago, who *are* these children you go out to meet? He might just as well have said, Behzad, you look unkempt and so do your friends. I could have said, They're left-wing, they're fighters, they're the bravest and most determined people this world has ever seen, and every day I spend with them I grow to be a little more like them. What I said was, They're the same children who've been in and out of this house since I was born; the ones whose fathers you sometimes drink tea and play backgammon with after work. Father didn't nod, because he was busy running the sharp metal over his Adam's apple, and the sound it made on the hard stubble was a substitute for any further words.

Behzad, he said a few weeks later, they're talking about you in the neighbourhood — and he could have sounded worried but he wasn't, and he could have sounded proud but he wasn't. I was sitting in the same corner of the tiled room where I always used to take up my observation post. He used to sometimes interrupt his humming and tell me things. Never when business was good in his little bookshop — but constantly when it was bad. Then he would tell me about the days when everyone took to the streets, because a man named Mossadegh wanted to ensure we were the ones profiting from our oil, and not the English. And then people were killed, on the streets, and at this point my father always said, It doesn't matter to me whether the money goes to the English, the Americans, or the Chinese, the important thing is there are no dead bodies in the street. With these words he ended his monologue about business being bad, about how few books in the bookshop were being sold, and how many books had been banned, and how the shop's owner had stopped reading. He has scarcely embarked on a single one of these monologues since the Revolution; instead, there have been more questions about me, my friends and the rumours. I said, Baba, they're always talking about someone in the neighbourhood; sometimes it's me, sometimes it's other people. Knowing very well that he hadn't talked about Mossadegh and the dead from that earlier time for a long while, although there had been more deaths, and remembering the dead from that earlier time was more relevant than ever.

These days, watching my father shave is mostly just the sound of the metal on the sharp little bristles of his stubble and his ageing, tanned skin. Take care of yourself, Behzadjan, he says sometimes; I'm old, and you need to look after the little ones. And I nod and don't say that staying at home would be the worst possible way of looking after the little ones. The smooth face that is revealed when my father's large hands splash water over his cheeks. The shirt that carries away little droplets, and the white chest hair that peeks out from under its collar. The brief nod in my direction as he leaves the tiled room, leaves the house, in his cotton slippers, carrying a little fruit, a little bread, a little cheese in his pouch. This is how he sets out into a day that won't bring any earnings, as the war rages on the streets. This is how he returns home in the evening, to eat dates and drink milk and ask no questions.

The Shah is a scoundrel, he used to mutter to himself sometimes. Really, he knows full well that we're doing the right thing; fathers always know what's right. My father, who always pays the full price when he goes to the barber, as if they'd shaved him as well. So as not to drive his barber to financial ruin, while also sticking to his principles.

A cool wind blows over the roof, and Sohrab clicks his tongue, as if what Peyman is saying about his face and the shaving boycott is childish nonsense. My beard can't hold a candle to your brother's, though, can it? he asks him. Peyman's eyes are sad, and they don't just grow sad then — they were already. How hard must all this be for someone who never actually wanted any part in it? Who only came to the meetings because all his friends were there. What would Peyman be doing if we weren't a political group, if he had grown up in another part of town, if he'd had other friends? He'd probably be sitting on some other roof and trying just as unsuccessfully to tease someone else who didn't take him seriously. My brother is only doing the same as most other people in this country, he says finally, without the bitterness I'd like to hear in his voice. Stupid people are in the majority, Sohrab says, and he knows that I know that this is a quote, and he knows that Peyman doesn't know it. You need the majority for your revolution, though, don't you? says Peyman.

You can't sit in silence on the roof. On the roof, there are too many noises coming from all directions; even the bright snick of the nail clippers is lost in the din from the streets, the people, the wind. We don't need everyone who thinks they have something to say, says Sohrab, and his tone of voice is sufficient to stop Peyman arguing back. When Peyman's mother has been to visit us, she will sometimes come up to me just before she leaves, and whisper in my ear. She can neither read nor write, and if her husband was later than usual coming home from work, she would appear weeping at my mother's door, constantly afraid that something had happened to him. Nothing has ever happened in Peyman's family. Peyman always notices his mother whispering to me, but he pretends not to. He isn't like you boys, she whispers, He can't join in with all the things you do, don't force him into anything. I've never told Sohrab this, because I've never told him other stories from the past, either.

When Peyman and Amin were children and got into a fist fight with some older boys who were pushing them around because of their worn-out clothes, making jokes about Amin's jug ears; when Peyman couldn't defend his little brother though he tried with all his might, I climbed the tree in the yard and threw moist, ripe dung over the wall at those older boys. I didn't just throw it, I literally bombarded them, as rapidly as I could — the dung was so fresh it splattered on impact, and I aimed well and hit my targets every time.

Peyman goes on humming his song with the wrong notes, as if the shaving conversation never happened. Sohrab turns to me: Why do you keep glancing over at me all the time? he asks. I take a close look at him. He didn't use to have these lines, or this streak of sullenness on his face. He was always more serious than the others, but the Revolution has left its marks, and I don't know if I like them, and I don't know if they will ever fade. When I don't reply, his eyes rest on me. Unwavering, almost challenging. I guess you don't want to stand out, I say, returning his gaze. There are those who played a part in the Revolution and there are those who claim they did. And then there are those who are afraid of falling between two stools, and deliberately dress and walk as unobtrusively as possible. Sohrab's expression doesn't change. The conversation is over. At some point, amid all these days of battle and victory, someone in the group decided that I get to decide when conversations are over. Sohrab can't possibly approve of this, but he can't do anything about it, either. I smile at Peyman, but he doesn't look satisfied with the turn things have taken.

When can we start making jokes again, he asked me a few days ago. When can we start teasing each other again without everything, *everything* always being political? And I said, Peymanjan, we're in the middle of a revolution, even farting is political.

I walked past the wall three days in a row. The graffiti from the early days of the Revolution has been pasted over with the clerics' pictures and posters. *Down with America!* is the only slogan you can still see everywhere. *Down with the clerics!* is the only slogan that appears afresh day after day and is immediately pasted over again. The further we get from the Revolution, the more pictures of Ayatollah Khomeini we see, and the more groups are banned and vanish back into secrecy.

I walked along the wall three days in a row to see if the chalk line, about a metre above the ground and barely visible to anyone not in the know, had been lengthened. Every day, there were a few centimetres more. Every day, I strode past at a brisk pace, hardly daring to give it more than a glance, because who knew who might be watching, who knew who knew how to read our signs. We did learn them from books, after all, and who knew whether the enemy had been reading the same books. On each of those three days, that fleeting glance was enough. The line was longer; everything was going according to plan.

Now, on the fourth day, I am waiting on the opposite side of the wall. The first two days, a yellow Peugeot was parked there with no flyers in the boot; on the third day, when everything was going well, it was replaced by the same model of car with flyers. Today, on the fourth day, I am standing here waiting for a driver, who will bring a child with him to identify himself, and will drive me part of the way before I carry on alone to Ilam. I've been invited there to speak about our local campaigns, and who will take the flyers, if not I?

As I am getting into the car, I think, if all this works smoothly, if the whole of life works out with such wonderful ease, how can anyone still be worried that this Revolution will come to a bad end, with the wrong people pulling the strings? This is the right car on the right day; this is the driver with the little girl between his knees, and he looks exactly like the fat comrade told me he would. If you know the feeling, you can't doubt. We are too strong for anyone to take the Revolution out of our hands.

The buses aren't running today, Agha, I say as I get in, trying to sound as routine as possible, as if this car is a normal ajans — only, the man behind the wheel has been expecting this precise sequence of words. Then I'll drive you, Agha, the man says, as agreed. He must be ten years older than me and has a magnificent moustache, thick hair, and I'm sure his wife is a good cook. Salam, Agha, the girl says. Her voice is light and clear, as children's voices are, but there is something challenging in her tone. Salam, Khanoom, I say. She turns her eyes away to look ahead, at the road, with such concentration it's as if she is the one driving. We will travel thirty kilometres, out of the city, to a bus station — that's what has been agreed. If there is a woman standing at the entrance with a newspaper, then all is well, and only then will

I take the car on to Ilam. Alone. The moustache and the little girl will get the bus back into the city, bringing with them the information that everything has gone without a hitch.

I haven't previously given any thought to what these thirty kilometres are going to be like. They have just been part of a political campaign, part of a plan that others have come up with and that I just need to understand and put into action. But political campaigns don't feel the way it feels to sit beside a stranger and a stranger's child. The man is a comrade, or we wouldn't be sitting here, but who knows at what point and in what company the child might blab about it? How much do five-year-olds understand of what is going on around them? However useful the little girl was for identifying the driver, I am finding her very disconcerting. She sits there quite peacefully, combed hair gleaming, neatly dressed, her hands in her lap. A little person like her could put him and me and all the others behind bars; you hear of more and more comrades being caught, vanishing without trace.

The man turns the volume down on the radio when she begins to speak in her light, clear voice, taking control of the conversation. It's only now that I notice the man is playing one of Khomeini's cassettes. They were sent from exile and distributed here, and they were almost a brand in their own right, these cassettes filled with lessons and warnings. Since the Revolution, since Khomeini's return, since his gnawing, growing power, I have begun to think of them as warnings from the pre-revolutionary age, which feels like it was decades ago. We should have started listening to them sooner.

Before we said *They are the first step*, we should have considered whether it was a step in the wrong direction, and whether we might have taken that step without them.

The girl asks questions, one after another, and the man answers patiently. It becomes apparent that he is her father. She asks clever questions, about the car, the engine, the steering wheel, and the father has an answer for them all. I stare out of the window. I am a revolutionary. I'm on an important mission. This is a car full of flyers, and I am the spokesman who — My name's Tara, she says. I nod and say nothing. We took my cassette out because of you and put another one in, she says. I nod. I could say: You didn't need to do that. I could give Tara's father a warning glance. What cassette were you listening to? I ask. Songs, she says almost sniffily, as if that much was obvious and it was simply wrong to listen to anything else. We quite often listen to stories, too, the man says. I turn my head to look at him. He is driving with great concentration, peering over the hair on the child's small head. His voice is deep and affectionate when he talks to her. But his eyes, fixed on the road ahead, give him away.

Do you know Samad's stories? I ask Tara in my teacher voice, and her father smiles silently as she says, Who's Samad? And I say, Samad Behrangi, he wrote the story about the little black fish, surely you must know that one. She doesn't reply, but she's listening, her eyes alert and looking into the distance, and the soft little ears beneath her thick hair are invitation enough for me to tell the story I've told so often before, to my sisters, to my pupils, to everyone who can learn — they must learn from this story. It begins with Grandmother Fish telling the little fishes the story of the brave black fish who doesn't listen to his mother or the neighbours and sets off to discover where the stream goes, because he doesn't believe the stream always remains a stream. And even though he dies at the end, helping someone weaker and killing someone stronger, he is right: the stream becomes a river, and the river becomes a sea, and Grandmother Fish sends the children to bed, and a little red fish is the only one who stays behind, lost in thought.

Tara's expression doesn't change. The moustache looks relieved. He knows the story, of course, and of course he knows Samad. And of course he's glad not to have to entertain the little girl for a few minutes. Why did he die? she asks, and she sounds sad; it's an unsparing story. *If someday I should be forced to face death — as I shall — it doesn't matter. What does matter is the influence that my life or death will have on the lives of others,* her father says in my place. The father says it as it's written in the book, and then all three of us fall silent.

The pelican isn't evil, the girl says eventually. I've just told her a story in which the hero and his comrades are swallowed by a pelican, but Tara still says, The pelican isn't evil, the pelican gives his children food, and if there's no more food he bites off his own flesh so no one will starve. I smile and say Ah and Oh, and I didn't know that, the kind of thing you say to strangers' clever children.

Tara nods very shrewdly and asks if we can listen to her cassette with songs on again, and of course for the rest of the ride, we listen to her cassette with songs on. It would be lovely just to stay sitting in this car forever, I think, with a father and a child who may not be my father or my child, but they could be, in another time and another life. A more beautiful time, a better life. Outside, the vast, never-changing landscape, rocky hills with dry plants growing on them, and hot air blowing in through the window. The man and I don't exchange another word, and yet we think about each other — we can't help it, we're part of a campaign planned by strangers in order to keep it secret from other strangers.

When we arrive at the bus station, it doesn't feel like relief, either for him or for me. Only Tara is excited. The man utters a weary Khob dige — right, then. Here and there, drivers are standing by their buses, hands in their trouser pockets, shouting across the asphalt to one another, waiting until they have enough passengers to set off. Our car passes the entrance to the bus station building. The air is full of dust, stirred up by the idling engines. The man and I glance casually at the entrance as the car's wheels keep rolling. There is no one in the doorway. The woman with the newspaper isn't standing there as agreed. What do I do if things have gone awry? Drive back to the city? Get rid of the flyers somewhere? Or is that too risky? The driver sighs. Then he parks up and starts bidding me farewell with the usual formulaic phrases as he helps Tara out of the car. They've played their part.

The woman with the newspaper arrives two hours later than planned, and she doesn't hesitate for long. For two hours I have been trying not to look like I'm waiting, going into the bus station at twenty-minute intervals to wash my hands, use the toilet, check the timetable, then spending another ten minutes strolling around the barren area, before returning to our meeting point. Feeling deeply worried that she might have been caught, they all might have been caught. Hardly has she arrived, hardly has she taken out her trembling paper, when she recognises me and starts chattering away. Sohrab would say this is why many women ultimately shouldn't be involved. But I don't give any more thought to Sohrab; I think, What a shame, if the comrades were sending a woman to stand here with a newspaper, whose sole job was to convey the news that everything has gone well, then why a stranger? Why not Nahid, the woman who loves books and language, and whose real name I have finally discovered through spending so much time eavesdropping on her friends? I listened to them laughing, and once her best friend forgot to use her alias when she said, Nahid, you look tired, what are you getting up to at night? And Nahid said she'd spent all night reading Shamlou's poems and couldn't sleep, and at last I knew: her name is Nahid and she reads Shamlou. And then a moment later, none of that matters. Because a moment later, the stranger is saying, Plans have changed, we managed to take over a barracks and we've occupied a country house, and we're preparing to do battle for the next barracks. Either you join the fight or you take the next bus back and leave me the car.

And then everything happens very quickly. There we were, still thinking our main job was to sit and discuss and read and speak and plan and plan and plan, and now our leaders' strategy has changed and we're taking up arms again, preparing an offensive against the clerics, wanting the streets back, wanting our rights back, and we're slap bang in the middle of the fight again. Suddenly you are asking yourself what on earth you were thinking, doing nothing but sitting and talking; did you think a revolution would drive itself forward, with just the knowledge in people's heads and the printed words in the car boot? Did you think political campaigns are political simply because they're secret? The others don't just have the voices on car radios, and they don't just have the cities. They don't just have the crowds at the demonstrations and the words in the media. What were you waiting for, and why did you think the flyers were important, when the other side has everything that used to belong to the Shah's army? When that's the strongest means by which they uphold their power, calling themselves the new secret service, the guardians of the Revolution, just so they can have our groups officially banned?

Suddenly you can't remember when the shared fight during the Revolution turned into a fight among ourselves to become the new rulers. But what immediately occurs to you is: fighting was what we originally signed up for, and so the question of fight or turn back can no longer be asked, and you get into the car and drive to an area you don't know, have never even heard of. The only thing you know is that it was abandoned by the rich landowners when the Shah left the country, and we will bring it back to life with the true spirit of the Revolution, to stop those who have no right to call themselves revolutionaries.

As the empty prisons were to the city, so the profiteers' abandoned houses are to the countryside. This house belonged to the area's largest landowner, who had the monarchy to thank for his riches and had to flee along with the monarchy, most likely to a country ravaged by capitalism, where he belongs. We distribute ourselves across the two floors. Our offices are his former study. We hold our meetings in his former drawing room. We sleep in his children's former bedrooms. Cigarette smoke hangs between the air-conditioned walls; our guns lie on the rugs; the cellars are an arsenal of everything we could scavenge from the Shah's barracks. Our arms are as muscular as they were in our military days, and we sleep as briefly and effectively as possible. Two people are always posted outside the house, keeping watch, with two more on the roof. By day, the village looks deserted; the farmers work their land with our help. Where at first the harvesting and weeding was accompanied by sceptical looks and furrowed brows, our songs now float over the hot soil. The air is different to back home in Tehran; there are no exhaust fumes, and at night the ground cools right down, only to charge itself with heat again the next morning as the first birds start to sing.

Summer has arrived without my noticing. The day I met Tara and her father was the first day of the summer holidays. My pupils had said their goodbyes to me and set off home just a few hours before I went to look for the chalk line on the wall, and so for the next three months, no one will ask why I haven't turned up for work. In three months' time, my pupils will have grown. In three months' time, they might be living in a fairer world. The other comrades have simply left their jobs as electricians, nurses, dentists. If we should ever leave this house, they will probably all have to live in the underground. But in three months' time, everything could be completely different; we could have driven the clerics out of the strategically important positions, and I could go back to my pupils and look forward to them asking, Sir, what did you do in the holidays? I keep thinking of phoning my parents, and then I keep reminding myself that it would be negligent. They mustn't know where I am, because I'm a danger to them. I always have been, but now that our campaigns are so focused and successful, the clerics will take more severe action against us and our families. But Dayeh and my sisters will go on filling a portion of vine leaves for me, because who knows when I'll turn up at their door again.

It's a hot summer evening. There are twenty-six of us sitting under the electric mock-chandelier, all involved in a jumble of different discussions. We are barefoot, and we smell of sweat. Some of us have spent the day on shooting practice, some helping the farmers, some in the office organising things, some guarding the house. The women stayed indoors, cooking, typing up our news and announcements, making copies of our newspapers. I was on guard duty for the second time in a row, because I can still handle a gun pretty well, and if I'd had someone with me I wanted to discuss things with, and not just Olumy, the yes-man, then I would have told him how good I think it is, how wonderful, that we are finally taking action and not just sitting around. Two hours from here, our comrades have taken another barracks, and we've been expecting another delivery of weapons for a few days now. The barracks we have our sights on next isn't especially large — not much longer now and we'll be ready. Olumy, the yes-man, would just have said yes to all this, which doesn't do much to liven up guard duty.

The drawing room is impressively large for a single landowner and his family, but there's no room to move when we're all sitting and chatting there in the evening. After the day on the roof, the sitting is too much of a strain for me. I've been here long enough now to know who is in which corner of the room, having what conversations, and what their views are. In the beginning, new people were arriving every day, and the odd one still turns up from time to time. They're excited and they pretend to be calm and collected; they want to see everything, know everything, experience it all for themselves, like people going to the cinema for the first time, their eyes probing every corner of the screen in the fear of missing something. The excitement and the pride last a day and a half inside or on top of this house, or out in the fields. Then they settle down.

I didn't have this initial excitement. When I arrived here, they knew who I was. On my first guard duty, the wind was cool and countless stars watched over us. I couldn't help but smile for a moment, hoping that the yes-man wouldn't see; I would have been embarrassed even in front of him. Anyway, you don't start laughing in card games when you're about to win, either. A revolution cannot be taken forward if we stand around grinning on the roof.

Since then, I've started writing letters to Nahid. I

42

don't really write them down — anything we post could be intercepted and give us away. I memorise the words that I feel are worthy of her. In my head, I can read them out and imagine her reply. When they've got you, Sohrab's uncle told us after the months he spent in Evin, they leave you to stew on your own for so long that you'll start to consider betraying your comrades just to have someone to talk to. That's hard training, conversing with yourself, fixing up your own memory to make it a worthy, good, and fair partner for those conversations. He told us this in the knowledge that, in a few years, we might profit from it, though he probably hoped that by that time it might all be over. Now we sit in this room, and if something somewhere had gone wrong and the false revolutionaries had got wind of us, the twenty-six of us would be filling a prison cell instead. And, after interrogation, in the worst case we'd betray at least as many people again. We would be a jackpot for the Pasdaran, the Revolutionary Guard, which in our minds is nothing other than the new secret service. Two days ago, a man came out from Tehran who said that, judging by how quickly Evin was filling up again, there were suddenly either an awful lot of criminals in this country or an awful lot of blabbermouths.

Nahid, I will write in my next letter, this world we're building is not for us. Nothing is for us. This world we're building is for those who will come after us, and may they share your perspicacity and your knowledge and may they value it.

How long have you been here? a dwarf at my side asks me just then. He doesn't seem to know me, or he wouldn't have needed to ask, and he's so unobtrusive that I hadn't noticed his own arrival, which must have been yesterday or today. I take my time answering, remove my pack of cigarettes from my shirt pocket, realise it's empty, and see that he is already offering me his. Like the rest of us, he is wearing baggy, Kurdish linen trousers, which look even baggier on his thin frame, and is probably still a teenager. He doesn't wait for my answer; he says, My older brother sends his regards. I take a closer look at him. I'm guessing you don't know who I am? he asks with a laugh. Well, at least you know who *I* am, I say, finally lighting the cigarette. Of course I do, he says boldly, half the city is talking about you, they're saying you're dead.

All at once, a great spasm grips my insides. What are you talking about? I say, raising my voice, and a few people fall silent and turn to look at us. The dwarf almost soils himself, and he brushes the reddish-brown curls from his forehead nervously. Ghader Nuri, he says, is my big brother, and he sends his regards — he knew you were here but he couldn't tell anyone, or he would have given you away.

I feel sorry for the boy now, and in a flash I recognise him. Comrade Ghader is five years older than me; he was in my cousin's class at school and agreed to be one of the three people I needed to vouch for me when I joined the movement. Ghader is a well-read man and level-headed, too; if half of our comrades were only half as brave as him, the fight would long since have been won. His little brother was playing with the hose in the yard a few years ago as I sat with Ghader and his friends in the shade, talking about the movement in low voices. The little boy couldn't hear us, but he was so awe-stricken that he didn't even ask if someone would play with him. He just sprayed water on the plants and his bare legs and kept his mouth shut. Years have passed since then, in which I've barely seen Ghader — who has taken up a more senior position in our movement — let alone his brother. And now he's sitting beside me. Still short and uncertain, but all the same.

Who's saying I'm dead? I ask, feeling a touch of pride, but then thinking of Dayeh. Dayeh with her loud weeping and wailing, when one of the neighbour women died; Dayeh and the days she spent apathetic, lying down and sleeping after her miscarriages; Dayeh standing in the doorway; Father shaving and saying, God protect you, Khoda negahdar, but there is no god, there is no reason for me to want his protection, and even if god offered it to me in person, I would turn it down. I'm pretty sure it came from Amin, the kid says now, and there is such a hesitant, serious tone in his cracking voice that I am starting to like him. That might be why I didn't believe the rumour, he adds modestly. Dead. They just think I'm dead. That's how easy it is to be dead in the world's eyes. You don't even realise it yourself. And how did I die? I ask. The kid smiles: Amin says you got caught with flyers in the boot of your car and, when they caught you, you made a statement against the holy revolutionaries. He reckons he was there but couldn't save you.

He tried to save me? I ask, thinking that Amin may have made that story up but it could easily have been true. A few weeks before the summer holidays, they really did stop me and search the boot, where luckily there was nothing to find.

Maybe he only said the bit about trying to save you when he had a more critical audience, the kid replies. He makes me laugh. Amin and the kid could be in the same school year. I don't know if they were friends, Ghader's brother and Peyman's brother; I didn't see these boys often enough to know that. I just know that this one here has some cleverness about him, and Peyman's brother is a rat.

Why do you think he would invent a story like that? I ask in my teacher voice. I can imagine, of course, why someone like Amin would invent such a story. But I ask the kid this question so that he feels his opinion is important, too, or will be one day. He is clearly agitated. Amin is a show-off, and a nobody — maybe that's why, he muses aloud. Amin is trying to make a name for himself in the area. He wants everyone to follow him or be afraid of him. And then you were gone. And that might just be the obvious explanation. The kid talks slowly, as if after every sentence he needs to consider whether he can really add another, as if he feels guilty about speaking. For the first time, the thought crosses my mind that being a new member of these groups, in these days, must be a genuinely hard thing, and that I'm lucky this isn't my problem. I nod and smile at him.

What other news is there? I ask. The kid takes a deep breath and lets off a firework of rumours from our neighbourhood, and I nod and laugh, and he grows surer of himself with every detail he gives me: the new neighbours, the deceitful street vendors, his growing family. He doesn't talk about my family, and I don't ask. Finally, he ends his disquisition, probably fearful he is boring me and trying my patience. Now I'm here, he says, to fight. I nod gravely and say, Now you're here to win. He throws me a quick glance: Yes. Then, after a pause, he says, That was another reason to come; after they recaptured the other barracks, I thought okay, now's the time — now that they're fighting back like this, we really all need to come here. The other barracks? I want to ask. Recaptured? I want to ask. But I merely assume a knowing expression — I've been practising that expression for many months — and I nod and say, It's been a real pleasure, and he nods hastily, too, over-hastily, seeming relieved that the conversation is over, and a little proud as well.

Thirteen days later, the kid is in jail, and the occupation of the barracks has been abandoned. The three leaders of our movement, the people right at the top whose names and faces we don't know, have been put under surveillance and arrested. Someone in a cell somewhere must have named names and locations, because important organisational bases, our offices and meeting rooms, our printing shops and weapons stores have been cleared out and destroyed. No one comes to tell us: Everything has been cleared out and destroyed. No one comes to tell us: They're torturing people in prison until they talk. But we can imagine it, because it is so very like what we knew before the Revolution. It's just that now we say other names when we speak of the enemy, the name of the judge who passes death sentences on everyone who comes before him, the judge with whom people are threatened even when they're just being pulled over on their way back into the cities. Khomeini is on television and he is speaking as Rahbare Enghelab, Leader of the Revolution. A chamber of horrors, full of demons and greed, is reflected in his lined face.

The fat comrade from Ilam arrived shortly after our leaders were jailed to seek refuge in our house, bringing with him the news that I will now take back to our local group. There are only a few of us left, sitting on the rug of the former drawing room and smoking nervously. The fat comrade takes quick drags as he explains, We've put the occupation of the barracks on hold for the time being, because we need to restructure. I blink as slowly and knowingly as I can, and say, Well, in light of the current situation, that seems sensible. And I think that only a month has passed, one month in this house and the surrounding fields, and we may have had guns in our hands, but all we've done is sit and talk, again, while in the rest of the country — apart from the areas we're fighting over — the propaganda of a religious system has become normality and we have become the new bogeyman. The fat man reeks of cold ash; he has probably dropped ash in his scarf, as so often happens with simple people.

At a stroke, I feel tired. Most comrades left our house quickly, in something of a panic. And it was then that I became aware of how many children there were among us. In nearby houses, true, but they were still part of the occupation. And children should really be protected from this kind of thing. They shouldn't be in the movement, shouldn't have to start fighting for their future yet. I can't imagine the children and adults travelling back to the cities after living in this house. They will never be able to sleep soundly again; I can't imagine that any one of us will live without a gun now. We were ready. We are ready.

The fat man says we should move on to new operations, and we haven't been preparing in vain. Then he says what I was already thinking. Comrade Behzad, he says to me, and his tone gives me an instant image of how he sees me: as a significant, strong, radical martyr. As you know, he says, it will be impossible for many of us to return to our old lives. Of course, I say, and my voice no longer sounds like a teacher, more like a company director, a bank manager, a politician, someone who is secretly afraid but knows how to hide it from laymen. The fat man is important, it's true, and well-read since the Revolution, but he is a layman when it comes to the expression of feelings, and that's lucky for me.

It's going to take a lot of time and energy to enable a few of us to live in the underground, he says. I nod, as if I'd already considered enabling a few of us to live in the underground a hundred times before. Anyone living in the underground is worth their weight in gold for the movement. We can deploy you and your comrades anywhere; you won't be missed, and you can do work for the movement and make it look like a normal job to outsiders, without drawing attention. You can be there for the movement twenty-four hours a day. I nod, still not looking at him.

I heard about the rumours in your neighbourhood, the fat man says casually, stubbing out his cigarette. There's no better way to go underground than to have people think you're dead, he says. And that's exactly what I've been thinking, too. And that's the point at which I don't dare pursue that line of thought any further. A jumble of sentences that I have put together for myself and the others over the last few months swirls around my head. I nod and say, Yes, that's worth considering, and the fat man nods, too, and heads off into the hubbub of farewells, into the uncertainty that hangs in the smoky rooms of the former landowner.

Everyone always used to come to weddings. My siblings, aunts, uncles, Peyman's siblings, aunts, uncles, Sohrab's siblings, aunts, uncles, the neighbours, their friends, and the friends' neighbours. Weddings were like festivals, holidays when everyone had a good time because everyone else was having a good time, and somewhere in their midst would be the bride and groom. But all that seems worlds and light-years away, when I look outside or even just at the newspaper. Now celebrations are quiet, celebrations are simple.

Only a few people come, and anything too flamboyant is avoided. The bride's hair is loose, combed, centre parting, no make-up; her dress is plain and white. Sohrab is wearing a beige suit, a shade lighter than mine, and new. The tailor who used to sew our school uniforms made it for him. We are sitting in Sohrab's parents' apartment; the few armchairs and bookcases have been moved temporarily to our house to make room for all the guests, and the bare walls are hung with little sprigs of blossom, pink flowers that the florist on the corner sells, for which he is finding fewer and fewer takers. We laugh softly, as if we have something to hide. As if someone might catch us doing something forbidden. Because it wouldn't surprise anyone if they banned marriage now as well. If the instruction came: *Citizens of this land, brothers in the revolution, cease starting families! May this country grow, but consider the immorality of copulation, avoid marriage, avoid the opposite sex.*

Sohrab, who actually did try to avoid the opposite sex, is now smiling quietly as he wears the ring his bride placed on his finger. He was quiet and abashed, too, when her sisters held the white cloth over their heads, the guests applauded, and his mother rubbed two sugar loaves over them. A sweet life for the happy couple. Never before had wedding guests looked so resolute at this point in the ceremony.

Sohrab had fallen in love quietly, married quietly, and it was in a quiet voice that he told me he was afraid. And I said quietly, Yes, of course, fear is our constant companion, it rocks me to sleep and it wakes me every morning. Sohrab nodded, a mournful expression on his face. I could have said I was happy for him, but that wouldn't have been true. I wished he had stayed faithful to the Revolution, and I wished I was the one marrying my chosen bride, putting the ring on her finger, looking into her contented eyes. Sohrab's bride, one of his sister's former classmates, is shy and educated. Her parents have money, and she has nothing to do with politics. Sohrab fell in love, asked her older siblings and then her parents for her hand in marriage, and then, once everything was settled, negotiated, and decided, he confessed to me that from now on, he wanted to take care of his family. I wasn't surprised. Not just because of his altered beard, which I'd noticed that evening on the roof. But also because of his fear, which he was increasingly incapable of hiding, and which seemed to be growing as the rules became more restrictive again.

Two months ago, when I and the others were occupying the country house, Sohrab was on summer holidays, too, and it would have been easy for him to come and join us. Sohrab didn't join us; at first, he didn't explain why, and then later he told me about his fiancée. Since the Revolution, all our decisions have had consequences, and Sohrab decided to put his new family first.

Sohrab's parents seem tired. Our parents look weak and fragile, I think, and we look as if we don't yet know whether to despair or to keep waiting patiently. Peyman is taking photos. In those rare moments when a smile creeps over people's faces, he presses the shutter release. He was the first person I went to see when I got back from the house, the first I wanted to tell about all that had happened in those weeks. Because, although the struggle might have needed me, I was longing for someone familiar. I'm not dead, I wanted to tell Peyman, forgetting that this is something you don't need to say. Not only because I was standing there in front of him, but also because Peyman knew already. Contacts had informed him, so that he could reassure Dayeh and my father. Nothing attracts more attention than your family searching for you.

Peyman asked no questions when I told him about the occupation, the arrests, and what followed. Nor did Peyman ask questions when I told him about potential underground operations. And when he still said nothing, I said, Peyman, I think I'm in love. And then his face changed, he looked at me and laughed and said, Oh, comrade, I've known that for a long time. Then I had to laugh, too, because I'd only known it since I went to the country house, since I'd stood on the roof and been unable to stop murmuring her name, and it was only then that I'd realised it was possible, alongside the struggle and alongside the belief in victory, to start believing in love as well.

And do you want to get married, too? Peyman asked, and, just to cheer him up, I said, Yes, I think so. Are you expecting her to go underground as well, out of love for you? he then asked with a laugh, getting up to look for something in a drawer. There were some photos on his table, and one of them was of me, Dayeh, my father, and the little ones, in the corner of our living room, on the rug, the fruit bowl in front of us piled with large, round oranges. Peyman had taken it when he was there for dinner, when he'd claimed that not even his own mother could cook as well as mine. The other photos on the table were of Peyman's parents, sitting by the well in their yard, and of him with his arm around his mother. But he had taken down the photos of him and his brother Amin that used to hang on the wall. Peyman finished rummaging in the drawer and pulled out two things. A photo of Nahid and a small pistol. Go ahead and get married, comrade, he said; I'll take care of the underground fight for you.

But today he is taking pictures for Sohrab's new wife's photo album. Pictures for her parents, who are losing a daughter and gaining another picture frame in the living room and an educated son. Meanwhile, the Revolution is sacrificing a fighter and my circle of friends a bachelor. Meanwhile, Peyman is hiding his face behind the oversized camera. Comrade Ghader is now providing him with weapons.

But I haven't told Peyman anything about the conversation with Ghader's little brother, or about his death, and I haven't broached the subject of the rumours about Amin.

Evening after evening, Peyman's mother would weep. Evening after evening, she and her husband would come to my parents' house. They had always thought the Ayatollah would be guarantee enough that their Amin wouldn't make any mistakes. Their little Amin, who since the Revolution has finally found his calling and stopped lazing around. They'd felt honoured to have a son who renounced vices and the West and chose to pray. Thought he would be in good hands with the believers. Now he's carrying out death sentences in the name of Allah, and no court in the land is going to stop him. At first, this was just something the neighbours said, having heard it from sources who wanted to remain nameless. Then Amin himself was heard claiming that opponents of the Revolution deserved to die, and certain death was in his hands alone. No court in the land is going to stop him, because every court has declared it lawful to kill the opposition. Peyman's and Amin's parents might be simple folk, but they still know that all this cannot be the will of any god, and they said as much to my mother every evening. Then eventually they stopped coming to our house.

Sohrab's bride is sitting with her sisters and girlfriends. They look modest and beautiful, with children wearing suits and sparkling dresses sitting on their laps. Nahid is among them, and I hardly dare look at her. Since our movement's meetings have become less frequent and more dangerous, we have seen less of each other, too. Although, following my return, I actually gave her one of the letters, one of those I did write down after all. When I look at her, because I can't help it, because there is no other face in this room and this country that I want to look at so much, she quickly looks elsewhere, as if her head had never been turned to this corner of the room where I am sitting and waiting, and there is a little smile on her lips, as intelligent and proud as the rest of her. I should have written down every one of those letters I composed in my head and given them to her, I think. Tomorrow, after dinner, when Dayeh has washed up and Father has had his nap, I will get them to take tea with me in another room and ask them to come and visit Nahid's parents with me. Her eyes wander back to me and at once she blushes, and we look down in mutual embarrassment, at our shoes — smart shoes, not the ones we wear on the streets.

1989
Nahid

We hid the books under her skirt. The Old Persian poems and the political manifestos, Maxim Gorky's works and the children's stories by Samad Behrangi. This stately old lady, whose hand I sometimes kissed, before whom I always stooped a little so I wouldn't be taller than her, whose hand always trembled in mine — and I couldn't tell Behzad; he needed to see for himself that his mother's hand trembled, always. His mother, who always smelled of carnations, always had a blessing on her lips, always tugged hard at my hand to kiss it, and we both knew she shouldn't do that, and that I should have been firmer and not allowed it, not dishonoured myself, but her small, wrinkled hand was strong, and sometimes she pulled so hard that she managed it anyway, and I would quickly kiss her hand, quickly kiss it and say, Thank you, kheyli mamnun, thank you. Her face — I still picture it so vividly, every day, as though I still saw her every day, as though nearly a thousand days hadn't passed without her. Without her, without her house, without the others. How close I was to her, as she sat in her chair in the yard, in front of the fire. I felt her breath, her warmth, smelled her scent, as I gradually hid the books under her skirt, so the neighbours wouldn't notice if they looked into the yard and recalled the Ayatollah's instruction to denounce anyone who kept counter-revolutionary thought on their shelves. They even class Saadi and Hafez as counter-revolutionary. The corncobs lay beside the fire, the alibi corncobs, and to this day cooking corn on the cob makes me think of Behzad's mother, because these alibi corncobs looked at me, gleaming dully and as pure and as yellow as could be, and told me they would not be eaten today and these were strange times we were living in. Just then, Behzad's mother burned the first book; she burned Shamlou, the poems of Shamlou, and the flames seemed to grow hotter, more scorching, painful. *These are strange times, my dear, they smell your breath to see if you have spoken of love* — Behzad had read it aloud to me so often. The smoke burned my eyes, everything was burning, and Behzad's mother looked at me from under the long black cloth that covered her henna-red hair, looked at me and whispered, Natars, azizam — have no fear, my darling. She didn't look away as her hand ripped out the pages, and I went back into the house, where my little Morad was crying, where we were trying to keep my clever Laleh from noticing anything.

Behzad drinks beer on evenings like this. He holds the bottle as if he needs to hide the label, clinks it against Walter's and

Ulla's, and takes a large swallow. He looks strange drinking from the narrow bottleneck; he doesn't tilt his head back, and appears oddly strained.

Drinking beer doesn't seem like something that takes up any space in Walter and Ulla's heads. Ulla has her knitting out and is creating complex patterns. The colours of her wool clash with the colours of the waxed tablecloth, and with the colours of the plastic chairs, and the balls of wool are lying in the grass and will probably start to get damp soon. I've never liked knitting. I could spend the mornings on it listening to the radio, the afternoons on it in front of the television; I could knit jumpers for the children, learn patterns, invite Ulla round for tea so she could show me. Ulla speaks very slowly, and not just with us — she always speaks slowly, even when she's talking to Walter. She would explain it to me patiently, and she would be as kind as she was with the children when she made straw stars with them a few months ago. Ulla and the children were sitting at the table when I came to collect them, and Laleh was proud. She looked like a little Ulla, like a woman in a body that was much too small, much too slight, and I wonder what I would look like if Ulla taught me to knit. Ulla is knitting slowly but beautifully, a little red jumper with black polka dots. I haven't asked her, but I suspect it's for Laleh's birthday. Just as she made the children jumpers for their birthdays last year. They are running about on the grass — there is so much space here for grass and trees and flowers — and calling out to one another, German sentences that come quite naturally from Laleh's lips and that Morad tries to copy.

I am a woman with two children for whom all people knit things, I think, and I glance at Behzad, who is deep in conversation with Walter. Walter has finally left the reeking barbecue alone, waiting until the fire has died down a bit, and is on his third beer while Behzad is still drinking his first. He doesn't speak as slowly as Ulla. Little beads of sweat drip from his bald head, and in conversation he uses technical terms whose meaning I have to try and recall before I can follow what he's saying. Behzad nods. I don't know how much he understands. He tells Walter that the GDR has missed an important point in time, just like the Soviet Union. I always understand him when he talks; I can understand anyone with a Persian accent perfectly when they're speaking German. All Germans should speak with a Persian accent.

Ulla's eyes are fixed on Behzad, concentrating on him as she knits, taking a brief drag on her cigarette from time to time. She is an astonishingly fast smoker. Why on earth does she wear her hair so short? I think, watching her out of the corner of my eye. Such a beautiful face, such a beautiful woman, but why that haircut? We used to have the Beatles cut — we would go to the hairdresser and say, Beatles cut, please, and now we laugh at the photos. But Ulla's haircut is like a man's, not like ours in the photos. Like a boy, a student maybe.

In Germany, I can spot students at a glance, while all the other demographics look too much alike for you to be able to recognise a teacher or a labourer. In Iran, I could tell a person's class instantly. In Germany, they look like they all belong to one big class. I have an image in my mind of Behzad, as we sat in our first apartment in Tehran and talked late into the night about our plans for the future. He proclaimed things like, The West is the epitome of capitalism — either you're too poor to feed your children, or you have more money than it's possible to spend in one lifetime. In West Germany, *this capitalist giant of production and export* as Behzad called it, I kept my eyes open and thought actually, no one here looks very rich or very poor, and actually all the groups here look very similar, in the way they dress, in their habits. The men who sit on the pavement outside the department store drink beer, just like Walter and Ulla. In capitalism, the poor man is too poor and the rich man too rich, Ghader used to say, back in Tehran. And Behzad always believed what his comrade Ghader believed, and forgave him all his arrogance. Because Ghader was older, because Ghader had been in the movement longer than Behzad and me. I imagined Germany as a place you saw in old films, like *Oliver Twist*, like *Little Lord Fauntleroy*. No one here is genuinely struggling to survive, I said, when I realised that — of course — these films bear no resemblance to reality. We live in a small town here, Behzad shot back, this part is very rural, you don't see the differences as clearly as you would in the big cities.

But the difference I do see straight away is between normal people and students, the young men and women who look like they've always had a lie-in, as if the rhythm of their day is made up of studying phases and cooking phases and communal-eating phases. And phases when they can hide away in the world of their books. The university is an opaque building. Men and women go to seminars together, like we used to; they get on the bus together, with me and my children; they go back to their flats together and then they cook together, too. It's nice to watch them, on the bus, laughing and having discussions, lighting cigarettes as they get off, greeting one another with little hugs. I imagine being one of them — I imagine that a few years ago, after the Revolution, when all the universities were closed, I was simply living here with them already, with a book bag and a student bus pass. I'd be in my early twenties, and weigh forty-seven kilos, and dye my hair with L'Oréal, not henna.

Ulla leans over to me. I read an article about this book, she tells me, speaking as slowly and softly as she always does. I nod so that she'll go on, nod so that she'll see I consent to us withdrawing from the men's conversation to have one of our own. It's about this woman, an American, Ulla tells me, who has an Iranian husband. Sometimes I wonder whether Ulla always talks about Iranian people because she thinks it's the only way to interest me in what she's saying, or whether this is what she's interested in herself. It always makes me feel a little odd, like someone is serving up a dish made specially for me and expecting me to enjoy it. And although I never quite understand her enthusiasm for these stories and feel odd as she's telling them, I am still grateful for every conversation she starts with me.

The Iranian guy, Ulla goes on, was a doctor, he'd been to university in America, he was an educated man, and the two of them went to Iran because the American wife wanted to get to know the country. I nod again, because what is there to say about American women who want to know our country.

Ulla pauses, not smoking or knitting, she is very focused, summarising the content of the article for my benefit, and I don't know where this article is heading, but I get the feeling that I don't understand its topic at all — I know nothing, it's something I learned at school and then forgot. In America, the husband was always nice and good-natured, they had a young daughter, but the minute they got to Iran he showed his true face, Ulla says. I don't know if I'm imagining it, but for a moment her eyes drift over to Walter and Behzad. *True face*, I think, such a lovely turn of phrase in such an otherwise uninteresting language. I always thought it was only Persian that relied on these metaphors. Ulla goes on: The husband wanted to keep his wife and child there; he would have let the wife go, but he wanted to keep their daughter with him, and he beat his wife and coerced her and locked her up.

I look at Ulla. She is telling me a tragic story of separation on a day that is sunny, sunny and cold, a spring day when we are sitting outside in scarves and coats. It makes me think of my mother's neighbour, whose husband was constantly beating her, coercing her and locking her up, of my brother-in-law's sister, whose husband was constantly beating her, coercing her and locking her up. I think about them both having happy marriages and successful children, loving and respecting their husbands, and being neighbours who welcomed people into their homes. My eyes, too, drift over to Walter and Behzad, more to Walter than Behzad. Walter is forceful and loud, and sometimes he gets angry at Ulla for interrupting him. I'm sure he isn't one of these pacifists; in his study, which is filled with stacks of newspapers and books, he has the emblem of the left-wing German terrorist group up on the wall.

The wife, says Ulla, wrote a book about it that was a big hit in the States. Where is she now? I ask. An obvious question, which comes out of my mouth with a strange melody to it. Ulla looks at me as if she's proud of me for noticing that she's left this part of the story out. She fled in secret, with her daughter, and they're in America now. Fled, just like that? I ask. Without the husband? Because that's impossible, that can only be a story invented by Americans, who have no clue about the laws of the Islamic Republic of Iran. A woman can't leave the country without her husband's permission. Yes, says Ulla, I don't know exactly how she did it, either, but they're back living in America now, and the woman wrote this book about it. My friend bought it; I'm going to borrow it and read it, and if you like I can lend it to you, too.

The only German books I've read are children's books, which Behzad brought home because that's how you learn the language. A Nigerian man in his German course told him that. So does he speak good German? I asked, and Behzad said, He doesn't talk very much. In the mornings when Laleh was at school and Morad at kindergarten, when the TV was just showing repeats of programs that had already bored me the day before, I looked at the books. Books about animal children who are like humans, and books about human children who play detective. Erich Kästner, Behzad explained, was a great opponent of the Nazis, and I can tell from his tone that he doesn't know any more than this one fact. This book isn't about Nazis in any case; it's just about little children who are constantly shouting the name of a boy. I was the one who read the whole book, struggling through the unwieldy language to the end and realising that the feel of a smooth book cover in my hands and the act of flicking through the pages had lost their magic thanks to the German sentences.

Wait a sec, says Ulla, I'll get the article for you, and she stands up, and at once I stand up as well to take the plates and the fruit peelings inside. Ulla doesn't take anything with her. She marches ahead of me in her gumboots, wearing them into the house although the grass was damp, although she leaves footprints. I put the plates down in the kitchen, not daring to wash them up. I would like to take the plastic cloth and wipe the sink dry, sweep the crumbs from the long, thin loaf of bread she cut earlier into my hand and throw them in the bin. Ulla hands me a magazine, a glossy magazine full of photos of German celebrities and actors, and heads wordlessly towards the toilet. I put the magazine into my handbag, which I have hung on the coat pegs, and wonder if I should wait for Ulla. I feel like an intruder, alone in her messy house that smells of wood and coffee. And so I go back outside, glancing at Laleh and Morad, who are sitting under the cherry tree and stroking the dog, putting their arms around his head, cuddling up to him. When we get home, I'll have to wash their hands, arms, and legs, and change their clothes, so they don't take the dog smell to bed with them.

The wind carries Behzad's voice to me; I would know

his voice among thousands, and when it reaches me it gives me that feeling of home that few things have been able to these past few years. It's only when he comes back from his German course or his casual jobs in the evening and I hear him through the wall, later on, telling the children bedtime stories — only then does our little flat become my home. I would love to know how the Germans see him. What they think of him.

Sometimes I imagine I am Ulla or Walter, seeing this Behzad for the first time after years of being surrounded by no one but Ullas and Walters. I try to hear him with ears that are used to different television, different radio, used to Helmut Kohls and Helmut Schmidts, ears that understand Nazi speeches, understand Goethe. But I can't do it. I look at Behzad, stare at him, hear him talking, and try to defamiliarise his words, his whole self. Then I can't help thinking of him ten years younger — ten years younger, badly shaved and with huge sideburns, thick black hair, and a deep, loud voice.

He used to listen to political discussions for hours without saying a word, and then he'd finally emit a long Khob — alright then — and all eyes would turn to him and he'd start slowly and deliberately summarising the arguments that had been put forward, cutting them down, weighing them up. His voice would grow louder as he spoke, not even seeming to realise that everyone was listening to him, as if a higher power had entrusted these words to him and him alone, or as if they were something he'd come up with for us and would put into action for us as well. When I think about that, I feel like my old self, I feel younger and thinner, light and lithe, I can feel my shoulder-length hair, the skin smarting beneath my freshly plucked eyebrows; I can smell Azar's shampoo beside me and feel her warmth, her fluttering breath. Then I feel my heart again, beating faster as he made his comments, so fast that later Azar claimed she could feel the vibration in her own ribs. Azar, who is younger than me, looks up to me, and yet was always a shoulder to lean on when she told me, with absolute conviction, that the modest, studious comrade over there kept looking in my direction, and that I should think myself happy.

And I couldn't fall asleep at night for fear that Azar might have been mistaken, or even worse, that he would never dare propose to me. Not because he could be shy, but because a true revolutionary doesn't harbour amorous feelings. How great was my relief when the two of us spoke alone for the first time, and talked not about socialism but just about him and me. When he asked me what my favourite books were, and I asked what his favourite food was, and we told each other about our families and siblings and made each other laugh with our hesitation. How great was my relief when I thought, What luck that not all left-wing men are hard-bitten, humourless fighters.

Walter opens another beer on the edge of the beer crate, makes some claim at which he then roars with laughter, and Behzad laughs, too, a brief, loud laugh, too brief and too loud, and I know very well it isn't politeness that has induced this artificial laugh; he just hasn't understood Walter's joke. He has let his facial hair grow again, his moustache, which is gradually turning grey. While Walter has gone bald, Behzad's moustache is turning grey and droops over his upper lip. When he shaved it off, so he wouldn't be recognised, Morad ran away from him.

You can't explain to a one-year-old that his parents are known as communists and so they have to live under a false name in someone else's apartment. Nor can you explain to a one-year-old why you are packing your suitcases and leaving the country. You can't even explain such a thing when the children are three and six, I think, looking over at the tree beneath which the two of them are sitting, still stroking the matted dog. Back then, when Behzad disguised himself by going clean-shaven, both he and I were surprised to find we liked it better, but Morad's fear of his own father was reason enough to let it grow back, as soon as it seemed safe to do so.

How can Walter and Ulla look at Behzad and not know the story of that moustache? And not know that the belly bulging under Behzad's thick woollen jumper doesn't come from beer, but from buttery rice and dripping barbecued meat, and stews that sometimes have to simmer all day? That his hands, resting on that belly, once held cigarettes, one after another, until Laleh was in my belly and later Morad, and then they never did again?

Ulla comes back, sits down beside me, resumes her smoking, resumes her knitting.

She interrupts Behzad, asks questions that he tries to answer, and my eyes roam across the garden, past the children and the dog. Walter and Ulla live on the road out of town, surrounded by cornfields and farms. They cycle to the shops because all the country roads around here are so flat that cycling is no effort. We were spending a day in the woods with the children when we first met Walter and Ulla. We had to find three specific leaves for Laleh's kindergarten project, without ever having learned anything about trees ourselves. We were standing under a tree looking at a German encyclopaedia and a dictionary when the two of them walked past with their dog, and used every gesture they could think of to ask if they could help. The speed at which the three leaves were found, and at which we learned the words sycamore, birch, oak, were matched only by the warmth they both showed us from the very start, inviting us for coffee at their house for the first time and at regular intervals from then on.

Bertolt Brecht, it was Brecht who wrote that poem, Ulla says, rousing me from my thoughts. Behzad thinks for a moment and concedes, Yes, Brecht not Tucholsky. Walter and Ulla nod eagerly, very eagerly, because Behzad has mentioned Brecht and Tucholsky. We studied that poem at school, Ulla tells us, and Behzad asks, So you're allowed to read Brecht in West Germany, too? Yes, well, that's how it is here, Walter replies. You pick up the things you like, no matter where you stand politically. Then he adds, Behzad — stressing the second syllable and drawing it out and making a great effort to pronounce it properly — Behzad, things here aren't as hostile as you might think, especially not when it comes to culture. Behzad nods.

Behzad always nods, and it's only when we get home that he tells me whether he thinks what was said is true or false, what he might dispute, if he felt like disputing, where the weaknesses were in someone's argument, and what they unwittingly revealed about German society. In the beginning, when we first got to know Ulla and Walter, I thought: he wants to build trust with these people first of all, see where they stand, if it's worth arguing with them, and if both he and they would benefit from it. Now we've known Ulla and Walter for a year, and Behzad still holds his tongue, still prefers to talk to me later and argue against me as if I was Walter, as if I shared his views.

Behzad goes on talking about the poem: I read it for the first time here in Germany, he says; I didn't know it before, though we often read Brecht in our theatre group. I see Ulla and Walter following his words. They must be thinking Behzad is a perfect Iranian version of them. He was obviously going to talk about the theatre group, because he knows how interesting they find these things. Obviously going to start talking about Brecht and Tucholsky. I would never have the nerve to speak about German writers in front of Ulla and Walter.

Walter laughs longer than the others, claps Behzad on the shoulder and roars, Oh yes, *you* people know these things, *you* know them, Behzad, but you'll have to tell my comrades, because they've forgotten them. Ulla shakes her head as she slowly knits on, giving a black polka dot another row of black stitches, and repeats the word *comrades* under her breath. Walter glances at her and then says, Behzad, don't go thinking the police are always friendly here, we have plenty of problems with them, and Walter and Ulla exchange looks. Walter tells us about campaigns where they occupied streets and railway lines because of nuclear energy, and were then forcibly carried away. Ulla and Walter have been telling stories like this as long as we've known them. At the start, I didn't understand what exactly this was about; they kept talking about Chernobyl, and I assumed they'd written an academic paper on it. But Behzad told me later it was activism; they were against the use of nuclear energy in civil society. Where were you carried off to? I ask, moving for the first time in what feels like hours. Suddenly all eyes turn to me. There is a pause, and then Walter says, To the other side. Further away from the tracks. And what did they do with you then? I ask. If they carry you away, to the other side, do you then just stay there, on the other side? is what I don't dare ask. Well, that was all; they could have taken down our names and addresses, but they didn't, says Walter. I wish I had some knitting I could look at now.

They have everything in this country, Behzad said to me recently. There's no reason to be political — what are they supposed to revolt against? I could have said, Yes, but they *do* have capitalism in this country, which is stealing from them, and why does no one revolt against the Federal Republic exploiting its workers? Surely they should be shouting and fighting back? But Behzad was speaking in such a long, drawn-out tone that I had no desire to remind him of the arguments they had all slung at me back then, when I dared to say that a free-market economy can bring progress, if it's managed carefully. How embarrassed he'd been that I, his wife, had said such a thing, and how long he had spent going on at me until I eventually conceded that all people were equal and their earnings should be equal, too. When you say a thing like that, no one can dispute it.

I don't believe they don't have any problems in this country. They're always talking about the GDR, where everyone has relatives of some kind and so many things are not allowed. But here, people like Behzad and me are stuck in reception centres, where you aren't allowed to work or study or do anything else. They don't even wonder at the people who collect money in paper cups outside McDonald's, when this country has such a strong economy. Behzad is definitely wrong on this point: there is a reason to be political; there's just no sense of urgency.

Ulla has turned to talk quietly to me again. She is telling me about her women's group, and the mothers' union who were concerned for their children after Chernobyl. Well, none of us knew what we could allow our children to have and what we couldn't, and how we might be putting them at risk, she explains. From one day to the next, you couldn't feed your own vegetables to your children. Ulla doesn't have any children. Her sisters do, and she cares deeply for them. She reminds me of Azar putting Laleh to bed and telling her stories for hours. I knew from the start that Laleh would never fall asleep listening to Azar's stories, because Laleh was clever enough to know that the longer she stayed awake, the more stories she'd hear, and that Azar's stories were much more exciting than Behzad's. Azar made up her own stories, so they were new every time. But Azar enjoyed it, and her stories went on and on until she fell asleep herself. Every summer, Ulla would set up an encampment for her nieces and nephews in the garden, and sing songs with them. When she told them ghost stories around the camp fire, the children hung on her every word.

I could join the women's group, too, she says; after all, Laleh and Morad are growing up in this air as well, which is polluted because all the politicians think about is money. I nod and think that Laleh and Morad are never going to die from this air. Even if it were to kill every last niece and nephew in the Federal Republic, my Morad and my Laleh have survived too many other things to be finished off by a little money-air. I say I don't know when I'll find the time: we're still active with the Iranians in exile. That isn't quite true, but I don't want to tell Ulla I have no desire to join her women's group. That I'm ashamed at her women's group and would feel terrible about joining their campaigns. I imagine Azar and my other friends frowning and saying, Nahid, is that really what women's activism means to you? Talking to other women about vegetables and air?

And your friend, Walter is asking, who went to prison? Do you have any contact with him, or is it too dangerous? Ulla turns her attention back to the men's conversation at once, as it promises to get interesting, and it hurts to see Behzad suddenly lower his eyes. Walter wouldn't ask that if he hadn't been drinking; he seldom asks direct questions about difficult things. It's pointless to answer questions when the person asking isn't in his right mind, and you shouldn't have to do it.

We shouldn't be so polite; Behzad shouldn't have to search for words to give Walter an answer. It's been weeks since we last heard from Peyman.

The last time we saw Peyman, we were talking, for the first time in ages, about the war. It had been raging for six years, and we had grown frighteningly used to it. Behzad and I had put the little ones to bed, and we were sitting in the living room of our alibi flat. I said that the war was dulling people's minds, and if the Islamic regime wasn't such a bloodthirsty, dangerous regime, then the war might have had some advantage: we'd have more courage now, and people would be persecuting us less, because you don't expect revolt in a nation that is waging war, and Behzad agreed. But neither of us really considered exactly what that meant for us, because we'd have had to ask ourselves that question every day, and I guess that was why we never asked it at all during this time, this strange time.

And then Peyman knocked at the door. The children were in bed, sleeping the blessed sleep that children do while their parents talk and all is well. Perhaps they slept like that for the last time that night, and are too young to tell us that from then on, they never slept the same way again. Peyman was quiet and polite, as always; he came in smiling, a little too hurriedly, and I offered him tea, which he took immediately and put down again immediately, to stand up immediately and then immediately sit back down. He gave us an uncertain smile and began to speak the dreaded words: Comrades, he explained, I don't have much time, I just came to show you the letter I received today. He held the letter out to Behzad; he looked brave and yet seemed ashamed as well, and Behzad took the letter and read it and nodded and folded it back up and asked, What will you do? Peyman, looking at his fingernails, said, There's no other choice, Behzad, I will go in three days' time as the letter says and serve my sentence.

Peyman swallowed, and I swallowed and thought, This is the moment. For years we've known that one day this would happen, and now it's all coming to that end we've been waiting for from the beginning, from the first protests, from the first visit to the villagers in the mountains, from the first evenings we spent singing revolutionary songs. I thought about our post always being delivered to Behzad's mother, because our address had to be kept secret, and I imagined her accepting the letter and doing her utmost to retain her proud posture in front of the postman. I was certain that no letter could have come for us today, or she would have told us when we called her this morning.

Behzad's expression was unchanged as he asked, What about fleeing the country? The organisation has helped others; why don't you flee, too? Peyman let out a bark of laughter, looked at us, still smiling, and said, It's too late. There's no legal way for me to take the overland route now, they've got lists of our names, and mine will be there, you can bank on it. A false identity takes too long and is too expensive, and anyway, Behzad, I have a wife and two children, how could I leave them here? And I asked, What about Simin, won't she go with you if you flee? Peyman looked at me and whispered,

You know how she is, she wouldn't survive that, she'll barely survive my absence, she isn't as strong as you are. And then he looked at his fingernails. It was unusual to see his face without a smile on it. Unusual, too, to see him without his beloved wife. Simin, the good-hearted woman who clung to Peyman, who never spoke a word in the presence of others, but when the two of us were alone together couldn't stop talking. Who nurtured the most progressive visions of our country's future behind her reticent, girlish exterior and who, when she didn't hear anything from Peyman for several days — as happened so often — promised me that she would strangle the clerics with her own hands if any harm had come to him.

Peyman cleared his throat and got up, then reached for his tea and drank it standing up. He said, I only came to say goodbye — and that it still isn't too late for you. The four of you could still take the overland route, Behzad, who knows how many days it will be before they find your name on some list, too. Khoda kone, he added, God willing, it will not be me who gives them names. He smiled awkwardly, looking at the floor, and I wanted to beg him to sit back down and drink his tea in peace and pretend we had never spoken of such things. Then Behzad and Peyman kissed one another, several times on each cheek. Behzad put his arms around Peyman and held him tight for a few seconds, and I was glad that the children were sleeping, that this scene playing out between Laleh's Baba and her Amu Peyman had escaped her watchful eyes. She didn't just call him Uncle out of politeness; he really was like an uncle to her. Because he talked to the children like he talked to adults: he was kind and took seriously the things they told him, as if the little ones were very wise people from whom he could learn. He had a real soft spot for Laleh, the first and oldest girl in our circle of friends, who all kept producing nothing but boys.

Look after yourself, Behzad told Peyman — it sounded like a throwaway remark — and then Peyman said, Look after *your*self. At least I know I have three whole days of freedom left, and you have no such security, comrade. His expression remained serious as Behzad laughed. We shook hands for a long time, Peyman and I, then Peyman gave me back the tea glass before putting on his shoes, his small, clean leather shoes, and once more he smiled before hurrying away into the darkness, as we closed the door quietly behind him.

Behzad and I were like abandoned children in our living room, which, although it was a hiding place arranged by the movement, was slowly becoming homely, with framed poems by Hafez and Rumi on the walls, and Laleh's paintings in among them. I clutched Peyman's tea glass, and as we sat down mechanically and the tears began to well up in my eyes, Behzad said, Nahid, this time we're going to do it right, this time we need to leave. Then finally we looked at one another, and in my mind's eye I could see all the situations in which Behzad and Peyman had sat in the midst of our friends, discussing things with serious faces. Peyman, the clever, quiet one, and Behzad, the one who called the shots, and the state probably didn't care which of them it threw into its dungeons first, but it would only be a matter of time before Behzad got a letter, too. And Behzad called the travel agent, bought four tickets for two adults and two young children, and was given a three-day wait and the prospect of a booking on the fourth. And I cleared up the tea things and washed the glasses and the plates from the children's supper.

Peyman tries to keep living his life, Behzad tells Walter and Ulla. To them, he probably sounds like he always does; only I can hear the pain in his voice, the same as when we were stuck in the reception centre with its walls covered in mould and drawings of naked women, and he called Dayeh to say, It's all fine, we're safe now, we made it. Behzad told her, Our East German comrades helped us get out of Istanbul, and then added a little more quietly, They sent us to the Federal Republic.

Behzad doesn't look at Walter and Ulla; he gazes over at the children. Peyman is strong, he says almost defiantly. If Peyman only knew his name was being spoken in this place, in the twilight of a cold spring day outside a messy house with a filthy dog. Doesn't he want to leave the country? Ulla asks. Isn't it much too dangerous for him there? And Behzad says, Yes, it's dangerous, but they'll manage, they're hoping for a development. He got the German word for that — Entwicklung — from me. We heard it often on the news, and I could see that he never understood the news when it involved that word. It took him a few days to ask, What does that mean, Entwicklung? And I explained it to him and tried to remember the other word I'd looked up that afternoon, a single word meaning gross domestic product, and I wished Azar was there so we could place bets on how many weeks

80

it would be before Behzad swallowed his pride and asked me about that, too.

It's madness, Ulla says, madness to stay in a country that locks you up and drives out your friends. Ulla looks from Behzad to me and back with an expression of horror, and to make her stop I try to look upset, and then we all fall silent.

A letter about Peyman arrived in winter. I was sitting at the window, looking out; the neighbours' windows were lit up with Christmas decorations. The year before, in the hostel, no one had had lights in their windows; it was only on the housing estate that I understood where all the light came from, and how important it seemed to be in this country. I was waiting for the yellow post van, like I did every morning, like a child on the morning of their birthday — the only difference being that sometimes there were no presents, that sometimes the van stopped outside our building, and I would wait, and a few minutes later I'd run down to the pigeonholes and find ours empty. But even then I knew it wasn't a bad sign; it just increased the chances for tomorrow. That day, there was an airmail envelope, and my heart leapt, though at the same time I knew that a letter today meant an empty pigeonhole and disappointment tomorrow. Unfamiliar handwriting on the envelope, familiar Persian characters, and Simin's name under 'sender'.

When Behzad got home, we read the letter a few times to consider what it might mean. A bomb, a prison, a hole in the wall, and Peyman on the run, living in the underground and waiting for everything to blow over. At least, that's what I read in Simin's letter, which spoke of a lightning strike, a crumbling wall in the backyard, and rats scuttering through the cracks and getting into her house. One rat hid stubbornly in her kitchen, enjoying a nice life of food and familial love, without Simin or her two sons ever catching sight of it. Her letter ended with the words, *Walls are crumbling everywhere, and they'll never stop!* Behzad and I read the letter together, again and again, and rejoiced like children when we agreed on its meaning. We recalled the news about the bomb hitting the prison, established that the date on the letter matched, and smiled for a long time and surreptitiously wiped tears from our eyes, though not many, and I said, Are you hungry? Behzad didn't eat in his usual position on the floor in front of his big, boxy radio, but at the kitchen table with the children, where for once he didn't ask about their homework. Instead, he let them sing him the advent songs they had learned at school and nursery, Laleh proud and conscientious, Morad babbling with his nose in the air. And they were both giddy with excitement, as if they'd understood the good news as well. It's a long time since we've heard anything of Peyman.

As we are saying our goodbyes, Ulla takes me aside. Hugs me tightly. She smells of lavender and slightly of beer, and her hand-knitted woollen jumper scratches my throat. They hug here and don't kiss, but Ulla hugs me and kisses me as well, and I kiss back as if doing both were a compromise, as if we're meeting in the middle. My dear, she says, it's high time we got together, just the two of us — if you'd like? I smile and say, Yes, of course, that would be lovely. She looks into my eyes, inches from my face and with such a serious expression that I want to look away, but that's impossible when someone is standing this close. You seem so absent today — is everything all right? she asks, and I'm aware that Behzad keeps glancing at us as he's putting on his shoes, as if he'd like to come closer and listen. Yes, yes, I reply, and Ulla says, If you want to talk, if anything's wrong, you can always come to me. I smile, and she announces, I'll pop round for coffee tomorrow, okay? I smile again and turn towards the door, to tie Morad's scarf properly and kiss the back of his soft, fragrant neck.

Later I will be annoyed with myself for not daring to ask at that moment when exactly she'll be coming, what time, and whether I should buy coffee or if she drinks black tea, because actually we never have coffee. While Walter is hugging me and I am turning back to the children and the door as quickly as possible, I wonder what *absent* means, a word I know from government officials — when they are on holiday, they're absent — and how do I appear absent to others? Especially on an evening when I've made every effort not to think about the unsettling feeling in my stomach and the fact that I've been putting off a doctor's visit for weeks.

Morad asleep in Behzad's arms, and Laleh holding my hand, rubbing her eyes. She is trying to keep up with us in her little white patent-leather shoes. We told Walter and Ulla we'd take a taxi, and then in wordless agreement set off on foot. It is pitch black and cold, like a winter's night. Their seasons are so interchangeable, Shirin told us in the hostel right at the beginning, when we first met her in the large dining room, and Behzad and I drew the same conclusions about her and her husband without saying anything. When we were still able to do that — to meet new people and categorise them, when we hadn't yet begun to move through the world like children, only distinguishing people by who is friendly and who isn't.

Shirin told us, The others say the seasons are all the same here, and without meaning to, we began to wait for what the others said. Whether the others had been given a council flat; whether it made sense to let people give you furniture, or if it was more dignified to buy even older furniture yourself at flea markets. When the others had their first interview to assess their claim, did they build their hopes up afterwards, or decide not to hope for anything? Had the others been rejected, too? Were they were also reading: ... *for the reasons cited above you do not have a right to political asylum in the Federal Republic of Germany.* Did the others also feel weak and exhausted after the decision, or did they say, Everyone gets rejected the first time, no one is accepted straight away, you've just got to go again, do the interview again, mention more names, tell more stories, maybe some lies as well, make up things that we all know could have happened to us, even if in reality they happened to our neighbours? The others have been through so much that was similar, and so much that was completely different, and we see them so rarely now. In the last few months, we've been to so few of the demonstrations and protests that we have lost track of where the other Iranians in exile are.

You were very quiet tonight, Behzad says to me, did you feel uncomfortable? And I say, No, I always feel comfortable at Walter and Ulla's, I was just cold. Behzad smiles: Yes, it was very cold, it isn't the time for sitting outside yet, and the meat was very fatty and still red in the middle, and I said, Yes, that's why I didn't finish mine. You've been eating so little lately, says Behzad. You've grown pale. I'm surprised he's noticed that I have no appetite, that I feel weak, too weak to eat. Behzad asks, Did I wake you last night? And I say, No. I slept heavily last night, surprisingly so, when usually even my own thoughts can wake me, and I'd done nothing but sit around the house all day — but in the evening, I was so tired that I fell asleep straight away and didn't wake until the morning.

I had bad dreams, Behzad says. I woke up and listened to the radio until it was time to go out. My eyes fall on Morad, who has laid his little face on Behzad's shoulder and is deep in a dream, his eyelids puffy and closed, far away from our conversation. I look at Laleh, who is taking large strides. I can see her thick, dark eyelashes from above as she looks at her feet and at our feet and tries to walk in step with us. What did you dream about? I ask, and Behzad says, The same dream again, and I say, Again. I feel fearful, feel my stomach clench with worry for Behzad. What do I do if Behzad can't go on?

What's on the radio at that time of day? I ask. No proper programs, just music, he says — I listened to the tape recordings again. I record the news for Behzad when he isn't there: if his language course runs late; if he manages to get work on building sites, off the books; when he's out. Persian-language newspapers are too expensive here, and so the news comes from the radio. From America, London, Israel. Iranians in exile report on the political situation in Iran, on the hour, on the half-hour, with various focuses and themes. I adjust my television-watching to Behzad's radio news, slot the black cassette into the black machine, switch it on and wait for the pips and the urgent voice of the newsreader, who presents the news in a cold, objective tone. Who wraps the familiar language of our parents and siblings, our aunts and cousins, our uncles and grandparents in a distant coldness, as if we may expect only bad news from him.

Sometimes I am overcome by the fear of recording bad news on the cassette, listening to it while Behzad is sitting at school desks with other adults. And so I turn the volume down, as if I'm doing it for the children's sake — they automatically fall silent, interrupt their games, sit still, as soon as the radio is on and their father wants to listen. They have developed a reverence for this talking box that I might have to explain to them one day. Maybe I should explain it to them now, but luckily they never ask. As if they've given up asking questions, and as if you can keep them from asking questions just by reading aloud to them as much as possible, painting with them, playing Concentration.

I imagine Behzad lying in the bare living room after his nightmare, listening to the news from three days ago, and I'm sorry for him, and I would like to take him in my arms, show him that I'm strong, that he just has to leave me to it. And

I save up all these thoughts for tomorrow morning, for my half-hour in bed.

Behzad asks, Why did you tell them we were still active with the Iranians in exile? I don't know, I reply, I didn't want to join Ulla's women's group but I thought it would be rude to say so. Saying we're active with them is the same as saying we approve of what they're doing, isn't it? Behzad asks me calmly and firmly, in a tone that reminds me of him as a young man. A young Behzad who had no Morad to carry, just a leather briefcase tucked under his arm and a cigarette in his hand, who let his sideburns grow and always tied his black cloth shoes with the red star on them neatly. I say, Behzad, I know, I know all these things, but I didn't want to hurt Ulla, I didn't want to turn her down without a proper reason.

Behzad gives me a little smile and says, I found some cassettes from last year and listened to them. I look at Laleh and realise she's not listening, that she is now stepping on every second paving slab, and so I ask, Which cassettes, where did they come from? I always record over the same cassette for him, I've been doing it for weeks, and Behzad says, I found them in the drawer with the slide-show photos, there was one from last year, and I listened to the news broadcasts and interviews, all the reporting from after the massacre, Nahid, it isn't all that long ago, and we act like it never happened — Peyman could have been among them. I say nothing, thinking, *we* could have been among them. A simple decision by a simple man, a simple Ayatollah is enough to have almost all the prisoners killed, just like that. Who is going to make the Revolution happen now? I think once again. Who will make the proper, real Revolution happen, if they've all been hanged?

But I say, Behzad, come on, we've spent enough time thinking about that. And Behzad says, The others, they haven't spent enough time thinking about it, your Iranians in exile, the ones you use as an excuse, they haven't thought about it at all, that's the whole problem. And I think about them, the others, who are also waiting for letters, also waiting for familiar handwriting, also listening to Radio Israel and the BBC, the others who put up the protest tent with us, *For the freedom of all political prisoners in Iran* was what the placards said, and back then we had to have it translated into German for us before we wrote them. They looked old, the women's hair was dyed, they wore tight leggings like me, and their children had grown, were pushing their own prams, and the Germans looked at us, and I wondered, What must they know already, and what are they only learning now? I had an image in my mind of the magazines that Ulla had showed me, the colour pictures of the Shah, an image of Ulla laughing and telling me she'd hung on to them because that's where she and Walter met, at the student protests against the Shah and the Nazis in the universities. Ulla always giggles when she talks about Those Days, as if the protests had just been two young people meeting and not something the Germans could chalk up as an attempt at revolution, at least.

Shortly after the survivors from the prisons went public, we were standing with the others in the large, colourful square in the capital, having travelled the three hundred kilometres there in an overheated coach. We had wrapped

Morad in several blankets in his pushchair, and prepared Laleh for a demonstration for the first time in a long while. We told her that when a lot of people want to change something, they all go out onto the streets together, and then they're strong, stronger than they are alone, and she looked contentedly at the crowd. I inhaled the air and tried to make it taste like it used to, tried to feel like I used to, like a twenty-year-old at my first protests, with their pervasive scent of new beginnings and possibility. But the air smelled of Germans, who had stopped caring if they still had Nazis in their universities, who looked at us and looked away, who were probably still carrying the image of the good-looking Shah and his expensively dressed wife in their heads. Just as I always see the image of the Führer and the image of arms extended in salute when I think of their capital city.

Behzad was sitting at a table covered in flyers and pictures, making conversation. He looked young and level-headed, and Laleh was excited and quickly found other children to speak Persian and laugh and play tag with, and I saw the creases between Behzad's thick eyebrows, saw him sitting with his hands folded between his knees, on the very edge of the chair, watching the passers-by. His cheeks, which had begun to sag wearily, his hair with its grey gleam, his moustache, which he had not shaved off. But no people came; he had answers at the ready, but no one asked any questions.

And so Behzad spent most of his time talking to the man sitting next to him, who used to be in our movement as well. His wife had been captured not long after the Revolution, and tortured to extract the names of other opposition members, but she'd resisted right to the end. One of the first women to be killed by the Islamic regime. They're even killing women now, Azar had said when we heard the news. She didn't give them any names, I said. Protected her husband. Her husband, who was then sent to prison himself years later and since then has been skinnier than is right for a man. Whose asylum application the Germans granted immediately, after a psychological evaluation. Sometimes I think we could all use a psychological evaluation; then we would all get our asylum applications granted immediately. Behzad talked to him, and I went for a walk carrying Morad, talked to the other women, learned where they got their saffron from, and that there was a cheap shop that sold good children's clothes, and told them about my father, whose name we gave to Morad, and who died not long after the Revolution, and suddenly everyone was talking about their fathers.

In the coach on the way home, when the children had fallen into an exhausted sleep, Behzad whispered, so he wouldn't wake them, Nahid, they didn't understand, they think things would have been better under the Shah, they didn't understand that spilled blood is never better or worse, fair or unfair, Nahid, they just didn't understand. And the coach kept moving, and Laleh woke up and was sick, and it reminded me of when we took the bus to Tabriz, in the hope we could disappear and head for Istanbul, but soon came back.

Your Iranians in exile haven't given it enough thought, Behzad repeats now, as we walk through the cold night.

They don't learn from their mistakes, one day they want communism and the next they want the Shah, they'll never learn that there will always be blood. I say, But communism brings bloodshed, too, Behzad, let's not kid ourselves about that. And he says, Yes, Nahidjan, why isn't the goal simply no blood, ever again, just no more blood? I'd rather you came up with a different excuse next time you don't want to do something with Ulla — don't associate yourself with these people. He sounds a little like the young Behzad again as he says this, and I think that next time I'll lower my voice more so he can't overhear.

We walk for a while, Laleh's clumsy leather shoes clacking on the pavement. She isn't hopping from one paving slab to the next anymore, and I wonder when she stopped and whether she stopped because she was listening, or because she's tired. We walk through the darkness, and I feel a longing for our little flat, which somehow always smells of paint, where the television produces an electric haze when we haven't been there for a long time; where I feel the children are protected in their room; where Behzad and I huddle together in our small wooden bed because the radiators don't work. And again, the thought that our flat has nothing to hide from the other flats — I'd rather live there than in Ulla and Walter's house, which smells of wood and mildew and cellar and dog. They haven't broken us down as much as we sometimes think, as much as the others sometimes say.

A man comes towards us, an older man with a grey beard in a threadbare winter coat. The hood droops over his forehead, and beneath its fur trim he is slurring and singing. I tighten my grip on Laleh's hand, and her little face peers up at him in fascination and puzzlement. The man stops and looks at us, all four of us, one after the other; he stops slurring, makes a deft bow with his arm across his belly, and calls out, Salam Alaykum. Then he giggles in a high, hoarse voice and Behzad stops, makes a deft bow with the sleeping Morad in his arms, and responds, Alaykum Salam, and the older man keeps walking, and Behzad laughs, and it makes me laugh, too, and the man keeps walking in the other direction, singing, and I only stop laughing when I see that Laleh is looking up at us, sad and bewildered.

So, half an hour from now: wake the children, get them washed, give them breakfast, and in an hour's time: leave the flat, take the children downstairs to the neighbours' cars and kiss their tired faces. In two hours, then: wait for the post van, and in three hours: wash and soak the rice. Another nine hours and twenty minutes until the latest episode of *The Bold and the Beautiful*.

Behzad was awake before the alarm today, woke me with his kisses, on my forehead and my hair, and I wished the alarm would never go off, never emit its buzz into the silent dark, never throw its orange light onto our bedcovers, never make Behzad stretch out his arm and press the large plastic button. If the alarm hadn't gone off, I could have believed there was no world beyond our narrow bed. I could have closed my eyes and imagined the cold language outside the windows didn't exist. Only the little souls slumbering in the next room and

Behzad's arm and his breath in my ear. Only the veins that show through the skin, only the pulsing beneath me. Only the thick, black hair on his body, only the head resting against my throat, the head that comes up with all these clever thoughts, the cleverest thoughts in the world, all the things that could save the world, that one day *will* save the world, one day, I'm sure of it.

My mind is like the display of video cassettes in the big department store: I can pick out individual tapes and watch them. Videos of our wedding. Azar doesn't have a husband yet, or a son; Behzad's neighbour Sohrab is sitting playing cards with the older men; his wife has pinned up her long, gleaming hair. Behzad's mother wipes the tears of joy from her eyes, and mine sits on her cushion like it's a throne. They clap and laugh and sing for us. The video cuts to supper at Behzad's family home; his little brothers have not yet become criminal adults, and the older ones have come to visit with their smartly dressed children. There is always someone with children, and there is always someone playing marbles with the children; it's always noisy, and one of Behzad's brothers always manages to sleep despite all this, in a corner of the room, on the rug. Peyman and Simin join us, their sons Nima and Yashar come running into our flat, tumble and play on the rug with Laleh and Behzad, and we four adults are the last to go to bed, because we're talking about everything: politics, films, books. Evenings in my family, when my mother has cooked without letting anyone help her, and then gathers her full-bellied children around her, and is complimented on the food and sits in contented, exhausted silence. And what doesn't appear in the videos are the constant reproaches in the eyes of Behzad's mother, the pains my mother suffers, her back crooked, her sleep deep and frighteningly long.

The department store in my mind also has this one video that I play over and over — the cardboard case is battered and the colours have faded — one particular dinner at Behzad's mother's house. There is rice and okra, a vat of pulpy cooked tomatoes, pickled vegetables, and there is dugh, the sour yoghurt water. Most people are there, but not everyone. We couldn't ask everyone to come; that would have been conspicuous. We eat and pretend everything is normal, and I wonder whether they eat okra in Turkey, too, and what then, where then, and I stop wondering and try to commit the taste to memory. I should have eaten more, I always think when I get to this point; I should have looked everyone in the eye and I should have eaten more. Particularly Behzad's little brothers — how old will they be when we see them again, what kind of people will they have become, I should have smelled them, I should have kissed them, instead of thinking about okra.

We'll behave just as we usually do, Behzad and I had decided beforehand, and then no one will notice anything and we won't be putting anyone at risk. Laleh plays with my leather handbag, gets the tickets out, holds them in her hand. We've told them we're going to Syria for a few days, shopping; the children remember their uncle who came back from Syria with bags full of sweets, and the adults remember the food he brought back, the jeans, things that coupons couldn't buy and didn't feel like war. And I think, if someone looks over at Laleh now, if someone sees the tickets, if someone notices that they say *Istanbul*, then that person will look at us and know, they'll cry out, we'll throw our arms around each other, we'll weep and curse this unhappiness, and maybe, just maybe someone will have some other solution, they'll say, Oh but you don't need to do that, we've got a better idea, and maybe we'll never get on that bus, the rusty, grey bus that looks for all the world like a normal passenger bus, although it signifies such a turning point in our lives. And I take the tickets from Laleh's hand, wordlessly, stash them deep inside the bag, put the bag on my lap, and kiss my clever little girl on the top of her warm head. We are like we usually are, and no one notices anything.

Behzad's head is bent over his full plate as he shovels rice into his mouth, some falling back onto the plate. His mother sits in silence, as she always does; she has always done everything for us and never said a word about it. Not a word about the flyers we stored at her house, or the comrades we hid there for a few days, not a word about the weapons. Not a word about her putting herself in danger just to know that we were in less danger. She, too, had seen the pictures of the mothers outside Evin Prison. Dozens of older women in black chadors, their faces twisted in pain, their hands raised, accusing the prison walls, every day, at every hour. Wanting their children back, even if it was only for burial. Behzad's father grew quieter every time we saw him.

And how glad I was at our final meal together that they had almost stopped speaking to us. As if they had an inkling they would soon find our apartment empty and fear our next phone call. An inkling that they and my mother would soon be selling our furniture, sharing out our possessions between them, having to give up our apartment. Behzad's mother with her reproach, mine with her fear, both with their own regal quality, Behzad's father staying silent all the while. Pulling the door closed behind them, standing outside it as they kissed and said their goodbyes.

Another film in my mind — it doesn't come from the department store, it just plays by itself — always brings with it a feeling of guilt. Behzad and I are tidying up the flat, and sweeping the floor makes me think of that musical about the Jewish village in Russia, the man who marries off his daughters against tradition, and in the end they all have to flee anyway, and his wife is sweeping the floor and he tells her off and she shouts that she isn't going to leave a dirty house behind. We laughed at that, Azar and I, side by side in the cinema, we laughed and then cried soon after. And at the end, the violin.

In this video, which gives me a nagging sense of guilt, although I can't stop watching it, there are no children whose hair needs combing, whose things have to be packed in our suitcases. In this video, Behzad kisses me and takes me in his arms. He takes the broom from my hands and goes on sweeping, while I walk through the two rooms saying goodbye, to the rugs, to my favourite clothes, to the view into the courtyard. Behzad sweeps everything up — there isn't much, anyway — and props the broom in the corner, the last sound in this flat. Our eyes roam over the walls, our hiding place, our home, and then we turn to the door and leave. Behzad wraps his scarf around my neck, because his greatest concern is anything happening to me.

We climb aboard the bus, the young couple in love who might be going on holiday to Turkey. The camera shows us taking two seats next to each other, without first asking if anyone is willing to swap so we can sit with the children. Close-up on my face, knowing I am secure between Behzad and the window, looking out at the landscape, feeling safe, excited, maybe as excited as I was at the first protests. And when the border comes, when the man with the list comes, when they walk through the bus checking the passengers, we hold hands and know that if they take Behzad prisoner, I'm going with him. And the man keeps moving, hasn't noted Behzad's name; he is waiting for other ghosts of this country, and that is the start of Behzad and Nahid's beautiful life in Europe, growing and studying and then coming back brimming with education and ideas, to continue the Revolution, to have children in Iran and teach them all the things you learn in Europe.

They are joyful parents, giving their children proper answers to their questions, and not prevaricating. In my film, we are strong at each other's side. Neither is weak, neither is sad; we are two strong, clever, twentieth-century revolutionaries. We used to say, There is nothing private, there is only the Revolution. Because we didn't yet know what it was to know there is a land of carefree, joyful games in the next room that you are endangering with your own actions.

Fifteen minutes left, and fifteen minutes isn't long enough to play the tapes that remind me of Behzad's father and his sayings, or his brothers and their tussles. Not enough time to let the morning tears flow and dry, to wash them away and let the redness fade from my face. And with all my might I fight back the images of Peyman. Sitting in a cellar, waiting for Khomeini's death just as we are. I wonder when Behzad gives in to these images, or whether he never lets them in, purely for self-preservation, but I can't stew over that now. I've only got fifteen minutes left, enough time to consider what has to be bought, what has to be cooked. To think that we still have courgettes, that I need to check if there are enough shelled chickpeas. We buy tomato puree and rice by the kilo, when Ulla or Frau Sommer takes me in the car. There is meat in the freezer. We were lucky with the fridge, not everyone gets one with a freezer compartment.

I imagine frying the meat and the smell is suddenly in the room, and I swallow because my mouth is watering, but not with anticipation; I swallow to make the unpleasant feeling go away, the churning in my stomach, but it doesn't help, and I can't swallow any faster, so: get up quickly, go to the toilet — just don't wake the children early.

I've never told Behzad about the time I spend with my videos in the morning, and I don't know when Behzad cries. What I do know is that he never lets me see it. When I read the poem in Frau Sommer's book, I cried, because I thought otherwise Behzad won't read it, otherwise he'll act like he doesn't need to read the poem, because of course he knows Brecht, knows the whole of communism by heart. And he actually does know everything by Rumi, too, without the two of us ever having spent time together leafing through the poetry volumes that he bought me for our engagement, though that was what I always wanted us to do. I wanted to share it with him, the rustle of the pages, the effect of every word. And now I'm the one who doesn't dare pick up the books, fearing that they might have lost their power, somewhere between Tehran, Istanbul, East Berlin, and here.

The poem in Frau Sommer's old schoolbook caught my eye because it used the word *exile*, and Behzad and I always say, Germany is our exile, and to me the word seems like a frozen state, in which I am supposed to try and move about all the same. In the beginning, everything I did here fitted inside that word; every perfectly shaped but tasteless peach fitted under the bell jar of *exile*, and I heard myself say every German word as though it had been frozen, to be thawed out in later times. We stopped using that word long ago, and the words we use more often now are *residence permit* and *lawyer* and *school board* and *appeal process*. 'Thoughts on the Duration of Exile', it said, and I felt I'd been caught out; I'd gone rummaging in Frau Sommer's youth and been caught in the act. As if the word had fled my mind because I'd used it too little recently, as if the word had fled, perhaps because I discovered that the Chinese grocers sell fresh coriander, or because I heard Laleh and Morad arguing over Morad's claim that he loved lavashak more than anything, despite never having eaten it, or because Behzad's large, boxy radio told us about ten thousand murdered prisoners, killed without trial, some of whom had already served out their sentences, and for an entire evening we couldn't move, he lying on the floor by the radio, I on the sofa. Perhaps the word thawed out, bid us farewell, and tried to flee, to find a place in Frau Sommer's dog-eared book.

And when I read the poem, I felt caught out again, and cried to be on the safe side. The weeping was deliberate, and Behzad came in and said, What's happened, did someone call? and I was suddenly ashamed, because of course in his place I, too, would think something had happened, another prisoner with a familiar name, another death perhaps, or his mother, or his father, or my mother, who can no longer stand upright under the weight of it all, or Peyman, whom he thinks about so much. I asked, Behzad, when are we going back? We've unpacked our things, we've hammered nails into the walls, we've even bought the children summer sandals now, Behzad, so when are we going back? And Behzad sat down beside me and said, Nahid, don't be childish, stop crying, it doesn't do any good, Khomeini will die and everyone will wake up, come on, you know this, you don't need to have it explained to you.

I showed him the poem and said, We're acting like we aren't watering the tree outside, but we are. Behzad just slammed the book shut and said I should occupy myself with something meaningful and not read such things, and I cried, this time not deliberately, and thought about how he always shrugs off the things that make me sad so that we can go on living here as if everything is fine, though I can't even help Laleh with her homework without being afraid that I'm teaching her errors, when she should have what every other child has here: a mother who can sit beside her and explain it all, who can turn the pages with her, maybe even look ahead to see what letters are coming next. Not a mother who has to have the different sounds of Ö and O demonstrated for her over and over again. Not a mother who, during homework time, sometimes toys with the idea of reciting the much more melodic Persian alphabet instead of those stupid Ös and Os, *alef, be, pe, te, se,* whose mind wanders during handwriting exercises, and who ultimately leaves her daughter to do her homework alone.

On her first visit to our ready-furnished flat, Frau Sommer brought me the schoolbook she had liked as a little girl. I only read the poems; the longer texts were too boring for me. A schoolbook without any pictures or explanations, just texts, like an academic university book. So this is the kind of thing they give their sixteen-year-olds, I thought, scanning the table of contents for names I recognised, whose German spelling I could relate to their Persian pronunciation. Frau Sommer had annotated the book, before she was Frau Sommer, when she was Marion Ulbrecht — underlining passages, drawing pencil hearts on love poems. Love poems by Goethe and Lessing and Schiller, which I know in the Persian translation, and when I tried to read the poems in German, they suddenly seemed dusty, just as I imagined loving was here: hidden and dusty and cold.

They would never print a poem by Hafez; they'd never understand it, even if it was translated. Everything in Hafez shines with love for others and with the love of words — it shines on the reader, shines out of the page. They could never package such a thing into a schoolbook and give it to little

Marions as homework, I think. Maybe they should try it, the Germans, maybe then the married couples here would go out together as couples more often, and not on their own. Frau Sommer is almost always alone, and Ulla even goes off to the seaside by herself for several days, and it's no wonder when you have to read this Goethe as a young girl, on dry, yellow paper. And the Germans who are young girls now are always alone, too, or in large groups. When they sit on the rocks by the fountain in the pedestrian precinct, pretty young girls with long hair and brightly coloured leggings and denim jackets, laughing and shouting and making a noise, such a noise that I feel a little ashamed, maybe on their behalf, maybe on my own. And when boys are there, they sit on the boys' laps for all the world to see, and yet: they are never in love and beautiful and in pairs. Just noisy and public and probably utterly confused, because no one has ever been able to explain to them what love is.

Then I think that I never want to walk down here and see my Laleh sitting by the fountain. My Laleh, on a boy's lap, without the love from Hafez's words. It's lucky that my Laleh will never be an adult here, and I'll never lose her to a fountain and brightly coloured leggings; by the time she's that age, we'll be back, Khomeini will be dead, everything will be different, everything better, and until then I will keep saying no when she asks for chewing gum — that might be how it all starts, first she gets chewing gum, and in a few years she'll want to sit by the fountain in brightly coloured leggings.

Frau Sommer takes a sip of the black tea. Frau Sommer always acts as though it's a very special kind of tea we drink. The first few times she kept asking how I make it. Her eyes were searching for a samovar, and I showed her the little limescale-encrusted water boiler on the wall. And then the teabag, bought from the supermarket that always smells of radishes and vinegar, where something has always been spilled on the floor. This time, there are little shreds of tea in the glass. A parcel from my mother, with birthday presents for Laleh and consolation presents for Morad, dried herbs and pistachios, dried lemons and barberries. And a packet of black tea that has not been hidden away in bags, smelling of cinnamon and cardamom, sent by Behzad's mother to mine, for her to send on to us. No letter from her, but the tea was greeting enough, worry and reproach and caress in one. The feeling is like stumbling between sleep and reality, like having to quickly decide what is real and what's fantasy, when the postman hands you a fragrant parcel and you open it on the factory-made rug, freeing the softened cardboard from the sticky tape, tearing the handwriting, and when the aroma that comes from the box is of everything there is, of Eid Nowruz and wedding parties, of suppers and school holidays, and in an envelope are the letter and the saffron, wrapped tidily in newspaper. Bland newspaper, bland news on paper that is only kept for a few hours and then used to wrap food. The letter in my mother's handwriting, the tender strokes and dots drawn slowly across the page. Words making an effort not to sound reproachful because they are actually worries. And they feel like warmth, until I've finished reading them and laid them aside. She is telling me that the parcel is the point, she has sent us a parcel and not just a letter, and we should think about the parcel more than the letter.

Frau Sommer smells the tea and says, This time, Nahid, this time the tea is different, isn't it? And I laugh and say, Yes, it's from my mother-in-law. Frau Sommer cries, That's why! And somehow all three of us are raising our voices, as if we need to drown out the sound of the children playing in the next room. I show Frau Sommer and Ulla the things that were in the parcel. They aren't familiar with any of them; they don't recognise the barberries, and I don't know the German word for them, Little berries, I say, goes on rice, and Ulla says, Oh, yes, you made that for us once, and there was saffron in the rice. I nod and quickly show them the herbs, so that they can smell them and to make it feel less awkward that Frau Sommer hasn't come over for dinner yet, although she's done so much for us, not just when she was responsible for us in the hostel, but even now.

But then I have to put the herbs away again just as quickly. They smell too strong; all the scents in our flat are too strong today. The mothers who brought their children here and smelled of either perfume or cigarettes. Then their children, who smelled of children's sweat, unwashed hair, and German food. When my eyes fall on my fingernails as I'm tidying the herbs away, I even feel like the smell of the nail varnish is in my nose again, the sharp chemical aroma, though it's two days since I painted my nails. And now the varnish is chipping again, despite the L'Oréal label on the bottle. I treated myself to it when I was buying Laleh a new party dress for her birthday, a light-blue dress with a white lace collar. And all at once I have such a desire to get dressed up, go to another wedding with a visit to the hairdresser beforehand, help another bride pick out a dress, laugh at the others' hairstyles.

There is an Eid Nowruz celebration here, too — some people Shirin knows hire a hall and organise a Persian buffet and a band, and a lot of interesting people come, as Shirin told me again recently when I called to invite her daughter Yasaman to Laleh's party today. I didn't ask — I don't want to know what people Shirin finds interesting, and I had no desire to tell Behzad about the idea, either. Behzad would say, They're all crooks, they have all that money and they flee to Germany, and when they're here they suddenly start claiming they were so very political and so very persecuted, and it's *their* fault our residence permit is taking so long, it's because there are so many of these slick, apolitical people. I agree with Behzad; what do we want with them? These are people we used to avoid back in Iran, so why should we suddenly start celebrating with them? But in the midst of this children's birthday party, while Ulla and Frau Sommer are puzzling over what the barberries might be, all at once I have a longing for these people. Not just for Shirin who, as superficial as she might seem, is somehow always slightly better informed than we are, or for her little daughter Yasaman, with whom Laleh and Morad love to play Persian games. But for all the people who go to those celebrations, for their excessive make-up, for their lilting language, for their laughter and the searching look around the group that follows it.

Frau Sommer and Ulla's conversation suddenly stalls and they listen to the children's voices from the next room. Morad's voice is louder than the others, and we hear him call out Police! Police! and it makes the three of us laugh, because earlier I told them about the time a few days ago when Morad sang out his alert from the children's bedroom, his shouts of Police! Police! ringing through our flat. At first, Behzad and I were alarmed, thinking, this is it: our child has been damaged by everything that's happened in the last few years, and it's all coming out in some brutal game. Until we realised that he himself was playing the policeman. He admires the police officers on the street, and that's why he asks for police cars whenever we're in the toy department. Behzad murmured that the last thing he needed was a fan of the police living under his own roof, but better that than a seriously damaged child, and we laughed. And it felt good to laugh with Ulla and Frau Sommer about it as well — not just because they had prepared special games for the children, but also because they were calming me down, amid all this hubbub.

As soon as the cake had been eaten, they got the children playing the game with the sweets and my largest cooking pot, the one that involves blindfolds and hats and gloves, and I went and sat by the kitchen window, to escape the smells and the noise.

For a little while there was only me, the chair by the window, and the view of the outside world, a brief moment in which to take stock: everyone is fine, I don't need to see to anyone, and outside spring is turning into summer.

I looked out at the rubbish skips, which overflow, which stink of fish, and the bin men don't come to collect them; I looked at the cars that are always there, with no numberplates, no owners, and I wondered what's worse — knowing your car is here in a car park like this without any numberplates on it, or just not having a car. Behzad told me recently about a man who wants to sell an old Polo. It hurt a little, when he was telling me about the old Polo; for a second it brought an image of our Paykan to my mind. The Paykan was our home, I said when we sold it, and today Behzad would say, You're being melodramatic. But he didn't say it at the time, didn't say much in general, sold everything he could while making sure that no one noticed, that we seemed normal, that we didn't stand out.

The Paykan had taken us north a few years earlier. Behzad, his mother, Laleh, and me. It was before Morad was born, and Behzad's older brothers drove other cars full of sisters and children and friends. We travelled from Tehran to the Caspian Sea, stopping along the way. We stopped at night in the mountains and put up our tents, and sometimes we found abandoned houses. The Paykan had also been there for us when we had to leave the city, when they said bombs were going to fall, when I was heavily pregnant and we called it evacuation. Now the Paykan belongs to someone we don't know, who doesn't know us, and who doesn't know that we only sold the car because of Peyman and the lists. And who knows if the person who drives it now also carries flyers in his boot, or if he works as a taxi driver or listens to the state radio station.

And right then, I hear soft music coming from the window of one of the neighbouring flats, a German man's voice with a guitar. On the other side of the block opposite is the meadow, and beyond that a vast cornfield, and beyond that a large wood. I imagine how my mother would enjoy being surrounded by all that nature; we could invite her, save up for her ticket; we'd have our residence permit and a work permit and money and the right to apply for a visa for her. I imagine the two of us going for a walk, taking the children and walking in the woods, my mother on holiday admiring the greenery, hanging out the washing with me, downstairs on the washing line, getting into our Polo — we will certainly have a Polo by then — getting into our Polo and showing her the little half-timbered towns in the area, and her smiling and keeping quiet, and perhaps thinking, What a shame about Dayeh and all the words she withholds from us. What a shame about the silence she has maintained towards Behzad and me since we fled. Perhaps out of grief, perhaps out of fear, or anger.

Nahid, says Frau Sommer, sipping her tea, you seem miles away — are you thinking about home? And I am suddenly no longer alone and no longer by the window and I realise that, much as I enjoy the company of Ulla and Frau Sommer, I'm suddenly dog-tired. A balloon pops in the next room, and I hear children's loud shrieks, with Laleh in their midst, Laleh's shrieks among the shrieks of her friends, as if there was no difference. I say, No, I was thinking, I need to make a doctor's appointment. Frau Sommer puts her cup down on the table and asks, What kind of doctor? I need the pill, I say — I looked the word up and doubted it would be understood, this word, *pill*, it's so vague, but Frau Sommer and Ulla nod quickly and simultaneously, and Frau Sommer writes down the name and number of her gynaecologist for me and explains that you have to make an appointment for an examination, and I sigh and think, Of course you do. It would be surprising if it was quicker here, simpler.

Did you take the pill before, then? Ulla asks, looking at me thoughtfully. I say, Yes, yes, in Iran. And Ulla asks, And what have you been taking here? I am ashamed to have feared the simplest question; here I am telling them about Mother and everything, and they are asking me personal questions, just like that, and I didn't dare to ask about the pill. I still had some from Iran, I reply hastily, so they won't see my embarrassment. More eager nodding, and I think how lovely they are, all of a sudden I think how lovely they are, sitting here at my wooden kitchen table, which we all know isn't real wood, which we all know was given to us by the welfare office, and won't last long and isn't meant to, because they're going to send us back, because we'll be back in Iran before it falls apart, but Ulla and Frau Sommer sit at the table and drink their tea and nod their blushing heads quickly, for my sake, so I won't feel uncomfortable.

I nod too, because anything else would feel strange, and then I pour more tea and straighten the serviettes that have been left on the table, from the cake. None of the children used a serviette, but all birthday parties need serviettes, as

Laleh assured me beforehand, with a serious expression on her face. She knew exactly what a children's birthday party should be like, led me by the hand into the little shop that sells postcards and candy shells and confetti, and chose the things she wanted. Chose the candles in various colours, went looking for sparklers and found some, spotted a cake mould in the shape of a mouse, half as big as she is, and announced that the cake should be baked in it. I bought everything, except those sweets in plastic shells, and I observed the shop assistant, who is usually always talking to old ladies, as she smiled at Laleh and asked her something and Laleh chattered back, loud and fast and cheerful, and the shop assistant gave me no more than a brief glance, but I quickly smiled, and she smiled back for the first time since I started coming to this shop, to this clean shop, and for that reason I bought a wreath of plastic flowers as well, blue plastic flowers with green ribbons dangling from them, which I can hang on the candle stand that Behzad bought me last Women's Day.

Ulla says, By the way, Nahid, I asked at the university, and the application period for the new semester starts next month, and Frau Sommer and I fall silent. Ulla read this book, brought it over, and for weeks it's been lying on the little table beside our bed. A book like a tabloid newspaper, I thought, and was pleased when later, Behzad said the same thing. The poor American woman and the wicked Iranian husband, and the little child stuck in the middle. But then I did read it after all, initially just to please Ulla, and then I understood the woman completely, was afraid for her, and for the first time in a long time I let go of the room around me again to hide myself in letters. Letters in foreign and unfamiliar shapes, but they still took me to a familiar place. And page after page I asked myself, How is it that you can make people stay somewhere they want to leave, and make people leave who want to be there?

Ulla has been asking different questions since she read the book; for one thing, she suddenly wanted to know exactly what I'd studied. When I told her that the universities were closed down after the Revolution and I couldn't study for two years, she was completely horrified. It wasn't the usual awkward head-shaking with which people respond when I tell them sad things from home; there was outrage in her face, and I explained that, after the new government declared the universities had now been purged, I went back, but it wasn't easy, with a daughter and a husband and all the rules that suddenly existed. A large proportion of the lecturers and students were missing, having been imprisoned, executed, or thrown out of the university; the more artistic subjects had been dropped and replaced by the teachings of Islam, and before every lecture we feared someone coming round to check we were wearing our hijabs correctly and didn't have make-up on. I kept going just to get my degree, but it was nothing like the institution that had once pulsed with ideas and the thirst for knowledge.

Ever since I told her that, Ulla keeps talking about me going back to university. I look at her and say, It isn't that simple, we don't have work permits, and we don't have permits to study, either, and Ulla interrupts me, saying, No, Nahid, you have to try, there are always exceptions, a woman on our street managed it, she's training to be a nurse, and if she hadn't she probably would have gone mad, sitting at home all day. Frau Sommer asks, What would you study — literature again? No, I say, so quickly that Ulla must be able to tell I've thought about this, weighed up the options. I think, what use will they have for a literary scholar when Khomeini dies and a new system is being built? With a scholar of German literature, at that? No, I say, economics, perhaps — or political science. But my German isn't good enough yet. Ulla says, Goodness me, Nahid. You're young and clever, and you have an emancipated husband who supports you, you can do this.

I take the cloth and wipe the sink; there shouldn't be any water or foam left in it. Laleh's joyful shrieks reach my ears, and behind me Ulla is telling Frau Sommer about the book, and Frau Sommer is asking questions and wanting to borrow it, too, and I think, When, when are we supposed to go back, if we're going to start being students again in this country, in our thirties for pity's sake?

1999
Laleh

Each person on a chair, each chair a country, and we are breathing the rain and mud stuck to our platform shoes. Maja is wearing a tight blue T-shirt, and I think my fat would stick out at the sides if I wore something like that, and her hair smells of mousse, hair cut short and dyed red, like on MTV, I think, the MTV studios must smell of mousse and never of muddy shoes. Maja doesn't have braces anymore, and since she had them removed you might almost take her for an adult. She looks at me and says, I did not have sexual relations with that woman, and her large white teeth flash — she is the United States of America, and everyone laughs. The teacher laughs, too, says, Alright folks, settle down. She is thin and smells of university. Maja needs to talk about Bill Clinton's policies, she says, not his personal life.

I don't laugh. I look at Maja and think, of course she chose the USA, I would have, too, only no one asked me, because everyone said Laleh should be Iran; everyone thinks that's logical. We are sitting spaced around this gym hall, ordered not geographically but by interests, which is the same thing, the teacher says. Israel is sitting opposite me. Israel's name is Patrick, but everyone calls him Paddy, though no one listens to the Kelly Family anymore. And the yellow presenter's card says seven, and it's seven's turn to speak, and I look at Paddy and say, We don't accept the existence of Israel, because that is what's on my card, but I say it quietly, because it doesn't sound good. And when Maja puffs herself up and shows her red Veto card, I say, But now we've got a new president, we're more reformist. That isn't on my card, but it's how Papa explained it to the neighbours recently, and I think, if I say something clever-sounding right at the start, then people might not notice if I don't speak again after that.

Paddy looks at me like he's wondering if he should care that I'm denying his right to exist, and I think Paddy must be rummaging around in his brain for what *reformist* means. Paddy says, Hmm, but they're not dangerous, are they? Right? I mean, the countries down there aren't rich enough to have really dangerous weapons? And there's a moment's silence, before France speaks up. France is called David and he says state and religion need to be separated, and beside me Syria puts a hand up and says, But that doesn't apply to Israel?! and then I stop listening. I think I really don't care. I still don't get what the thing is about Israel. A soup of information, of suicide bombings, of old men, of attacks, of news items, for about the last hundred years, at least. A soup of the same words over and over on the eight o'clock news, before we can turn over to watch films on the other channels.

Maja keeps her eye on me, as if I understand very well what Syria has just said.

David turns to me. When David speaks, it's slow and gentle and so clever that it almost tips back into being boring. I don't trust myself to look at him, because when I do all I can think about is what he looks like when he's kissing and I'm watching him. And hoping he doesn't notice. Marie, who has lucked out and is an international group of observers rather than a country, is wrapping a strand of blonde hair around her finger and giving me a conspiratorial smile as David talks. David is delivering a monologue, and I don't understand any of it, but I nod, nod eagerly in his direction, because I do know that what he's saying has something to do with me. David is saying, Even a fanatical state in the Middle East is a product of imperialist power struggles in foreign territories. I nod.

The teacher gives me the speaking card. I'm supposed to respond to France. And she points out that David has just been speaking as David and should actually be speaking as France, and David says that makes him sick and it's democratic idiocy, and the teacher says, Alright, Laleh, do respond to what David's said, but speak as Iran. And I think, Crap. What David said sounded so good. But what is there to add? Victim. I'm a victim. Iran is a victim. We're the victim of America, I say quickly. Can you be more specific? the teacher asks, pen in hand, writing it all down on the thing she refers to in English as a *flipchart*. In my whole school career, the whole of the last decade, I've never had a lesson that involves coloured cards and marker pens and flipcharts, and the only reason we're doing it now is because this is a little show we're putting on for the men from the ministry, who are sitting in the back row.

I say, The people are the victims in this country. The teacher is holding the pen on the spot where she wants to write next, but she isn't writing, she's just looking at me. It's like David said, I explain, all the other countries have their fingers in the pie. I think that's always true. If you're not talking about, like, a world power. The teacher lowers her pen, turns to the class, looks at me for a while, and then says, Are you talking as Laleh now, or as the Islamic Republic of Iran? I don't say anything, because the Western states sitting opposite me are holding their cards up. And then I take the card from my lap and read out, *For a long time, under the monarchy of the Shah, the country was an important exporter of oil to the USA and Great Britain, and enjoyed great wealth. Since the revolution of 1979, the country that used to be known as Persia has been a religious state with restrictive laws.* And as I'm reading, I hear the teacher's pen eagerly writing this down, and I wonder whether anyone has noticed that really, I'm completely clueless. That really, I just learn what I've copied off the board in history lessons. That I don't really follow the news, although it's constantly on at home.

All I know is that when I was little, we were supposed to be going on holiday, but then suddenly we were here and it was just the four of us, and my brother got proper milk instead of powdered, and scented Nivea cream, and my mother made cakes for us in a pan, and the children in the hostel called themselves and me and everyone else *kanaken*. I know Iran consists of baby chickens and blue doors, of people and smells and a backyard with a barefoot grandfather in it. And lately of three plane tickets, pinned to the kitchen board, ordinary bits of paper with ordinary words on them. Which all at once are going to give back what was suddenly taken from me all those years ago.

At the airport duty-free, the newspapers, in different scripts and different languages, have different front pages, because it's July and July is silly season, as our social-studies teacher explained to us. *Peace? The price, the risk, the consequences.* I leaf through the magazine. Damp fingers on glossy paper; Bill Clinton is smiling at me and saving Kosovo. I got the second highest mark in the test on NATO, the best results in my year, and I don't know exactly what's going on in Kosovo. The girl on the front cover looks like the child from Michael Jackson's 'Earth Song'. *The price, the risk, the consequences.*

The price was nine hundred marks for a plane ticket. Tara is only nine, so her flight was half-price. Mama is still enrolled as a student, though she's already had her graduation, but her student ID is valid until October, and the discounts are as well. I'm at school and I pay full price. Iran Air could have earned more from us if Mo hadn't already been booked onto his sailing course. Iran Air could have earned even more if Papa had said he was coming, too. If I'd dared to ask him the real reason why he wasn't coming. But I didn't. Instead, when Mo asked me, I acted like it was obvious. It's too dangerous for Papa, I said, and he believed me, because of course I'm older and, like the adults, I never talk about what happened in the time before Germany. When I answer Mo's questions, I'm also answering my own in a way, and am then satisfied that I've resolved the issue for both of us. All the same, I'm pretty glad he isn't flying with us and I can spend at least a few weeks without him getting on my nerves.

Iran Air doesn't need the income from Mo and Papa, I think; Iran Air is already making the biggest profits of all time since Helmut Kohl left and German citizenship arrived, since this Khatami arrived, with a shorter beard than the other Ayatollahs, since the first people dared to fly back. Since Khale Shirin started coming to visit us in the afternoons and telling us over and over about progress and developments and how simple the forms are to fill out, and then showing us photos of her and her daughter Yasaman at sunset barbecues in the parks of Tehran, thirty people gathered around them, even though they've been living in Germany for twelve years just like us. Yasaman was insanely proud of the photos, which made me think all the more that we should do what the others were doing, go to the embassy, sort out the paperwork, book the plane tickets, and go. In the last year, Iran Air's profits must have increased fivefold, I think. Iran Air must have had to build new planes. Because who actually flew before? Refugees with visas and tourists with nerves of steel. Now the market is booming; now each time I go to the cinema with Yasaman, she brings a different handbag, covered in little crystals and gold bells, and she bought them all there, in Iran.

I take the copy of *Der Spiegel* to the till — maybe it can explain to me what I didn't understand at school. In case one of my relatives wants to talk to me about Kosovo. Or Bill

Clinton. Anyway, apparently Bill Clinton has nearly resolved the Middle East conflict, although in my head his grin automatically becomes Maja's grin. The woman in the shop looks at me as if she's wondering whether I understand the language the magazine is written in. All these languages being spoken here, in Germany's largest airport, Europe's largest international airport, and my head is just filled with useless information and I don't know where I got it from or why. I'm wearing the manto, but the hijab is still lying casually across my shoulders, so of course she's looking at me and feeling confused, and I put the magazine on the counter in order to press the last of my change into her hand. *The price, the risk, the consequences.*

Is it dangerous? Frau Sommer asked. I don't know, I thought. But we probably wouldn't be doing it if our lives were at risk, I thought even more quietly. No, I said, straightening Paul's raincoat on the hook and arranging his gumboots more neatly on the doormat. She gives me ten marks an hour for looking after Paul, but she talks so much after the kids have gone to bed that I have to factor in those hours as well. The woman at the till gives me my change, I take the magazine, and turn my back on her and the Bill Clintons on the other papers. No, it isn't dangerous, everyone's doing it now! I told Frau Sommer, like it was an obvious fact that everyone knew, only once again she didn't.

When we booked our plane tickets and it was clear Papa wasn't coming with us, I imagined there was a list of names and a row of fat-bellied men who sit at border control with the list. They look at some names and say, These are dangerous, and then for others they say, These aren't. But recently the fat-bellied men have started wearing glasses with frosted lenses, frosted and slightly tinted, and so they have some trouble reading the names. If they were to take the glasses off for a second, it would all be over: they'd see the lists again and start putting people in prison. But recently they've been wearing these glasses day and night.

And is your papa staying here all on his own? Frau Sommer asked. She must have asked Mama exactly the same thing, I'm sure she did, but she wanted to hear it again from me. She turned her small, shining blue eyes on me, and I looked at her blue eye shadow, which was much darker than her eyes. Someone should tell her those are two different shades of blue, I thought. Well, yes, I said. But Papa will survive, it's only three weeks. It's a shame he can't go back, said Frau Sommer, I'm sure he would have liked to. I moved my hand from Paul's boots straight to my Dockers, so she would get that I really was leaving now. Frau Sommer looked at the flowery material I've sewn into the seam of my trousers, a large triangle of orange flowers, which turn my old Levi's into flares. I hastily started telling her about my new sewing machine and the evening class, and she didn't ask any more questions.

Maybe there are names that aren't on the fat-bellied men's lists — names that the men keep in their thick heads, behind the frosted glasses, or in their hairy ears; those names aren't going to get past them, and there'll be no fooling around with lists and glasses when it comes to them. Maybe Papa has one of those names. Behzad Hedayat — the words echo in their minds. But how come Frau Sommer knows that? I think. If Frau Sommer was sitting on a wooden chair in the school gym, she'd be Germany. She seems to know things from the past that Mama and Papa have never told me. Because they're over and done with, maybe. And because I was kind of there, too, as a four-year-old.

Mama and Tara are sitting opposite me on the airport's rows of cold plastic chairs, and I am looking intelligently at the pages of *Der Spiegel*. Tara is talking in her Mickey Mouse voice, and Mama says, You can't take that magazine with you. And her face is stern, as stern as it is when you've done something that isn't allowed, or are just about to. I say, Yes, of course, I know. And am annoyed that I just spent money on it, when Mama had already taken away Tara's Spice Girls tapes. The rules are actually very simple. Things that are fun are not permitted. Films, music, nice clothes. And politics. You just have to keep this in mind and keep tucking your hair back under your hijab. But if it's that simple, then why is Mama staring at the ground? Not talking to us, apart from to tell us off, not listening to Tara's Mickey Mouse voice, as she talks about her kid stuff and tries to make Mama laugh? But Mama isn't laughing.

At the start we laughed. Put the hijabs on at home, in front of the big mirror in Mama and Papa's bedroom. Put a hijab on Mo, and Mama's long coat. The only thing that could hide

Marie's blonde curls was the tablecloth. We lined up in height order, looked in the mirror, and laughed.

But we weren't laughing in the photo booths outside the supermarket. Only Tara was still laughing then. Tara, who we had dressed in a long-sleeved checked shirt and a small black headscarf. Tara was the first in the photobooth, and when she was finished, four photos of her little face dropped out of the box. Four times Tara, smiling uncertainly and looking strangely pale, but very cute with it. She didn't even look at the photo, just took off the hijab, gave it to me, didn't laugh anymore. Then she walked to the toy department without saying a word. At first, Papa was puzzled, and then he went after her without speaking either. Mo cursed and asked why he had to go in there, too, when he wasn't even flying with us. Mama told him he needed an Iranian passport all the same, and I said, Count yourself lucky, at least you'll look normal in your photo. Mo went in and came out holding his Game Boy. I waited for the Game Boy to appear in the photo as well, but the photo was just of a pale, morose Mo, the fuzz of hair on his upper lip looking dark. Have a shave, I said, and he said, Have a shave yourself.

Then me in the photobooth. Me alone with my face on the screen. Not pale, but green. The hijab slips, and while the machine is still doing the countdown, a few strands of hair fall across my forehead, and I quickly tuck a few strands of hair back under the hijab. What happens if there is hair in the photo? Does it get rejected by the embassy? What if the photos aren't rejected, but we still get turned away at passport control, because an embassy worker wasn't paying attention, because I wasn't paying attention, because the machine started the countdown too quickly? The clock is ticking, the numbers are going backwards, for a second I think of New Year's Eve, and then suddenly the machine is making its noise. The screen says, Print your photos? I see one large, wide-open eye and a hand covering half my face. See half the fuzzy hair on my upper lip and think, Mo is right. Wonder what will happen if I select the photo. If I just say, Well, if hair isn't allowed in the photo, then that rules out half my face. If the hair on my head isn't allowed, then I'll put a hand over my facial hair, too. The machine looks back at me and changes its message. Print photos. It made that decision without any countdown. Please be patient: your passport photos are being printed. I step out of the booth and look into Mama's reproachful face. I need another five marks, I say. It was no good. And Mama waits for the photos and says nothing.

At the start, we laughed. But last night, Mama cried louder than usual. I woke up, scared, my heart racing like something bad had happened. I thought, if I stay lying down and keep quiet, no one will know I'm awake, and if I'm not awake, then I don't know anything, and if I don't know anything then I'm not to blame if I don't go and help. Like in school, when I'm really sure that someone else's group-work grade is lower than it should be, and mine is higher than it should be, and I think, Well maybe I was only listening when they said my grade and not the others, and if I only listened to my grade, then there's no way I can know that anything was unfair, and then there's no way I can feel guilty or put my hand up and say something, and there's no way the teacher can think I'm disruptive.

Mama cried, and it was really loud, and then I thought, that's almost too loud for me to pretend I haven't heard it now. I was all geared up to go to her, though as usual I had no idea what I could do to console her. Mama has been having these crying episodes ever since we applied for our Iranian passports, ever since we bought the suitcases. As if we'd suddenly broken open something she'd kept tied up securely for the last few years. And there has never really been anything to say to these outbursts, and so none of us said anything, plus they were just too frequent and too inexplicable for Mo and me to be able to think of anything better to do than just hold her hand or sometimes stroke her shoulders.

I wondered why I wasn't crying. Papa and Mo wouldn't cry, obviously, and nor would Tara, because she's much too little, and she doesn't know anyone but the two uncles and aunts and the grandparents who have come to Germany. But I don't cry, I just think a lot; there are all these jumbled thoughts and fragments of thoughts about everything that has happened. There are the five of us in Germany, our flat, the new corner bench, the new video recorder, the dinners when we tell stories about the old days, about Mo when he was little, about me and how I used to look after him, and sometimes stories about my cousin Ava, and Mama's friend Khale Azar, and my grandparents — and then something will tighten inside me. There are people and smells and images that sit so deep and sometimes come to the surface so suddenly, feeling so right that I have no idea how I could have forgotten them on all those days at school and evenings in Marie's room. They sit so deep because they're bound up with childhood and security and safety. Until I go back to school and immediately forget it all. And then eventually it catches up with me again, and I think, Why is it that I have to carry these things around with me and Marie and David and bloody Maja don't even know what that feels like? I really don't want to know what it feels like to be Mama.

Last night, just as I thought, okay, I'm going to go and see if there's anything I can do, I suddenly heard Tara sitting up in bed and stretching. Taking a deep breath, sounding almost annoyed, and then putting her little feet on the carpet and leaving the room. Wordlessly, completely ignoring me. Brave little Tara, I thought, and the crying stopped, and in the morning Papa drove us to the airport, not saying anything. With the suitcases under a blanket so no one would see them. The suitcases he'd already taken down to the car in the night, so no one would see him. So that later, no one will ask. So that later, we won't have to give anyone any answers. So that later, no one will think we were lying if they don't let us into the country. So that maybe, we could pretend none of it was real until the very last minute. Tara was squashed in between me and the suitcases, her head with the Walkman headphones on it swaying from side to side and finally coming to rest on my shoulder, digging in a bit because of the headphones and surprisingly heavy for such a little head. Her deep breathing sounded like an adult's, only turned down very low, to the minimum volume.

They had a blue door. But never just blue; blue with sunshine, and when we got near, the blue door would disappear inwards and Madar Bozorg, Mama's mother, would come into view. She always opened the door to us slowly, cautiously, and at the same speed the sweet smell of her sweat came to greet me. Each time, she would put her arms around me at once and say something like, Little daughter, is it me you're all coming to visit? Then she'd kiss Mama and the others, and inside the house Ava would be waiting for me. Ava was a little beast, sometimes, and she was the best friend anyone could have, but also only sometimes. And everyone was always there, in this room, and sometimes we went on holiday to the Caspian Sea, all of us together, and then Ava and I argued about who got to sit on Madar Bozorg's lap, which was larger and softer than Mama's or Ava's mama's. We argued for so long that we both got to sit on her lap, and Papa said, Look after my mother for me, but she wasn't his mother at all, she was Mama's.

I try to picture Papa's face younger, but I can't; the Papa I see in my head is the one sitting over the books for his electrician apprenticeship, coming home from work and sleeping, watching TV with his bare, calloused feet on the coffee table. Going for walks in the nearby woods on his own because no one wants to go with him, and coming back relaxed and content.

In my memory, they are all still like they used to be, Madar Bozorg, my cousin Ava, my youngest uncle Amu Mehrdad, Mama's friend Khale Azar, all like they used to be, like they've been preserved in jars of sugar water the way Marie's grandma preserves apricots. Amu Mehrdad gave me a chick once, and I raised it, and I hated them all for the first time when I was ill and there was chicken soup. I hated them again when I was ill but no one brought me chicken soup; we were in one of these flats that were all the same colour, and later no one could tell me whether it was in Germany or Turkey. Mama got into bed with me because I had a sore throat, and was almost as feverish as I was, or maybe Mama was sick and I wasn't, I can't really remember now, and where was Mo? By that point, it was also clear to me that we weren't just on holiday: that had been a lie the adults told us. But I'd been thinking that when we were on holiday, they'd buy me a doll that could talk, just like in the story that Papa always read to me at bedtime. But there was no doll and no holiday and no chicken soup, and I was so angry that Madar Bozorg wasn't there that I thought, she's a mean, mean old woman who has chickens slaughtered and sends children away, and I'm going to tell her that on the telephone.

But when I spoke to her on the phone later, and I don't know, I might have been four or seven or thirteen, and wanted to tell her that, Mama and Papa were sitting beside me and dictating what I should say. Kheyli mamnun, merci, I had to say, thank you very much, I'm well, Kheyli mamnun, be hame salam beresoonin, best wishes to everyone. When what I wanted to say was, You left us on our own, all of you, but Mama and Papa were sitting beside me, and they seemed small, like children themselves, and I let it go.

I didn't get angry after that, or only at Mama, and I still get angry with her, every second time I have to write to the insurance people and speak to the phone company because she doesn't want to do it and claims she can't, she makes too many mistakes with her German. Being angry with Mama works out pretty well. I have a rant, and when I've finished blowing off steam, no one mentions it again.

When we went in, I completely forgot to check whether the door is still blue. We went in, and it was only walking into Madar Bozorg's house that made it feel like we'd arrived in Iran. Walking not of my own volition, though these are my feet stepping on the floor. I'd removed the purple nail varnish before the flight. It's like being carried, not walking, with drum and santoor music around me and people kissing my cheeks and stroking my hair, while I take off my hijab, my shoes, put my feet on the soft rug and feel like these people are carrying me. Kitschy, I think, it feels kitschy, like the point in Hollywood films at which Mo gets annoyed and stands up and disappears off to his room.

As we walked in, I lost track of where Mama was, if she was in front of or beside me. You don't miss your Mama, I think, when you have so many other people around you. People who are holding your hand, leading you to your seat, cupping your face and telling you you're the one who is so soft. Who is so beautiful, so thin, the one everyone has been waiting for, for weeks, for years. Amid all the bustle, all the non sequiturs, they suddenly start showing you childhood photos of yourself that are completely new to you, hanging on the wall like a commemorative plaque, for you, for your father. It's funny, suddenly seeing him here, and for the first time you realise that he looked really different before, with his hair still thick and carefully blow-dried, a bit like Roy Black dressed up as a revolutionary. They show you letters you wrote, which you have no memory of. And just then you stop seeing the little girl in the photos as you and start seeing Tara — and where is Tara, anyway?

Ever since you finally got out, out of the aggressively air-conditioned plane, out of baggage reclaim and passport control, you haven't been aware of your noisy little sister. Once your relatives were no longer looking at you through the glass but were beside you, around you, everywhere, the aunts and uncles by marriage, the newborn babies and the children who only come up to your shoulder. The flowers that people gave you and then took away again when there were too many, the biscuits you were offered, although dry saffron biscuits in a dry mouth are absolutely disgusting. They kissed you and hugged you, and then you barely opened your eyes, because you didn't recognise any of them, and your face was pressed to their black-fabric-covered shoulders, and you could only tell them apart by their perfume. For a second, you thought what a silent sea of glowing jewels Tehran is from above, as silent and peaceful as a shining, glittering, sprawling palace, and was it your tears or theirs you were wiping from your cheeks — but where was Tara in all this? Who has been looking after Tara, who none of them know and who doesn't know any of them, either?

I look around. Tara is sitting in the middle of a group of children, throwing M&Ms in the air and catching them in her mouth. She explains, These are M&Ms, and the other children say they have those here, too, but not with nuts in, and Tara calls out, Maman, what are nuts? The children laugh and say, Don't you even know what nuts are? Mama says the German word, she says Nüsse, and the aunts around her laugh at the strange sound, and the children laugh at Tara. Tara laughs, too, lobs two M&Ms in the air, catches them, and says, They melt in your hand, not in your mouth, and of course she's got it the wrong way round again, but I keep that to myself, because I'm already getting enough attention here without saying anything.

Everyone around me is looking at me, talking to me, listening to me, going suddenly quiet when I dare to respond and address my faltering Persian words to them. But all this attention doesn't really have anything to do with me; it's about Mama and Papa. Who isn't just my Papa, but a brother, an uncle, a brother-in-law, a friend, a son. Above all, someone they haven't seen for a very long time, and don't know when they will see again. For me, he's someone who is home alone, and was waiting for us to call. He'd probably been waiting since the moment he got back to the empty flat that will stay empty for the next three weeks. And he sounded happier just now when we spoke on the phone than everyone here put together, though he might really have been sad. Coming from the green plastic receiver, his voice sounded very quiet and very far away.

You're so beautiful, how beautiful she is, what a beautiful face, the women say, winking at Mama, rousing me from my thoughts. I don't know how you respond to that — do you say thank you, or do you say oh no, come on, that's not true, or do you just keep quiet and say nothing?

Mama, who answers for me because it takes so long for me to think of the Persian words, says, Your eyes see beautifully. A stock phrase that people wait to hear when they've said things that sound like compliments, although they could just be lies that you say to everyone. Only I don't know these stock phrases. Where was I supposed to learn them? I'd love to say, Your eyes see beautifully, like Mama, but it would feel wrong, because I'd just be parroting it. Though it's so true. I look at them: the tired faces, the aunts with shadows under their eyes, the uncles with their laughter lines, the plucked eyebrows, the feet with dark hair sprouting from them, never larger than a size thirty-nine, no matter if the feet are male or female. Well sure, your eyes see beautifully, I want to shout, because *that* would be something true. Truer, at least, than the answers I'm giving when they ask me things.

Morad is doing well at school, I say, and yes, of course he speaks good Persian. Our town is pretty and clean, and my school report wasn't all that brilliant, I claim, feeling slightly uncomfortable and aware that I've done this a thousand times before: overstating and understating things at the same time. Does your father still not swat away the flies that settle on his feet? my cousin asks. My cousin, who was such a pretty little girl, and yet has got so impossibly old, put on weight, looks tired, and I shake my head. Because I don't understand what flies she means, or if that's something improper for which I need a polite response. But the others treat this as an entirely normal question; they say, Your father, such a good-hearted man, he never even used to swat away flies. It takes me a moment before I say, I don't know. Although I *should* know — I mean, I do see him every day. But why would I take an interest in his feet?

He's a gift, your father, my cousin says, like she is so much older than all of us. She takes my hand, which is resting on my thigh, and calls me azizam, darling, and I look for Tara and the M&Ms and her laughter, which strikes me as rude and too loud, even for a child of her age. But Mama's mind is elsewhere, Mama's cheeks are glowing. Not like she's ill or flustered, but like she's bashful, suddenly recovered from illness, newly in love. Mama talks and gesticulates, and her eyes are so wide and alert that for the first time I can see real similarities between her and Tara. She sits in the midst of her friends and sisters and tells them things and asks questions without drawing breath.

What *is* that manto you're wearing? Khale Azar called out as Mama was taking it off. Mama said (sounding wistful), The same manto I travelled to Germany in twelve years ago. The other women instantly burst out laughing. No one wears those anymore, they cried, it's so old-fashioned! Khale Azar put an arm around Mama's shoulders and said, That coat is so conservative the Islamic government is going to send you a thank-you letter and a medal. Now Mama is sitting with them and laughing about it, too, the way people laugh when they've just belatedly got a joke. But now and then she turns serious again. Our house is scarcely recognisable now, I hear her say, and she looks around and shakes her head slowly. I find it odd that she's trying to recognise Madar Bozorg's house — she may have grown up here, but she only lived here until she got married. The two large, interconnected living rooms, with rugs everywhere, a little kitchen, a little bedroom, and the yard outside. Khale Azar says with a laugh — she says everything with a laugh — True, before the war you had smaller rooms and smaller windows, you did well out of the reconstruction.

They talk about the war and the reconstruction as if these were completely normal things, and somehow Mama doesn't fit in, with that sentimental look in her eyes. It's a look that doesn't belong to the woman for whom I have to fill in insurance forms, either. She drives me insane with the form-filling. No one here would believe I sometimes get angry with Mama, though, or with people in general. Since the plane touched down, I've been an angel. An angel who is sitting on the rug, having pistachios and grapes and figs put in her mouth, who places a lump of sugar between her teeth and then slurps the black tea, like the men do.

When the first person brought the tea round, an older cousin, I swallowed, took the glass, said Kheyli mamnun, merci, and thought, Why is she handing the glasses out, why doesn't she just put them in the middle, why doesn't everyone take their own tea? How come I'm sitting here, while the other women are busy dishing out and clearing away? But I stopped feeling guilty the moment I realised that nothing in the world feels so right as when someone hands you a glass of red-gold tea. It's the same feeling I sometimes get at home, listening to the old stories. All I should be doing, I thought, is sitting here leaning on a floor cushion, surrounded by loud people and loud music. And I should never again sit in a classroom with people who only know this country from *The Naked Gun*. Everything here sounds like music, even the big old television in the background that everyone is ignoring. The men are playing cards, the women smell of hairspray, and everyone is barefoot. The heavy scent of rice and saffron hangs in the air, it's oppressively hot, and I can't feel my body anymore, though everyone is admiring and stroking it.

I answer their questions, a confusion of questions about everything in my life. This must be what it's like to come out of amnesia, when everything you say feels new. I tell them that I like drawing, and they laugh and say, You used to do that as a child, all the time, the whole day, do you remember when I looked after you and you sat in my kitchen all day, drawing? I say, Yes, I remember. Because just then I do think I remember sitting there in her kitchen. So I smile at the aunt who asked me that, and I recognise her laugh. Deep inside my brain, where the forgotten dreams are stored, I've seen it before. How beautifully you speak, she says, How beautiful your Persian is still, what a lovely accent. They kiss my throat and the back of my neck, and it gives me goosepimples and a strange kind of excitement that has no place here, as little as David's beautiful face does; it suddenly pops into my head and I push it aside for later, when everyone's asleep and all these eyes aren't focused on me.

David's chin is a little like Kurt Cobain's chin. His shoulders and his hair, too. No way, Marie said, You're just into hippies, that's what it is. Because every man who doesn't bleach his hair and spike it up with gel is always a hippy.

David's forefinger on my belly, which I am holding in; a straight line of fine hair running between my breasts and down my abdomen, a line like animals have, when the fur on their back is parted into two halves. David's finger, walking along it, and I guess this is something he's never seen before. I mean, in the changing rooms I've seen that the others don't have one, a thousand times over. Marie and Maja have pale, flat stomachs, and the most you can see is a glitter of gold in the swimming pool. I considered just shaving everything that could be shaved, even if it's the skin on my belly. Because I knew what David had in mind, because it wasn't for nothing that I told my parents I was staying at Marie's, and then caught the bus to David's brother's house, to watch *Wetten, dass ... ?* and his *Mission Impossible* video together.

And to have David's arm around me, when he switches the TV off, puts his leg on my tense body, when he closes his eyes and snuggles into me and suddenly breathes on the back of my neck like a child. You can be tall and broad but in the end still childlike. I can't fall asleep when someone's pressing against me like that, with my bare arms around him as if I could protect him. And when the whole time I'm thinking, what if his brother does come home after all? In the TV dramas, they always leave their bras on so that viewers can't see anything, and I would have preferred to do the same. And I pulled the duvet up, so as not to be completely naked. But no one does the bra thing in reality. Still, I'm always glad about the bras on TV, because otherwise it would be even more embarrassing to watch *Unter Uns* when Mama or Papa happened to be around, and it's a shame you can't pretend that's normal. Being totally naked is weird; when you're totally naked your breasts lie weirdly and no one should see them the way they look then.

The next day, David asked if I wanted a shower, because he'd just had one, and I said no and wondered if he would think it was weird I wasn't showering, if it might be disgusting or dirty. But what would Mama and Papa have said if I came back showered from Marie's house? When Mama knows that I wash my curls every second day, and knows exactly which day that is, because she washes her hair the same day. I could have given them some excuse, but I couldn't have lived with the idea of it making her suspicious.

David's forefinger on my belly, I think, as they kiss the back of my neck; David's forefinger in the air during a class test, to ask if he can go the toilet, where he'll cheat; there's a crib sheet in the toilets, but I didn't put it there. David's forefinger, tapping my nose and saying, Ski jumpers could come down that, you've got a ski jump on your face, and I laughed, although there were so many jokes about my nose, at primary school, at secondary, always. The same nose as my mother, the same nose as my aunts, who have had operations, because plastic surgery is commonplace in the land of large noses. David's fingers in my curls, David's hands on my arms, asking if I ever get sunburned, and my reluctance to answer; the weird feeling of being with him in the first place, and then such a reluctance to go home, where no one knows about it. Back to our seventy-square-metre flat, where there is lunch and supper and they're eaten as a family, everything always done as a family: we watch the Sunday night police drama as a family and go shopping as a family, and Tara and I even go to bed at the same time because we share a room and she won't accept the idea of saying goodnight earlier than me. That night, when I was back in my own bed, she went to sleep at once, as usual; I could hear the voice of the newsreader on television through the door, and I lay awake and thought, is the lie about wearing a bra in bed just as much of a lie as falling asleep in someone's arms?

No one ever told me it would be my arms that someone else would fall asleep in. And I would never have imagined that someone could fall asleep in my skinny arms and feel protected. Except my brother and sister, when they were little, I suppose. But not at home, only when we were on holiday — like the first holiday we went on. It felt like an experiment, and it was only later I realised that this was the first time we'd planned anything in Germany as much as nine months in advance. Months before, as a ten-year-old, I had filled in all the paperwork for the family to get tickets for the ferry to Sweden, where we were going to visit Amu Ghader and his family. Amu Ghader is Papa's friend from way back. They used to be neighbours, and he always looks very serious. He's a bit older than Papa and so he talks more than the other adults, but anyway, the only thing I was looking forward to was seeing his daughter.

In order to catch the early morning ferry, we spent the whole night in the car, Mo's warm head resting on my shoulder, like he was a toddler again, although he was going

139

to start school after the holidays, and Tara lay across Mo and me, with the most room, breathing peacefully and softly, and I was the only one who was scared someone would come. Mama and Papa in the front, each in their own seat, and I thought, What if someone knows there are foreigners in here, what if someone sets fire to the car?

On the ferry, we were safe. Safer than ever before. On the ferry, the five of us were an island, sitting around the plastic table of the on-board restaurant, Tara wanting to go and play with the other children in the ball pool, and Mo wanting more Coke, and Papa asking questions like, What's the capital of Sweden? What language do they speak in Sweden? Asking, Who is the queen of Sweden? And always alternating between a hard question and an easy one, so that Mo could answer, too. But Mo didn't answer, he just wanted more Coke, and I thought, if the boat sinks, then all five of us will sink together. And I thought, if someone tried to hurt us now, he wouldn't be able to get away, because he'd be on a boat with nowhere to run to, and so no one will hurt us. And that was a nice feeling, a safe feeling, the greatest feeling of safety.

The nights are quiet in Tehran. The days, so loud. The people in the house so loud, talking so loudly about unimportant things and hesitating so loudly about important things. Their laughter so loud, the names they call out so loud, the way they say those polite sentences so loud, throwing them out like breathing. Their presence so loud, fabric-swathed bodies in a protected space, the clatter of crockery so loud as they cook, eat, drink tea — a constant silvery, dry clatter of one thing against another. Outside, the streets: a horrible racket, traffic backed up, horns honking despite the no-horns signs, people yelling and cursing, the heavy air that seems to create the racket in your head, the exhaust fumes you breathe in, the abiding feeling of being heavy and carrying something heavy. Hands constantly touching hijabs, constantly holding coats in place, pulling sleeves down. They look beautiful in their clothes; they follow fashion. I feel misshapen, a feeling that was normal up until a few years ago but which, since I left year eight, I'd actually forgotten.

The nights are quiet in Tehran. For the last week, we've been spending every evening outside, strolling about, idling — bummeln is what we'd call it in Germany. Evenings of picnicking in the park, surrounded by so many other families and children. No one worries about bedtimes. People sell barbecued corn on the cob, and the corn tastes of the days when someone would carry me around on their shoulders. At night, we go home to Madar Bozorg's and spread the blankets out on the rug. The blankets smell of fried onions and fried herbs, of dill and parsley and fenugreek and coriander and chives. By day, it's the freshest scent in the world, but at night, when it clings to your bedcovers as they lie sticky and heavy on you, it's the stalest smell you can imagine. We hear breathing and snoring, and the air conditioning unit, and, when we can't sleep and are just dozing, the singing of the muezzin.

And until then, I'm aware of the human bodies, the warmth they give off in the drily cooled room, the way they sweat and roll over. They are recovering from the day, which has been an unusual one for them as well. Since we've been here — Mama, Tara, and I, the visitors from Germany, the exotic foreigners, the cute little cartoon stars, Fievel Mousekewitz maybe — since we've been here, their life seems to have switched to holiday mode, too. We're all together, all the uncles and aunts and their children from all over the country, staying here as guests of my Madar Bozorg, who must have been about a hundred even when I was little, and still is — a hundred, and not a day older. Her short legs carry her body into the kitchen — a body that has been through an early marriage, eleven pregnancies, and widowhood at a young age, too — to fry kilos and kilos of meat and herbs and onions and eggplant, to soak the rice, to stir the rice, to keep the gas on almost all day, to stir the oily sauces, let them simmer, so that each ingredient releases precisely the amount of flavour it should. And then she is the real centre of things; it isn't about us so much.

The first few days after we arrived, they all stayed at Madar Bozorg's, Mama's relatives and Papa's relatives, but now the ones who couldn't stay any longer have gone. My other grandparents, Papa's parents, came for the first two days as well, although they rarely leave the house since they got old and set in their ways, as my uncle says. It was only for us that they made an exception and travelled outside their familiar neighbourhood. They ate with us, asked me about Papa, played with Tara, talked and laughed with Mama, but they still looked so thoughtful the whole time.

There are a few people left, though — people we usually

talk about at home over dinner, whose photos hang on the wall of my parents' bedroom, the subjects of stories we never tire of hearing. People I still have mental images of from my childhood, which are now being overlaid with new images. New ones every day. They sleep on the floor with us, on the rug where we sit and eat during the day, where I sat and drew pictures as a child. The rug where my grandparents were eating when my father came to ask for my mother's hand in marriage, and where they had dinner when my parents left without saying goodbye to anyone. The rugs are woven by children, I would have thought in Germany, and I'd have gone round collecting signatures with Marie against child labour. Here, every home we visit has a huge number of rugs on its floors, but it feels like another universe.

They sleep and snore, and it's funny how meaningless sleeping bodies are for a waking body, how meaningless when they're lying asleep beside you — I might as well be back in Germany then, I'd get just as little from them. We're here for twenty-five days, Mama said on the first night, but if I stay awake through the nights, then it's fifty days, so don't you go sending me to bed. She said it sadly, although it was a joke, and everyone looked sad, because it wasn't funny, and in the evenings they keep talking until they can't talk any more, until their eyes start to close and another day is already over and the next one is beginning.

Madar Bozorg's doorbell always rings in the morning. Then the little boy from next door comes in with the bread, a pile of huge, hot flatbreads that comes walking into the house as if there was no little boy behind them. Every morning, my uncle tells him he can stop coming; there are lots of visitors here who can go and get bread themselves, so Madar Bozorg doesn't need help right now. Then the little boy smiles and looks around, for Tara and the other children, says a polite goodbye to my uncle, and runs off to play with them.

I do as the adults do and sit around. The heat presses in on the windowpanes from outside, herbs are prepared for the day's meals, plans are made and discussed with other people on the phone. I never quite know what the day will bring, and am always dependent on what the adults plan. My cousin Ava is sitting beside me on the floor, slicing fruit and cucumbers for the children, and telling me about the family who want to come and see us tomorrow evening.

To begin with, I tried to keep the visitors separate in my mind, but the more people want to see us, the more confused I get. Papa's neighbours and people who were at school with him, friends of Mama and Papa — they're all allocated their own time, either popping round to visit us here or, if they're a bit more important, inviting us to their house for a meal. That means the adults call a taxi, we put on our mantos and hijabs, pull on our dusty shoes, and venture out into the dome of heat and smog that covers Tehran. This morning, there were excited phone calls, not just about the visits, but about a hair appointment that all the women are keen to attend, which is fixed for this afternoon.

Ava cuts cucumbers lengthways, scoops their seeds out, salts them, and calls the children over. As if she was much older and responsible. The children come and take a piece and run back to their dice game. It would never occur to me to offer the children cucumber and fruit without being asked. I wouldn't know if people would think it was appropriate. But no one asked Ava to do this, she just did it, and no one was surprised. So I pick up her knife and start cutting cucumbers, too, which is better than sitting around waiting for someone to fire the starting gun for the next visit. Ava slices open a peach, it releases its perfume, and now that I've learned what real peaches taste and smell like, I never want to eat a peach in Germany again.

When the phone rings, Ava only glances up. The adults are in the kitchen — Madar Bozorg needed help — the children are playing in the corner, and her own hands are sticky. Can you get that? she asks, like it's an annoying but obvious thing. I look over at the green plastic phone with its rotary dial. We used to have one like that. But I don't want to get it. The call won't be for me. I don't want to speak to a stranger in Persian. Ava stares at me impatiently, already slicing into the next peach without looking. I try to act like it was my own idea as I lay the cucumber aside, pick up the receiver and say, Bale? Yes? There is a moment of silence on the other end of the line. I hope it's just Papa, or Khale Azar calling about the hair appointment.

Allo? I hear a man's voice saying. Allo? I say, wishing I could hang up. Ava, is that you? the voice asks, and I can hear it must be a very young man. No, I say, this is Laleh. There is another silence on the line, and then all at once the boy sounds cheerful, almost excited. Laleh! he says, Laleh, how are you, did you have a good journey, how is your mother? Yes, I say, thank you, we're fine. The stock phrases come out of my mouth now quite naturally. Laleh, it's Nima, do you remember me? Yes, I say, how are you? And while Nima is responding with his stock phrases, I wonder who the hell Nima is. All the cousins on my mother and my father's sides have already been to visit us. None of them is called Nima. I haven't heard that name since we've been here. But this Nima seems to know exactly who I am.

Laleh, my mother has already tried to reach you; she's not very well at the moment, but she'd love to see you all, it's important to her. Thank you, I say, kheyli mamnun. Because that's usually the right response. Nima doesn't really know what to say then, and I'm sorry about that, but I don't, either. I don't even know who his mother is and why she wants to see us. Could you pass that on to your mother? That we'd love you to come round? he asks eventually, and I think, I could go and get my mother now, but then I'd have to walk into the kitchen and say, Nima's on the phone, and everyone would see that I don't know who Nima is. I'll tell her, I reply, kheyli mamnun. Nima hesitates, and then says goodbye in a significantly less hyper voice.

Ava looks at me, amused. So who was it? she asks. Nima, I say, as if that's perfectly normal. His mother isn't well, but she'd like to see us. Ava nods, as if she has been expecting something like this. She says: later on, let's not take the taxi to the hairdresser with the others — we can walk. I say, Good idea, and wonder whether I have, in fact, heard the name Nima before.

The air conditioning in the taxis never works, and hot air blows in through the windows. When you get to where you're going, you're drenched in sweat, no matter how much or how little you're wearing underneath your manto. But walking down the street is even worse. So many people and so many cars in motion, but the air doesn't shift even a centimetre.

Do you wear make-up, at home? Ava asks. At my side, she is walking purposefully, because she knows the way, and yet I have the feeling she might fall over at any moment with the rapid, uncontrolled way she moves. She's tall and lanky, with big, dark eyes that look even bigger under her hijab. I imagine Marie seeing her — imagine us sitting in class together, and this new student turning up, and Marie and I would think she could be in our friendship group, and we'd think about whether we would get on with her. I think Marie would get on with Ava, and vice versa. The Ava from before, who I remember so well. But the only thing that Ava has in common with this one walking beside me is her name; there's nothing else, though I do know it's her, and she doesn't seem to have any problem connecting me with the child from before, either. Or maybe she doesn't care, as long as I'm walking beside her and talking to her. I don't like make-up, I say, and that makes me think of Marie's eyelashes stuck together with black, and how funny she looks when she isn't wearing make-up and instead has short, spiky bristles for lashes.

Are you allowed to wear it at school? Ava asks, turning her saucer-eyes on me. They're almost too big for me to find them beautiful, I think, and it's a good job she doesn't wear make-up on top of that. Yes, I say, we're allowed, and talking to Ava I feel a bit guilty for never doing it even though we're allowed. Because from the school's point of view, of course I could, but it would be weird to wear make-up in front of Mama and Papa — I'd have to explain, give them reasons, find convincing arguments for why going to school in make-up is a good idea, on an adult level, a theoretical level. And that's just too stressful.

A friend of mine painted her fingernails, Ava says, and they pulled them out. She says it without any emotion in her voice, and for a moment I have the horrific image of fingers without nails and how painful that must be. And because I don't know what to say to that, but silence also feels uncomfortable, I say, But you wear nail varnish, too, right? It was the first thing I saw at the airport when they came to pick us up: they stood in front of us, and they said, Here she is, your Laleh; here's your Ava, as if we'd once been a married couple or were going to become one, and then she held out the flowers to me, and I found myself looking at a set of red fingernails.

Ava spreads her fingers in front of me, suddenly and boisterously, and it takes some concentration to focus on her fingers and the street at the same time. The nails are normal again, with no colour on them. All gone, she says. It's only for special occasions. So picking us up from the airport is a special occasion, I think, and feel guilty once again.

You could make up your eyes really prettily, says Ava, and get your eyebrows plucked. Sara Khanoom is really good at that. Sara Khanoom is a name they've been using a lot since yesterday, since a firm plan was made to go to the hairdresser's, to Sara Khanoom: Miss Sara. I imagine her as a kind of queen, to whom the women go when they want to be saved, and then Sara Khanoom uses her wisdom and her skill on them.

With every step we take, dust whirls up from the street, and there is a smell of hot asphalt and petrol in the air. We're walking along uneven pavements, past little grocery shops, which sell brightly coloured plastic toys alongside drinks and pistachios. Ava walks quickly, and I try to follow, and realise that moving in the heat doesn't make me feel good, that I'm sweating under my manto, and later people will be able to see how much I've sweated. My heart is racing and I am breathing faster, inhaling this thick, heavy air. I can't see the sun, but I can feel it reflecting back at us from every paving stone, from every stone wall; every window of every car throws heat back at us. I don't know if everything around us is really frantic, or if the noise of the cars is what makes it feel like that.

I try to act like I belong here, like I walk down these dust-whirling streets in my canvas shoes every day, like I know where I'm going and this is all completely routine. Like I know all secrets and keep them to myself, the way Ava does. Everyone here has their secrets, I think, and how could they not. I've heard so many secrets just in the last few days. Where they get their alcohol, who meets up with whom to drink it, who got what amount of money from whom to launch some risky enterprise, and who plans to start looking for a husband, right away. Everyone has secrets, and they are only spoken of quietly. I walk behind Ava, thinking they must be able to see a mile off that I don't have any secrets like those.

You should make up your eyes, Ava says — then they'll look bigger. I don't reply. I'm a bit hurt. It isn't even an important statement for her; it seems like just one incidental bit of information in a conversation. We walk, and I look people in the eyes. Women wearing chadors, the same large, black cloth my grandmother puts on when she leaves the house. Wearing a chador over their hijab and manto, one hand clamping it under their elbow, and a shopping bag in the other, their eyes on the ground. Mama says chadors aren't compulsory in the street; women only wear one if they want to.

I imagine having one of these chadors in Germany and being able to just hide my body under it, like being under a blanket, and spending the whole day surrounded by that protection you feel when you wake up in bed in the morning, protection from looks, protection for my body. I imagine it would be nice, actually — if I didn't already know that in Germany, wearing a thing like that is what would really attract looks. More looks than I get already. Or Tara. Mama used to put Tara in these little dresses, and slide colourful hairclips that Khale Azar had sent over into her thick hair, and take photos of her. Tara hated it. She used to cry.

People would stop and look at Tara in the street, and tell Mama what a pretty little girl she had. Once, a man asked if he could take a photo of her. I got massively angry and was scared one of these people was going to take Tara away from us. And Mama and Papa might just say, Well then, Laleh, Mo, we're giving Tara away, she's too beautiful for us, it's just the four of us again — and you know, it was fine before, when it was just the four of us. And so I always wanted to be the one to hold Tara's little hand when we went shopping, because there was no way I would have let her go, and sometimes I was quite pleased when Tara yelled and pulled out the hairclips in the middle of Aldi, and people stopped looking like they wanted to steal her.

Ava says, We need to cross here, and she hooks her fingers into the sleeve of my manto and stops at the kerb. Before us lies a three-lane road, with traffic hurtling past, five or six cars deep. When one car gets too close to another, they speed up, honk their horns, and the drivers shout insults at each other — and I think, I'll have to remember these, so I can teach them to Mo when I get home; he'll be ridiculously pleased. It didn't use to be like this, Mama said on the first day with a shake of her head, when we were in a stifling taxi; she was looking out at the honking cars and then ahead at our yelling taxi driver. Khale Azar smiled and said, What did you think, Nahid? That we'd still be helping and supporting one another on the streets, like we did during the Revolution? And Mama's sisters laughed, a bark of mean laughter; Mama was the only one looking in disbelief at these moving heaps of junk, and shaking her head. The traffic doesn't surprise me any longer — but there's no way I would dare cross the road on my own.

Ava cranes her neck forward — her white hijab doesn't have a single crease in it — takes my arm, looks to the left, waits for a few speeding cars to pass, then suddenly sets off, dragging me firmly behind her. The approaching cars don't slow down even though there are two living humans in the road, and halfway across Ava suddenly slows her pace and cranes her neck again, to let one of the cars right in front of us go past. Faster now, she hisses, pulling me after her, and I'm unbelievably glad when we reach the pavement on the opposite side. The cars never stop; somewhere, traffic lights flash helplessly.

Ava keeps up her cheerful chatter. Telling me that Mama always sends such good lipsticks, for her mother, and she was hoping we'd bring another one that she could use as well, in secret. I have absolutely no idea whether we've brought a lipstick for her mother, and it makes me feel uncomfortable. We had three suitcases full of presents. Men's shirts, ladies' slippers, toy cars, swimsuits, and jars of Nutella. Things Mama has bought and saved over the last few years, in a crate under my parents' bed, which she and Papa then emptied and went through to decide who should get what. There must have been lipsticks in there, but as to who was given which present, I don't have a clue. Because presents are given in secret, like you're doing something indecent. Packed into shopping bags and given to the families when they've said goodbye to us, in the evening. So it's best if I say nothing.

I wonder what Ava would be like if she was in Germany and in my class. She might be loud and funny, and then she'd sit with Maja and the boys at break time. Or she might rant at everyone all the time and offend them, and then she'd have no friends and everyone would be scared of her. But here, she's the person who still sleeps over at Madar Bozorg's, to stay with me. Who sits beside me in the midst of this soup of relatives and explains to me which cousin belongs to which aunt, where they all live, who has got married, who used to share a bath with us, and which doll it was that her brother and I always fought over. The person who always explains everything to me in other, easier words when I haven't understood.

When Sara Khanoom plucks your eyebrows, Ava says now, your eyes get bigger; it opens up your face. She looks at me as we walk, nodding at each word. I nod, too. She doesn't just use tweezers, Ava says, she uses a thread as well, have you seen that before? I shake my head. She laughs and says, You're going to tell all your girlfriends in Germany about this, and then they'll want to come here to get their eyebrows done as well. I laugh, too, and because I'm laughing I smile at a woman, a girl who might be the same age as us, but she frowns and looks away, like she should know me but doesn't know where from; like there must be a reason for my smile and she's racking her brains for what it could be. And the woman next to her, older, wearing a chador, answers me with an angry glance. I keep walking and think about Yasaman and how, after she and Khale Shirin had shown us the photos, she told me never to look people in the eye, and it reminded me of all the nonsense things you hear on TV.

There it is, says Ava, heading for a large, metal door painted an indeterminate, faded colour and set into a crumbling stone wall. She rings the bell and we can hear the sound from outside. I'm drenched in sweat, not daring to check under my arms. When we first got here, I was surprised at all the women wearing black mantos, because they must make you even hotter. Now I think how nice it would be if my manto was black and not grey, because no one would notice the sweat. Next time, I just won't wear anything under it, no shirt, no bra. Ava is breathing heavily. She must have found the walk hard going, too, and I'm reassured by her panting.

Ava talks to the telephone voice coming out of the intercom, and then I suddenly recoil because a hand is sliding across my back and slowly down to my bottom. I turn around — there are countless people walking past us, paying us no attention — and then the door hums open and Ava drags me through it.

Ricky Martin is singing about Maria. Incessantly. Every so often, it goes quiet, and then we hear the cassette recorder rewinding and he starts up again, about her. Marie and I watched Ricky Martin, too, on *Bravo TV*; we danced along with ironic expressions, to give us the justification for bursting out laughing, though I think both of us secretly wondered if the way we were moving looked good. Here, we listen to Ricky Martin and no one has an ironic expression — except me, at first, when an uncle asked me if I knew the song. I laughed a little bit at that, and rolled my eyes, and he nodded, as if all he'd wanted from me was the information and he was disappointed by my behaviour. Everyone here loves Ricky Martin.

Sara Khanoom is tall and broad, and her hair has been

bleached so often it looks yellow. It stands up from her head in such a perfect halo that she must have spent several hours blow-drying it this morning, and can't possibly have put on a hijab and left the house. There is one electric fan in her lounge, and two more in the room where she does our hair. The doors to the other rooms are closed. The cooler packed up this morning, she says in a voice heavy with meaning. She takes a deep breath, and my aunts sigh and are outraged, as though that was the most important thing on the country's mind on this particular morning, and I wonder whether a woman like Sara Khanoom can actually sweat, whether a face so plastered in make-up can get wet, when it looks about as dry as the landscape around Tehran. My aunts say, Sara Khanoom, you need to look after yourself, you should get your blood sugar tested, and Sara Khanoom combs my mother's hair, snips a few final strands, sighs gravely, and enjoys everyone's concern for her — the only person in this room standing rather than sitting.

When I take a seat in the chair, she calls me azizam and asks me what shape I want my eyebrows, and in a soft voice I say, I don't know. This voice gets more childlike when it speaks Persian, because I now know that I have an accent, and people can hear there is something not right about me and my words. I'd been thinking that what I could do as a child, I could still do now. But either I couldn't do it properly as a child, or that was a false assumption, and acting more childlike doesn't help, either, but I haven't come up with a better solution yet. Mama plants herself right next to Sara Khanoom and says things like, Her forehead is so high, it would be good to lift the brows a little; she says words for eyebrow styles that she can't possibly have known from before, words she must have learned while Ava and I were walking.

Sara Khanoom nods and smiles and says, Where is she from? And Mama says, Alman, az Alman. Weird that Germany sounds like a foreign, exotic place when you say it in Tehran and in Persian. Alman is a word I don't associate at all with our home, with our flat, my room, my route to school. But for Sara Khanoom, this word seems to spark a whole lot of associations. She raises her head and breathes in deeply, takes a long look at my face in the mirror, much too long, and I suspect she's thinking I should look different if I'm from Germany, I should be much more modern than all of them and much better put together.

She asks me incredulously, Do you not pluck your eyebrows there? I say, No — because what would Mama and Papa have thought if I'd suddenly started plucking my eyebrows? And how do you even do it? I could have asked Yasaman; none of my other friends would have been able to show me. But then if Yasaman had shown me, she'd have felt superior again, like the better Iranian. Sara Khanoom turns my head to the side and narrows her eyes. I am starting to suspect she's making a special effort with my face, now she knows it'll be flying back to Germany with me.

And then the confusing procedure begins, whereby in the space of a few minutes a face is transformed into a grown-up doll's face without any annoying little hairs and with perfectly shaped eyebrows. A procedure that involves combing, trimming, and shaving the eyebrows, taking a length of cotton thread, forming it into a triangle, holding it in your mouth and running it across my face, my whole face, cheeks, temples, forehead, the narrow area above my upper lip, tearing out masses of fine hairs with each pass. I close my eyes from the very start, not wanting to be constantly looking at the thread and at Sara Khanoom's plump fingers, or at myself in the mirror as I try desperately not to pull faces. Everything Sara Khanoom does hurts; she pulls out little hairs from above my eyelids, what feels like an incredible number of them, and I think this is the worst pain I've ever felt in my life, there cannot be any part of the body more sensitive than the one she's currently plucking, and I imagine I can hear the hairs being torn out of their roots. But my eyes are closed and there is no going back, and in a way I quite like the thought. I sit there, saying nothing; a stranger is fully in charge, and I'm not going to struggle.

It feels good to keep your eyes closed, to just close them against everything that impinges on you. Eyes closed to Mama, who is talking like I've never heard her talk before, laughing and joking and scolding and discussing things like she's never done at home, and sounding kind of wrong, kind of like a fish that has hopped out of the water, wet and gleaming, and can't incorporate itself into the dull colours of its new surroundings. But she isn't making sure I'm in her line of sight like she usually does — although she translates for me when (once again) I don't understand things right away, and answers for me when my own answer takes too long. But she doesn't tell me off when, despite my best efforts, I do something wrong again. And I stick out more here than I ever have before; I'm probably the only woman in this country who hides her body and yet is more visible than she's ever been in her life. You walk differently, they say, You look at people differently.

Sara Khanoom works her way right down under my chin, to the fine little hairs I always thought maybe no one would notice, but Sara Khanoom has noticed them. If Sara Khanoom has noticed them, then maybe David has, too, and that makes me blush, although I know my face must be red anyway, my nose must be red, because the tears are starting to well up in my eyes from all the stinging pain. A simple reflex that makes my eyes grow wet and my nose run, and I feel the tears slowly slide down my face. I find it an odd idea that the others can see that, though I can't see anyone, but I let the tears flow. They can't touch me if I can't see them.

The others see me being inept all the time, I think, incapable of giving a straight answer to shopkeepers, incapable of ordering myself a bottle of water. I don't even have my own money here. And now, when I can't see them, when they're hidden behind my eyelids, behind the shadow of Sara Khanoom's arm, behind the occasional flash of sunlight, behind the hum of the fan and Sara Khanoom's stories about her relatives in Sweden, weirdly, I feel sympathy for them all. How overjoyed they are that we're here, day after day. The way they kiss and squeeze Tara as if she was the cutest little thing there had ever been. The way they think I must be a really great person, even when I don't say anything. The way they always find everything exciting and make so much effort to look beautiful, only to then hide themselves under a hijab. And the way I just can't take what they're doing and how they're doing it completely seriously, because I'm always kind of thinking, Sure, you're ridiculously nice and you're fond of me, but actually you're not leading a real life here; real life is in Germany. There, you can make decisions about your own future, you might be able to change things that aren't going well, and if you break the rules in the process, they call it individualism. And the thought instantly makes me feel bad.

Tell me something about Germany, Ava said to me last night. She was lying beside me on the rug, and in the dim light I could sense her breath and the expectant look in her eyes, wanting stories of adventure. I complied and told her what she wanted to hear, and as I was doing it I was thinking of the things no one wants to hear about Germany. I told her what the people in my class are like, and that in the afternoons we meet at the pool or in the ice-cream parlour; that we organise birthday parties together with other people who have birthdays at the same time, so that we can invite as many guests as possible. That we have barbecues and bonfires and dance to Bravo Hits CDs, and then I explained what Bravo Hits are. I didn't tell her that when we wanted to move from our small rented flat into a larger rented flat, so that the three of us wouldn't have to share a room anymore, we just never heard back from most of the landlords we contacted. I didn't say that when I go to the hardware store with Papa, I always have the feeling that the hardware-store men don't take his hardware-store questions seriously, as if he could have no idea about screws and machines, just because he makes grammatical errors and it always takes a while for them to understand what he wants.

Tell me something about your father, was the other thing Ava asked last night. He must be a very brave man, right? she asked, because that's what she had heard from her parents and everyone else here. Yes, I said, probably. And he has a very big heart, right? she went on, probing further, and I considered saying that he never swats the flies away from his foot when they land there.

When the woman next door complains because Mo's music is too loud or because Tara is skipping in her room, Papa isn't all that brave. Then he stands in the doorway and says, Yes, you're right, we're too loud. He never says *you're right* otherwise, neither to people nor to arguments. He doesn't even let his own arguments stand, because of course you always have to bring in several different perspectives, several truths. When Papa explains something, it's always as nuanced and neutral as it could possibly be. This gets on Mo's nerves whenever he needs Papa to help him with his homework, because obviously it takes longer than someone just telling you their opinion. Mo doesn't find it brave or big-hearted.

Azizam, the pain, is it really so bad? Sara Khanoom asks, and I open my eyes again. The light in the room is dazzlingly bright and I can see only a blurry image of her — I have to get used to seeing again first, and I look away, straight at my own reflection. There I sit, solemn and tear-stained, a revolutionary's daughter in a Keith Haring T-shirt. With thin, straight eyebrows. Kheyli mamnun, I say to Sara Khanoom, my voice sounding hoarse and breathy. She smiles and says, You can greet the whole of Germany from me with those eyebrows, azizam. I will do, I say. They have such good cosmetics there, in Germany, don't they? she asks, a serious expression on her face. I nod and say, Yes, especially the lipsticks, and am glad that this answer came to me. She isn't really listening, goes on talking straightaway, turning to the others: Everything is good in Germany, the hospitals, too, the medicines, the schools, it's not like it is here, she proclaims. I don't have to say anything else, because the other women are agreeing about how good hospitals and medicines and schools are in Germany.

I take off the plastic gown and get up; it's the next person's turn. Sara Khanoom takes the gown from me without looking, as she probably does fifty times a day. When she then turns to face me once more, she suddenly breaks off in the middle of her conversation. How pretty you are now, she says, and smiles. Listen, my pretty one, enjoy your youth, your freedoms, enjoy being abroad! And she gives a little laugh as she adjusts the chair for the next person and arranges her scissors and tweezers on the cosmetics table.

When I was little, I sometimes had to go with my parents to translate. To the doctor, for instance. Or the immigration office. That's nothing special, lots of children have to do it. Whenever I told Yasaman about it, she'd raise her eyebrows. Eyebrows that she plucks just like her mother taught her, because Khale Shirin wants to be beautiful at any price, and she wants her daughter to take after her.

In any case, Yasaman smiles condescendingly at all my memories and everything I'm annoyed about, and always manages to go one better. *She* even had to translate for her mother when she secretly went to get sterilised. She had to translate things about her parents' sex life for the doctor, and she was only eleven at the time. I never know quite what to make of this. She used to lie quite a lot even as a child, so I never really liked playing with her, but every time, Mama would say I needed to be understanding; Yasaman's father lied a lot as well, and maybe she'd just never learned any different.

So when I told Yasaman that I had to go to Mo's parents' evenings and talk to the kindergarten teachers about Mo, although I was only a child myself, Yasaman shrugged her thin shoulders and said, So what? I had to translate at my own parent–teacher day. And according to Yasaman, at her own parent–teacher day, she'd had to translate all the things she had carefully concealed from her parents until that point. The fact that the other children had laughed at her, snatched her schoolbag and thrown it in the bin, and that afterwards Yasaman had beaten a boy up.

In year six, for the first time, I took home a piece of work that had been given a five. I have no idea how that happened. I always get good marks, because I find it embarrassing to stand out for getting bad ones. Especially when you're the only girl in the class who doesn't have the words Roman Catholic beside her name in the register, but Musli, and so you already stand out for that reason. Someone left off the final letter of Muslim and never corrected it over all those years. Maybe it was the same secretary who explained to my parents when I started school that I had to have a religion. And so my parents, who had never mentioned any god at all to us, thought that if everyone was something, then we probably had to be Muslims. And what is more embarrassing than being the only Musli and then getting bad marks on top of that?

It's actually quite easy to get good marks when your TV doesn't have the cable channels. And when spending lots of time with other people from school isn't that attractive, either, because you'd have to tell your parents everything about these potential new friends. The new friends who somehow always do something wrong, even when they're the nice, well-behaved ones in your class. But then they suddenly sit down at our kitchen table and start talking about how their younger siblings recently asked what sex is, or something like that, and then I'm ashamed in front of my parents and decide not to invite anyone else back to our place, and don't even bother asking if I can go to theirs — apart from Marie, who I've been friends with since primary school — and so in the afternoons, after school, I have all the time in the world.

When I got that five, my parents were concerned, and when the note about parent–teacher day went out, they filled in their preferred appointment times, working around job and university and college times, and I had to show the note to my French teacher. And Herr Meise, who is a funny, cheerful teacher, looked at my note with my parents' times on it and said, Really? Is that necessary? He stopped short of saying, Please, no. Like what he meant was: But they never really understand what I'm saying, they always take everything so very seriously, you have to explain everything to them, they're so much more stressful than normal parents. And then I kept quiet, because my belly was filled with a mixture of shame and sympathy — sympathy for my parents, whose image I suddenly had before me again in meticulous detail, the way they looked sitting in the classroom with Mo's friendly young kindergarten teacher. They looked small and sad and a bit like everything around them would collapse if they made one false move. Then Herr Meise said there was really no need for him to speak to them, and if my grades should continue to fall then my parents could make an appointment to see him outside of parent–teacher day.

I told my parents that. They didn't respond, probably wondering for a moment if I could possibly be making this up, but then they realised that Herr Meise had only said it because he had so many appointments to make with the parents of the genuinely bad students. From then on, of course, it was clear to me that my French grades mustn't slip again under any circumstances, irregular verbs or no. They must never be bad again, and no grade in any other subject must ever get so bad that my parents want to come and speak to my teachers but can't get an appointment.

Though it would actually be fine if they did come to parent–teacher day. Now that I don't have to translate for them all the time. But since that has been the case, there haven't been any more appointments. No immigration office, no employment office, and I'd almost forgotten what it was like to sit somewhere like that with them, wanting to get home again as soon as possible. Here, in Iran, some visits feel like these appointments. As if we're doing them for the record, and Tara and I need to be there because that's the correct protocol. As if we have to ensure that Papa is always the subject of conversation at these appointments, which sometimes makes it feel like he's dead, like he lived hundreds of years ago and is kept alive by people saying his name over and over.

We are sitting in Madar Bozorg's living room again; another day has passed that is so like all the other days, I can no longer separate them in my mind. It's just that since yesterday, since we went to see Sara Khanoom, all the women have new haircuts, new hair colours, new eyebrows, and that's all anyone talks about.

My eyebrows still hurt from the plucking torture, and my body is narrow and out of place. The clothes I wear here are things I wouldn't even wear to exercise in at home. Relics from a time when I listened to Nirvana and Marie liked Guns N' Roses. When we wanted to hide our bodies because they weren't doing what we wanted. Here, now, I suddenly want to hide my body again, because I get a funny feeling that it's a big issue, for everyone.

You spend the days and evenings sitting on the floor, and you're never allowed to turn your back on anyone while you're sitting there, and if you do, you have to say, Sorry for turning my back on you. It means you're never allowed to stretch your legs out, though you're bursting to do exactly that and feel like you're going to go mad if you don't do it immediately, because more than three hours of sitting with your legs bent and propped on your own feet is painful and drives you crazy. You have to always make sure your body is doing the right thing.

When a new visitor arrives, you have to stand up. The door opens, and all at once everyone gets up off the floor, even the old people, and of course the visitor says, Oh no, please do sit down, but you still have to wait until they've been round and said hello to everyone in turn, and only then do you get back into your original sitting position, and carry on the conversation you were having as if nothing has happened.

And the saying hello bit has the most pitfalls. Women shake hands and kiss each other three times on the cheeks, but then sometimes there will be a woman who we only shake hands with, and how embarrassing would it be if I suddenly started kissing her. With the men, we only shake hands, but then there are the uncles, the blood relatives, older gentlemen who keep their distance from all women, but then give me three kisses, too, and so do their wives, who aren't blood relatives. Children are the most confusing. Pretty, angelic little things with immensely long eyelashes, politely holding out a hand and at the same time offering up their cheek to me. Because they're used to the adult women kissing them. But I don't feel like an adult woman; I stand facing a five-year old in a little white plastic-lace dress and feel like she is the older one here, and I have absolutely no desire to kiss her. Though it would be the rudest thing in the world if I didn't.

Tara has it easy. Tara doesn't have to do anything. Everyone else does to Tara what the rules say you have to do by way of greeting. Sometimes Mama will tell her off for something, but then Tara isn't a child who gets upset when you tell her off. She just does as she's told for a minute, and then goes straight back to playing football with the other kids. Whole sections of the street are occupied by them, and Tara comes back sweaty and dirty and talking just as fast as the other children and using words she's never used before. I envy her all that, and for the fact that no one is interested in her bony little child's body. That she wears the same clothes as boys her age, and that it will probably be at least another year before she has to start covering her hair in the street.

Sometimes I would like to be her. But sometimes, I just want to take her aside for a minute, be alone with her for a minute and tell her: Tara, this here isn't real. This is a dream. Right now, you've got everything. But in a week and a half, Tara, they'll take it away from you again. When I hear Tara laughing, in among the other kids, I think, it's weird; that laugh totally belongs in Tehran, with all the other treasures I've rediscovered here. And yet it's the laugh from Germany; how can it survive in this heat? How can she have imported her laugh, and how can it fit in so seamlessly? And how can her complaining fit in here so seamlessly, as soon as she's dissatisfied?

In the beginning, Tara diligently came to visit everyone with us and was glad of their kisses. But since she's begun to feel at home here, she starts complaining when appointments are coming up, and earlier, when the phone rang again and Mama picked up and everyone suddenly went serious and silent, I had an inkling it would be another of those visits-for-the-record that Tara would complain about.

Mama told the others: That was Nima. She said it quietly, and everyone stopped talking. And I thought, good job I didn't pick up again; I couldn't help this Nima the last time he called. It was only then that I realised everyone was looking sad, and Mama said, He was calling on behalf of Simin; she isn't well, but she'd like us to come over.

Simin is not the person she used to be, is all Khale Azar said, with a rueful shake of her head, as if sadly, she had experienced this all too often, and was at the same time glad it wasn't happening to her.

Mama raised her shoulders a little. No wonder, she murmured, and I suddenly remembered the name Nima again, Nima and Yashar, Amme Simin's and Amu Peyman's sons. I thought I would like to start complaining like Tara now. I'd like to moan: Oh no, not another one of those visits that's just designed to make everyone sad.

My body, small and narrow, is sitting on a black leather sofa. Everything here is black, with glass features. Only the large, delicately patterned rug has the usual red in it, the usual brown, a little yellow, and a lot of dark green. Green carpets are the most expensive, my uncle who works in the bazaar explained, green wool is dyed with pistachios, and what is more expensive than pistachios? This rug looks like it's sad about all the wasted pistachios, and the soft yellow doesn't glow anymore, either. Yellow is dyed with saffron — and as my uncle said that, he probably realised himself that there absolutely is something more expensive than pistachios, but this rug is sad about all the wasted flowers picked for their saffron, too.

Tara is also looking at the rug. She is being petulant. This morning, at Madar Bozorg's, she made an embarrassingly loud fuss because Mama told her she had to come out with her and me and she wasn't allowed to play with the other children. And that she had to get changed. And that there was no getting out of it. Tara shouted that she wanted to go back to Germany, right now, and then all the aunts suddenly started crying, because they blamed themselves for Tara's home not being where they are.

I imagined that Marie had a camera and was able to see us; Marie would be sitting at home and looking right into the room. She would definitely be wondering why people here cry all the time. I got changed into my long black trousers and one of my smarter long-sleeved shirts, and was ashamed that people were crying because of my little sister, and in fact I understand it just as little as Marie, sitting at home in front of the TV she doesn't have. And then I thought that Marie would think a lot of things here were really good, as well. She would like the abundant dishes of oily food, and she'd like how the hosts would come up to you beaming as if each meal was a feast. Driving at night through the shimmering city, music booming in the car, barbecuing in the countless parks under the smoggy sky. Strolling around the shopping streets or the bazaar with its thousands of stalls, and there is a smell of roses and a smell of pepper, and somewhere they're selling sheep's heads, and there is nothing more colourful than the piles of sparkly fabrics. The parties at night, the dancing and singing and drumming when my mother's brothers come to visit. Playing cards and napping after the meal, when everyone spreads out quietly on the floor and falls into a food coma. It would be the best holiday Marie could imagine, for sure.

Amme Simin invited us in and brought us tea. We've drunk so much black tea with so many families. When you're visiting, when you're sitting together, things are always served up in the same order. First there's a cold, sweet syrupy juice that no one likes, but everyone drinks to be polite, because everyone serves it to be polite. Then the plates come out. Then the knives. Then the fruit. Then the tea. Then the nuts and pistachios. Actually, every family works the same way. But at Amme Simin's, the tea came straightaway. The large fruit basket and a pile of plates are sitting on the glass table. Befarma, help yourselves, she said at the start in a weary voice, gesturing at the impressive array of colours, but no one took any fruit except Mama, who put two plums on her plate out of politeness and then set the plate to one side.

I look at Amme Simin's tired face and try to locate the woman from my vague memories. Vague memories of her and her husband, Papa's best friend, as I always called him when I told my friends about him, when I wanted to tell them how brutal it is, this country about which people know little more than that it beat the USA in the football world cup. Amme Simin was one of the lovely aunts, back then, one of those who didn't harangue you, whose attention you wanted. And she used to comb my hair, because she only had sons, two cheeky, curly-headed boys.

I only have memories of Amu Peyman being in the background. In the background, looking serious, with Papa. Always with Papa. But sometimes — and these were special days and special moments — he would be our playmate, inventing thrilling stories for our games about mysterious lands under the tablecloth, or stories in which we were the heroes: me, Mo, and Amu Peyman's sons. Sometimes they came to visit us, and I would look forward to those games so much — but then we wouldn't play at all; he would just give us a smile and spend the whole time talking to Papa, and what they talked about was nothing to do with me. Things that adults do. Things that I can't say when I began to understand. My parents did forbidden things in a country where everything is forbidden. That's how I would explain it to Tara, if she asked. But Tara doesn't ask. Maybe Tara understands without asking.

Amme Simin greeted us very quickly, with few words, and ushered us into her flat. I don't know exactly what we were expecting, but I know it wasn't that. Mama talks politely about the flat, praises the location, talks about how Tehran has changed, has got larger and noisier, so many tower blocks all over the place suddenly, a lot more cars than there used to be. Amme Simin's beautiful, tender face is pale. She nods tentatively, speaks calmly, rolls her eyes a little at the end of every sentence, and all at once I'm really frightened for her. A woman who was so beautiful and now has white, undyed hair and whose eyes never seem to open fully. She is slender but still looks like her body is much too heavy for her. She looks as though the small talk she is currently engaged in is the most tiring thing she could be doing. Mama grows quieter. Looks at the walls, the photos. Photos that are old and yellowing, in between current family portraits of various young people I don't know. And a single photo that looks like the standard martyr portraits on the walls of buildings. Men who fell in the Iran–Iraq war, soldiers who died for the Islamic government. This soldier looks insanely young, barely a few years older than me; he is carrying a machine gun and his large jug ears make him look like a helpless child.

When it gets very quiet, and everyone has stopped talking, I can hear Mama sobbing. Amme Simin, who is looking at me, smiles. You've grown into a real lady, Laleh Khanoom, she claims. I smile sheepishly, blink, and tilt my head to one side, a gesture I have copied from Ava — except Ava doesn't look this helpless when she does it. What are you doing now, are you still at school? she asks, looking right through me, and I say, Yes, I'm in year ten. She nods and says, That's nice. Then for a while she looks silently at Mama, who is crying. I wonder what Tara is thinking now. Tara, who is seeing something like this for the first time, probably. People in a room talking seriously, talking about nothing, and yet completely broken by it. In my mind, my whole childhood — in Iran, in the migrant hostel, in our first flat — is like this: friends of my parents coming to visit, talking seriously, bringing news. No one puts us to bed; we're just sent there. Papa lies in front of the radio, Mama has red eyes in the morning, and no one talks to us, to Mo and me. Always yet another pale, thin uncle coming round, or yet another angry aunt, and always lists of signatures being sent to the UN. I was six, and no word was uttered more often than UN, and in the end they're killed anyway, despite the list of signatures. Before Amu Peyman was killed, they collected signatures more busily than ever before.

Papa suddenly stopped just lying in front of the radio; Papa suddenly stopped being Papa. Maybe he was the person he'd been before Germany again, maybe he was a person without a family. I came home from school and there was no lunch. My parents asked if I'd like to go and play at a friend's house today. I went along with that, but really I wanted to stay with them, to know what had happened. I wanted to make sure I'd understood it all properly: first Papa had a friend, and then the friend was in prison for a long time, and then they collected signatures, and then he was dead anyway. And Papa was alone. Amu Peyman's name wasn't spoken very much after that. Nor Amme Simin's.

Now we're sitting here like strangers, with Amme Simin looking at Tara, looking at her for a very long time, and then saying, She's the spitting image of Agha Behzad. She asks me if Tara speaks Persian, and I say, Yes, better than I do. Amme Simin laughs, a bright, clear laugh like a young girl's. Your German daughter, she says and admires Tara's curls and her pretty face, the black eyes, the soft skin. Tara looks at her and says nothing, because she's still being petulant about having to come here.

Amme Simin asks her the same thing everyone always asks — she asks, Is it nicer here or in Germany? Do you like it better here or in Germany? Would you rather live here or in Germany? Tara and I always answer politely: Nemidunam,

I don't know. Because we have to give some kind of answer, and because this question is on everyone's mind except ours. But I look Tara in the eye and realise she is so petulant that she isn't even going to force out a Nemidunam; she looks at Amme Simin, takes a breath, and her childish eyes grow so hard and unyielding that for a second I'm afraid of my little sister, and then she says, That's a silly question, of course it's better in Germany, everything is better in Germany, in Germany people don't die, and they don't put kids in jail there, either. Amme Simin smiles and whispers, I know that, Tarajan, I know that, believe me. And then she says, I was just hoping that you might like it a little here even so, with your family. They've missed you so much, they talk of nothing else.

Mama doesn't look at Tara, and I know she's ashamed on her behalf, and then she asks, Have you heard from Yashar? Amme Simin nods and says, Yes, and the outlook for him isn't too bad, Nima has been in touch with a good lawyer. And Tara, still petulant, asks, How old is Yashar? Amme Simin gives her a long look. He'll be nineteen soon. Tara groans — Oh, I see, so he *isn't* actually a child anymore, and Amme Simin says, That's true, but he's still my child. She rubs her eyes and apologises: her new medication always makes her so tired. She asks how old Mo is now, and what he's doing, and whether he looks like us, and eventually she and Tara and I fall into friendly conversation.

I find Tara's questions kind of silly and childish, and so I start asking the questions that I could have been asking the whole time, ever since we got to Iran, but never had the chance, in among all the invitations and outings and picnics and cuddles — when was I supposed to ask questions like, What time do the shops shut in the afternoons and at night? And what are women's favourite shops here? Amme Simin seems to like me, and that seems to be because of the everyday questions I'm asking, and so I ask more and more, and it's only as we're putting our outdoor shoes back on that I realise Mama hasn't spoken for a long time, and only when we're getting into the stuffy taxi in our hijabs does it occur to me that Amme Simin didn't ask after our father, not so much as a word about him.

She was suicidal, Khale Azar hisses. Unlike Mama, she's incapable of really whispering. The first few nights we were here, the two of them whispered secretly to each other for a long time, and there was an extraordinary amount of giggling. They giggle less now, but whisper all the more. I can hear every word, even though I'm actually trying to think about David. Night is the best time to think about him. To imagine him on top of me, caressing my arms, my face, my body. In the daytime, I get the sense that people can see these thoughts.

I've got quite good at thinking about something else and blocking out Mama's and Khale Azar's whispering, because I have no interest in what they're talking about. But khodkoshi is a word that makes me prick up my ears. *Suicide* sounds much gentler; *khodkoshi* actually sounds like a violent act, and maybe that makes it the right word. Mama says she heard about that. Khale Azar speaks quickly and through her nose, telling Mama that it wasn't when they killed the husband, but later, when one of the sons, Yashar, got addicted to drugs. I turn onto my side — maybe I'll hear less if I'm lying on one ear.

Everyone is always so friendly to one another, and we have these polite visits that leave me with a sense of contentment. But that contentment only lasts until it's night-time and someone is filling everyone else in. Because then behind this friendly exterior there will be another terrible, secret story, which they talk about in agitated whispers. Which makes all the nice, laughing people suddenly seem like characters in a huge, horrific soap opera, where death and grief, intrigues and drug addiction are all par for the course. I would give a lot not to know these things.

The drugs here cost less than a litre of milk, my uncle said disparagingly. It's a way to keep people stupid. Religion is the opiate of the people, but these people need opiates to escape from religion. Then everyone nodded, but this information seems completely removed from my own experience here. Just as far removed as the torture in the prisons, and the destruction of Persepolis, and the names of the Old Persian poets.

I think the best way of not hearing about any of these things might just be to ask as many questions as possible, question after question on everything but these subjects I don't want to hear about. The strategy that worked so well at Amme Simin's house could work just as well everywhere else.

Amme Simin's son Yashar once told me that at night, when they're asleep, adults turn into little kids. Usually, he would just run around like a wild thing all day, causing havoc, destroying things, pushing me, hitting my brother, hitting his own brother. But there was this one time when he calmed down and said, Adults become children at night, and children become adults. It's just that no one notices, because they're all asleep. And I believed him for quite a while.

It would be so good if the two of us could go out together, Ava said to me, it would be good for you to see what it's like being around totally normal young people here. Ava opened her eyes wide as she said this and smiled at me, and I thought, she's so kind, my cousin, but for all the care she takes of me, she also keeps letting me know that I don't really have a clue, that I don't truly belong here.

The totally normal young people are sitting at the white plastic tables of a cafe that smells of old cooking oil. They call the place a kafishap. No one seems bothered that it doesn't even serve real coffee, and that they're drinking juice and milkshakes instead; everyone talks excitedly over each other, sitting on their wobbly chairs in groups of various sizes, screeching with laughter. Isn't it great here? Ava asks, and I smile and say, Yes. But the best is yet to come, says Ava, pointing to the door. What's the best, I wonder, and is it really the best or is it actually going to be boring, and I'll still have to act like it's something special? Like the clothes my aunts give me, like the gold earrings that must have cost a lot of money, but I would never wear gold, no one wears gold, except here.

Here he is, says Ava, tilting her head towards the door. A boy comes in. He's quite short, like everyone is here, and he's wearing a white shirt and has gelled his curly hair. Ava grins and says, Well, do you recognise him? He nods to us, sits down nearby and then slowly shuffles his chair in our direction. He is a boy, and we are two girls; he has to disguise the fact that he's arranged to meet us here, as I've already observed with the people around us. The group at the table understands the principle, understands that he's with us, opens up the circle, and while this is happening I take the opportunity to ask Ava, Who is that? I don't know him. I'm slightly impatient; I'm constantly being taken to places where I can't figure out who people are. Your boyfriend, from before, she giggles, the two of you wanted to get married.

I look at this boy from the corner of my eye as he greets the people around politely, seeming to know them, and talks shyly to them, though he keeps looking down, smiling at his fingertips. There is always a hint of a smile on his face. No one there seems bothered by it; they're pleased to see him, like he's a child coming to join them. A child, a little curly-headed boy — the thought goes through my mind, and suddenly through my body, too. His brother winding him up and hitting him, and him crying and then afterwards smiling again at everything his brother does. His father playing games with him under the table, picking him up when once again, all the others are quicker and older than he is. His father, the man who discovered the secret land under the table and knows all its legends. Nima, I say. Nima was the name the adults called out after they'd called Yashar. When they talked about Amme Simin and Amu Peyman.

Nima's chair comes ever closer, the women next to us

move apart to let in the men from the next table, and Nima is among them. Suddenly he is sitting beside me. Salam, he says. He nods to Ava, nods to me; Laleh, he says, what a coincidence, how are you? As a child, he didn't look like his father. But now his cheeks are sunken and his eyes are sad. I'm glad we can't greet each other more enthusiastically, that we mustn't attract any attention, being people of the opposite sex not related by blood. You're Nima — the words fizz out of me, though that probably isn't polite, but suddenly I'm four years old again. He laughs his shy, childlike laugh, exposing a gap in his teeth and a lot of gums. Do you want a drink? he asks, getting up. The milkshakes here are really good. He heads for the counter, sits on a bar stool, and swings his legs as he waits to be served.

You remember, right? Ava asks, following my gaze. I always used to say you were bride and bridegroom, and then you always started an argument. He wanted to speak to you, she says, it was really important to him, but he felt like it would be a bother when your mothers were there. Why? I ask. An extra person might have made the visit to Amme Simin more bearable from the start, I think. His mother can't cope with too many people at once, Ava says, but he was so keen to see you. She smiles at him as he comes back to us, looking like he has brought not just milkshakes but new energy for this strange reunion.

He sits down with us and sucks contentedly at his straw. When would David look that happy drinking a milkshake? David wouldn't ever drink a milkshake, I think. David would drink bottles of beer, in one of the pubs where the students go, so that we can pretend we belong in their ranks already. Here, in Tehran, it's probably a kind of belonging when you go to kafishaps and sit under neon lights sucking liquid ice cream through a straw.

Ava is much more relaxed and easygoing here than she is at home. She leaps up delightedly when she knows people, kisses her girlfriends on both cheeks when they come in, introduces them to me, and keeps glancing at Nima, who tells us about his journey here, the usual funny anecdotes about other taxi passengers who are complete strangers but start arguments about the most trivial things. Then he begins asking questions: what we've been doing so far, how I'm liking Tehran, a new question following promptly after each answer.

He's attractive, I think, he has watchful eyes, a straight nose, and delicate features. I like looking at him. But at the same time, I am wondering if I'd find him attractive in Germany. In Germany, would he remind me more of the boys Yasaman hangs out with, guys who strut around at the Iranian parties with their shirts unbuttoned, showing off their mobile phones? It always feels weird to laugh about these guys with Marie; it would feel better to laugh about them with Yasaman. But Yasaman is obsessed with finding all German men awful; she claims that having relationships with German men is assimilation, and subjugating yourself. She wants to take Iranian studies at university, become a journalist, become better than this cringy white middle class, as she calls it. Here, I keep thinking what a good job it is that Yasaman and Marie have never met.

So tell me, Laleh, how do you go about getting a place at

a German university? Nima looks at me as he sucks on his straw again. He's a student, hoping to get his bachelor's in mechanical engineering, if all goes well. And he's popular; a lot of the people here seem to like him. While he's still talking to me, he suddenly gets up, lets out a loud, hearty laugh, and hugs some newcomers, only to then sit back down beside me and keep asking me questions with an earnest expression on his face.

I'm not at university yet, I say, I don't know. It makes me think of Mama, the first night here in Tehran, telling her sisters and friends about her degree in Germany. About the professors whose handwriting she couldn't decipher, and lectures in which she sometimes hadn't understood a single word, and study groups where she couldn't be any help to the others, but did cook for them, and then they'd explain everything to her. An air of respect spread around Mama. They admired her diligence and her courage and above all her academic qualification from a foreign university. A degree in political science, passed with a below-average grade, admittedly, but she'd done it, and no one here asked what marks she got.

There is a soggy doughnut on my paper plate. Just don't eat anything, Ava's mother warned us, because she was making dinner; we needed to come home early, and Ava was not to take me anywhere I might feel uncomfortable. The greasy doughnut is a big, flabby mass of wheat with sugar on top, and is probably the most unhealthy thing I've eaten in the last few weeks. But buying it is one of the few decisions I've been allowed to make for myself here, and that felt good.

I can't tell you much about German universities, I say —
but why are you asking? You're studying here, right? Aren't
you satisfied here? And somehow even as I'm saying it, I think
it's a silly thing to ask. Satisfied. Sure, we spend the whole day
eating and we play cards and joke with each other, but words
like *satisfaction* take on an absurd quality when you say them
out loud. Probably because as you say them, you realise you
only use them when you're calling them into question. Nima
laughs through his teeth.

Ava looks at me. Here? Satisfied? The three of us couldn't
be sitting here together if the windows weren't tinted, if there
weren't so many other people around us, if we didn't happen
to be in a more moderate phase than we were a few years ago
— is that really not obvious to you? Ava says it in the same
tone of voice as when she asked me earlier if I really hadn't
noticed how insanely noticeable I was, that I move differently,
that people can tell I'm foreign just by looking at me. Is that
really not obvious to you? That's a question you don't expect
an answer to, for which reason we fall silent for a little while.

Nima acts very grown-up, and he sounds like my Papa,
like all the Papas around here, I expect, when he asks, You've
heard about the student protests, though, right? And I say,
No. Ava and Nima don't look disappointed; they actually
look quite pleased that they're getting to tell me about them.
They tell me one of the pro-reform newspapers was banned,
censorship, everyone had high hopes for Khatami, and for a
while everything really did get better, and then there was the
night in the student halls of residence — they stormed the
halls, Nima's halls, threw students out of the window. And

182

it's embarrassing but a laugh rises through me when I hear that. Because it's so ridiculous that I wish it was just a joke, something made up and not to be taken seriously.

I think about my strategy of distracting people with questions, but I can't come up with a single question that might distract anyone. I notice a man sitting behind Nima who is constantly looking at us, awkward and shy, glancing over again and again.

And after that came the biggest demonstrations since the Revolution, the streets were packed, and it was all us, all people our age! Ava says this with such a sense of importance, such seriousness. When was that? I ask, and they say, A month ago. And now it's all over? No, says Nima. It's just that no one dares take to the streets anymore. The government planted rioters among us, and they were so out of order that the police were able to take action against us at once. Officially, they said only one person was killed, but I know so many who've disappeared. What, personally? Nima nods. My roommate's brother disappeared, and my roommate himself was in prison, and among the students there are far too many people that know someone who died for it to have been just one. They hit them with cables, beat them, with TV cables.

Nima pauses, and then he says, It's impossible to keep studying here now. And I find it strange that he doesn't lower his voice as he says it, that there is no fear now about saying the words out loud — maybe because everything else is already forbidden, and because there are too many other things to fear for you to fear everything. I would like to know if they really were all students on these protests that I'd heard nothing about in Germany, because it was summer and I was at the pool.

Suddenly I see myself in the school gym, sitting on my chair and saying, we're more reformist. And when I look around here, I no longer even know if that was a lie, despite everything Nima is telling me. The fashionable clothes around us would have been unthinkable a few years ago. So many women with plasters on their noses, because so many women are having nose jobs. Ava told me that some of her neighbours stick a plaster on their noses from time to time without having had an operation, just because it's cool.

It isn't worth doing a degree here, says Ava, jolting me out of my thoughts. Especially not for women. Nima lets out a little laugh. There are so many women in my lectures now; they used to be dependent on either their husband or their father for every decision, and now suddenly there they are at university. There are more women than men in almost every lecture. I suck on my straw and say, But that's good, isn't it, if women are going to university? Ava and Nima nod and roll their eyes and say, Of course it's good, but who does it benefit if they aren't allowed to work anywhere afterwards, because either their husbands or the system won't let them? What good did it do all the women who studied law after the Revolution? It was only a few years ago that they started being allowed to work in it — though only as lawyers, mind you, not as judges! Ava turns her big saucer eyes on me; they are bright and angry as she says, Going to university here is like taking a little time out, just waiting for when you'll no longer be allowed to do anything.

And I don't know if I'm going too far, but I ask, You won't marry a man who'll stop you doing anything, though, will you? And without hesitation Ava responds, Well, I'm definitely going to have a proper relationship with a man before I marry him and before, in the eyes of the law, he has more rights over me than I do myself. I would really like to ask Ava what having a proper relationship with someone means here. Does it mean sitting at neighbouring tables, looking at each other? Or does it mean sleeping together?

Yasaman has told me so many stories about her cousins, who slept with all these men and then on their wedding nights had to invent elaborate tricks to leave virginal marks in the bed. But I'm not sure whether Yasaman's cousins are like Ava — if, like Ava, they say that they'd still wear a hijab even if they didn't legally have to, because they love their faith and because they love their hijab. I'd always thought you couldn't like a hijab. But of course you can, of course you can love your faith, and I'm sure you can love your faith and still have sex before marriage, too. Sitting here beside me, Nima and Ava seem like the most honourable and innocent people in the world, and I think, even if Ava and her boyfriend did secretly sleep together, it would just be one more secret on the list of secrets that this country has racked up. A secret that carries the death penalty. I picture David's face, but that suddenly seems stupid and childish.

Nima looks sad again, stirs the liquid in his glass. As a child he wanted to play dolls' tea parties with us, and we didn't let him. I need to try and get a student visa, as soon as I can, he says, not looking me in the eye. It's getting dangerous for me here; no one knows whose names have been mentioned in the prisons. At the next table, they are laughing loud and long, six or seven young people. But I don't want to go without a student visa, says Nima, I don't want to be a refugee. And I think it's good he's said that. What could I tell him, otherwise, what advice could I give? That refugees in Germany aren't allowed to study or work and can never leave the town where they live? That they're housed in barracks that get set on fire by neo-Nazis while the police look on?

Ava grins at me and imitates her mother, her aunts, my aunts, as she asks, So? Is it better in Germany or in Iran? I laugh awkwardly, and we fall silent again. I'm proud of the conversation, and yet I have the feeling I'm not worthy of it. I sit here, unable to help, and fiddle with my hijab because the man at the next table is looking over so often, and I wish I had the courage to ask Ava if she, too, keeps feeling hands on her backside in the street, or if they only do that to foreign women. We get up and put the plastic chairs back where they came from. Ava booked the taxi in advance, and we want to wait for it outside. I don't dare look at the man; I walk out right behind Nima. And then see him give the man a long look, and blink his eyes at lightning speed, before he turns away and strides towards the door.

Frankfurt am Main international airport, a place made for the transfer of human beings, where people are on the move, onto planes, away to distant lands, where people arrive and travel on, really nothing more than a transshipment point.

But for me, it's a museum of people, a museum of feelings, preserved and packed away and always there to be called up, involuntarily called up when people come to visit, from Iran.

I've only ever been an onlooker, waiting at the metal barriers in the arrivals hall to meet our guests, having been told: Amu Mehrdad is coming, you remember Amu Mehrdad, don't you? Or Khale Azar is coming — and feeling pleased. Not because I associated those names with actual people, but because the names had woven themselves into my childhood, had become entangled with the knowledge that there would be presents, and happy parents, and good food, the scent of rice and foreign cigarettes, loud laughter around the sofreh. Exciting, that drive to the airport, like a little trip away, the five of us in the car and Tara with her own seat for the time being — on the way back, with the new visitor, we took it in turns to have her on our laps so that we all fitted into the little Polo.

At the airport, adults lost control of their emotions. Older gentlemen walked towards one another, each pressed his face into the other's shoulder, their bodies quaking, and the trembling went on until the airport staff asked them to move along and make space for the next arrivals. Mo and Tara standing in front of me. Mo quieter at these moments than I'd ever known him, and Tara with countless clips in her thick hair. They were only excited because I'd told them so much about the guests, because I'd acted like I knew them really well and they were the greatest people on the planet. I always thought how weird it was that all these people walked out of this one door, this sliding glass door, and I wondered what might lie beyond it, and what would happen if I went through the door. Would it be like the *Mini Playback Show*'s magic ball — would I come out transformed?

There was only one time I didn't go to the airport, but stayed at home to look after Mo and Tara, when Mama and Papa went off in the Polo alone and came back with Papa's parents. No crush in the car, no Tara on our laps; Mama preferred to leave the three of us at home all by ourselves, though she was usually scared to do that. Because they wanted Maman Bozorg and Baba Bozorg to travel like gods, in our Polo. Maman Bozorg sang to us, baked bread for us, cooked us fereni, and I didn't even know if the pudding tasted like it used to, because I'd forgotten what it used to taste like, but I acted like I was really happy and was annoyed with Tara for not liking it. Maman Bozorg did the laundry with Mama and sat out on the grass by the cornfield with Baba Bozorg, watching us fly kites. Two weeks later, they went back; there's a photo of us kids and our grandparents at the airport, just before the flight, and we're the saddest kids you can imagine. For a time, Frankfurt airport was a sad place for us.

Until the next visit: Amu Sohrab. He was a mystery to me, and his visit remains a mystery to me still. He wasn't a real relative, just a friend of Papa's. He was on a business trip to Europe and kept his suit on even inside the house. Everyone was polite to him at all times, and we didn't go on a single outing while he was there. And then he left again, because he had business to do in Luxembourg and Switzerland, and he told me the names of his hotels and asked if I'd heard of them.

Visitors' final days in Germany would always be an orgy of

packing, with all the souvenirs that had been bought — there was a great folding and unfolding, removing the purchases from plastic packaging that would add to the weight, showing them off once more, comparing them, piling them up beside the suitcase. On those final days, I always had the feeling I was losing our guests already, and hated them all for their souvenirs. On those final days, nobody took any more photos, and Papa didn't film everything we said and did like usual. The final days were just to be got through and put behind us, and not to be remembered by watching videos.

We put Papa's video camera to one side, right from the start. We put it within reach, so we could film at any time. But only now, as we were putting the presents for Mo and Papa into the suitcases, did we suddenly remember the camera, because we felt so guilty about it. Papa had told us to film things, keep diaries, take photos of people and landscapes and the city streets. But so far, we hadn't filmed. We'd felt like we were in a film ourselves.

A square of plastic with rounded corners is stuck to my eye; my skin is sweating under it, and I zoom in on Baba Bozorg's face. When I was little, he was always working; now he's an old man, whose tanned, wrinkled face could be pictured on postcards in Germany. When he wraps his arms around Tara, picks her up, and presses his stubbly chin against her soft cheek, he laughs with delight and calls his wife's name, Maliheh, until she listens to him and he goes on: Maliheh, zendegi! Maliheh, life! But since I switched the camera on, he's stopped laughing. He looks around the room, an old man, a very, very old man, and I wonder if he knows I'm filming him, if he's forgotten that Mama asked him if I could film. I wonder if he's forgotten that we're here; I would like to take a step towards him — it wouldn't improve the picture, but it might remind him.

He turns his head. His neck is scraggy, and thin white hairs stick out from under his thin shirt as he looks at me and rubs his eyes, then looks at the floor. As if he's embarrassed by me filming him. But then I've seen him like this the whole time, every one of the last few days when we've been in this house and not with Mama's mother. Like picking up a camera would change anything. The camera does change things for the aunts; they have all disappeared to put on long-sleeved clothes, because who knows who might see my film in Germany. But that must not be important to my grandfather, my Baba Bozorg. He looks into my square lens in silence for a long time.

Behzadjan, he says eventually, Behzadjan, salam. His voice sounds so weak. Behzadjan, how are you? I hope you're well, my son. He falls silent and swallows, and his swallowing is so loud. Behzadjan, what pearls you have, what daughters. And then he falls silent again and looks at the floor. My grandmother comes into the frame; Maman Bozorg is proud and majestic as she sits down beside him and begins to speak into the camera with a serious look on her face. Starts with the polite phrases, the replies to which are absent because Papa is at home trying to cook for Mo, and will only see the film in a few days' time. But Maman Bozorg is resolute; she keeps talking even without getting any replies, and really I should zoom out from Baba Bozorg, I should focus on her, but it seems wrong, somehow. I don't move away from him, and he looks at the floor and rubs his eyes, and then his shoulders start to twitch, gently, in a regular rhythm. Maman Bozorg stops talking, and I see him twitching in the bright square, and I hear her silence in my picture, and Mama says, Alright, Laleh, switch it off. And I turn away.

No one comforts Baba Bozorg; no one does anything, says anything. Lalehjan, he says finally, his voice old-mannish, creaky, soft, but so kind. He puts out a hand to me, and I sit down beside him. Has he noticed how they've changed us here — that Tara and I wear different jewellery and hairclips every day, that I've acquired a doll-face? Does he know that I wear sleeveless tops in Germany? And I don't even dare think about David while I'm sitting beside him. Pahlavi was wicked, he says, he was a wicked man, a bad man, but these clerics, they just make everything worse. Khomeini was a murderer, Laleh, this country is ruled by murderers.

I want to comfort him, but I can't, and so I want to ask him to hand me the old photo album from the shelf for the twentieth time instead, the album with the photos of my parents inside. For years, I was jealous of Marie, whose parents look happy in their hippy photos, beautiful and sunny and youthful. And here, they have fat albums of my young parents tucked away, like they've been held captive here all these years. Papa in his military shirts, with an easy smile, looking off into the distance, sitting on the dusty ground with his friends in the mountains, sometimes in casual suits and plimsolls, sometimes in an almost ridiculously philosophical pose. Mama is quietly beautiful with a knowing expression, sitting among her friends, all wearing homemade clothes in loud colours that I believe I can see even though the pictures are in black and white: checked flares and corduroy blazers and henna in their hair.

Leave the girl in peace, Maman Bozorg says now, telling her husband off as she always does, as if he's simple-minded because he sleeps all day. But I smile at him, he holds my hand and I hold his, and I think it doesn't matter what he says and how much of it I want to hear, as long as in the end we hold hands.

Everyone has said goodbye, and beside me I can hear Tara snoring. Children don't snore, I always thought, but now I know that children do snore when they've spent the whole evening crying and haven't blown their noses and then they're so exhausted that sleep catches them unawares. In the beginning, I thought I'd have to look after Tara so she wouldn't get lost, or be scared of anything, to make sure she'd feel safe. Then I realised that everyone was looking after both of us, me and Tara, no matter what we were doing. And only now do I realise that other things would have been much more important for her.

We should have prepared her differently for our trip here, and given her different warnings about what going back would be like. She has spent the whole time sitting on someone's lap, has had her hair done by a different aunt every morning, and someone has bought her toys on every outing. She's been sleeping beside me every night for the last three weeks, radiating calm and warmth like a baby — though she's older than I was when we left, and no one told me we were leaving.

When I was Tara's age, I sometimes cried in secret when *The Fresh Prince of Bel-Air* was on, because the prince of Bel-Air reminded me so much of my youngest uncle. And then there was the checkout girl at Aldi: I always imagined she could be Khale Azar's twin sister. Whereas Tara met the aunts and uncles for the first time when she was ten, and I envy her for that. It's better to start missing your uncle at ten than at four. Maybe I should have told Tara much earlier on that it would hurt to meet them and then have to leave again — maybe that was my job.

Now, they've gone. Everyone but Madar Bozorg, Khale Azar, and her husband. We have to set off so early in the morning for Mehrabad Airport that it made more sense to say goodbye tonight. And I was ashamed that in the last few days I've been thinking I want the days to go faster, before the hair on my face that has been plucked a second time grows back. I want it to look perfect in Germany, not in Iran; it won't do me any good in Iran.

Tara's snoring sounds like Papa's snoring. Papa's snoring would never have entered my mind if everyone here wasn't constantly discussing every little detail about him. Like they're talking about a martyr. Three weeks have passed, and I'm no longer surprised they take him for a martyr. A hero who fought for everyone, and who became innocently guilty.

One night, when everyone was asleep apart from Mama and Khale Azar, Mama said he would never come back. He doesn't want to go on holiday to a place where they wanted to kill him and did kill his friends, she whispered, and certainly not after Peyman's death. That would make the murder seem legitimate. And then Mama said, He keeps dreaming about coming back, coming back to his old neighbourhood, and everyone saying, But, Behzad, you're dead, what are you doing here? And then he himself is suddenly frightened and doesn't know why he's back, and tries to hide. And in the dream, they always say, But you died together, you and Peyman, you grew up together and were killed together, too. Khale Azar talked about Papa like he was a film star, admiring, reverential.

I can already picture him, picking us up from the airport tomorrow. He'll be excited, waiting for us, abandoning his usual air of calm for a constant checking of his watch, glancing around all the time. Among the tourists, he'll look strangely short; he'll stand out in the brightly coloured jumper we got him for Christmas. He will patiently endure Mo's moodiness, occasionally asking him if he's sure they're standing at the right exit. He'll crane his neck to spot us as soon as the sliding door opens. And beam when he sees us, the way he used to when we picked Tara up from kindergarten together. That kindly, dedicated father, they must have thought there; he's so very different from the other foreigners. Always has a smile on his lips, always kicks off with a question, looks interested, follows up with a joke. Who would think that this is a martyr coming to pick us up? Not in the Polo now, but a Toyota, with a bigger boot but not a lot more room inside.

2009
Mo

Don't call it a taxi, call it an ajans, because ajans means an ageing man with grey hair and a smoked-yellow moustache flying along roads with ditches either side in his rusting Paykan, and changing the money you pay him into bread and cheese at the end of the day. I'm in the back, sweating; my sweat stinks, and the car is passing black cloth statues with people concealed inside. Fumes and smoke and smog, grey buildings with pictures of martyrs on them, martyrs wherever I look. Voices, noise, air flowing in through the window. Roll the windows up, the driver says, or we'll suffocate, and I roll the window up and can't breathe. He slots a tape into the tape deck and sings along, Russian ska-punk. I can't breathe. Where did you get the tape? I ask, and the man says, From you, my young friend, you smuggled it in, and he grins, and I can see torsos in black shirts with hairy chests, the men have cudgels, and I feel hot and nauseous. When? I ask. When was that? The driver spits in his car and says, It was entirely at your own risk. The whole country is out on the streets and you're smuggling ska-punk. Funny that he knows the term ska-punk — and then I realise that the driver is going to throw me out as soon as we get into the woods. But what woods? I wonder; we're in the middle of Tehran, there are no woods here, and when I look out, the cudgels are hurtling down, into faces I can't see. Until I say, Come on, bro, I'm paying you, just take me somewhere. And the man says, I am, don't you worry, it'll be fine. He laughs as he says it and spits in his car and says, We've got a few still to collect, people like you, like you, like you. You'll see.

Tobi hammers on the door; Tobi never knocks. He comes in wearing boxer shorts, and I look away with half-open eyes, because I don't want to see Tobi like this, but Tobi doesn't care how people get to see him. Mo, he says, acting like he's out of breath, did I leave my phone in here yesterday? And I have to think what happened yesterday, and I say, No idea. Listen, bro, says Tobi, sitting down on my bed, did I message Maryam? Definitely, I say. Tobi always messages Maryam when we're drinking and smoking and he's talking about her, and everyone is relieved when he finally just messages her and stops doing our heads in telling us about her arms and her walk. Shit, did I? asks Tobi, and I say, Tobi, man, I have no idea, and it doesn't actually matter anyway, does it? Yeah it does, says Tobi, it might fuck everything up, she's already having, like, second thoughts. Oh no, what if I wrote some bullshit to her again?

I turn my head away and close my eyes. Eventually Maryam is going to dump Tobi — the sooner the better, and the more stupid texts he writes her, the sooner it will be. I'm fairly sure I saw how this whole thing was going to play out from the start: this much-too-pretty, much-too-intelligent girl feels drawn to Tobi, because everyone always feels drawn to Tobi. Tobi is kind of weird-looking, but when he's on the bus, women talk to him, and when he's drinking beer, women sit down and drink beer with him. Because at first he has this aura of being a nice, uncomplicated guy, and most importantly really interested in them. And so a Maryam arrives on the scene and thinks a Tobi would be good; he's someone her friends will like and whose roguish charms even her parents will get used to eventually. Someone who just needs a little re-education and then he'll be a keeper. And then Tobi is a potential keeper for about a week, until he starts being Tobi and sleeping until lunchtime and not showering and not caring about anyone or anything except sleeping and smoking and banter, all day long. Maryam has no truck with this, and I've told Tobi that a hundred times.

Hey, you look rough, man, says Tobi, because he now wants to banter with me. Correct, I say, and as I roll onto my side, I realise it isn't Tobi who stinks, it's me. My mouth tastes of stale beer and my tongue feels like it's spent the night in a puddle of alcohol, soaking it all up. Tobi, searching for his phone, asks, Do you want to go out in a minute, go and see the döner man? Tobi always says döner man. Tobi also says Chinaman. And when you pull Tobi up on it, Tobi says he thinks political correctness is retarded. Sure, I say. When's your mother going to come and visit and make us dürüm? Tobi asks, and it almost makes me laugh, because Tobi is too stupid to realise that my mother has no idea what dürüm is, because Turkish food and Persian food are *not the same thing*. Tobi doesn't want an answer to that, though — his phone rings, and he picks it up off my rug and disappears from the room, leaving behind a sickening silence.

My bedclothes are wet, sweated through just like my vest and boxers. I run a hand through my hair, the curls sticking together, and think about ska music. I already know that this feeling is going to haunt me all day, a kind of angry-chickenshit feeling that comes when people say absolutely insane things and you're on the point of thumping them, only unfortunately they're your parents' friends or your friend's parents. Or in the past, when teachers didn't want to continue the discussion. Or when you get caught travelling without a ticket. Or when you've already told Papa about the bad grade you got at school, and you're scared because Mama is coming home from uni and you'll have to tell her as well.

I close my eyes and wait for the leaden feeling to subside, the feeling that spreads through my body when I think about the dream. I switch on the laptop that's lying next to me and press the remote control with the other hand. Flick through the channels to see if there's any news on, stare at the computer until it's finally booted up and found the wi-fi. Click open the browser, which loads my home page. Since the protests started, my home page is no longer yahoo but a proper news site, tagesschau.de. The page takes forever to load.

It's summer outside, and Tobi trots along the overcrowded streets at my side and grins dopily to himself, as if any minute he's going to ask if he's allowed an ice cream. And people keep grinning back, there's a perpetual exchange of grins going on, and I find the weather-dependency of this general mood almost too transparent to be able to join in. Everyone everywhere is getting more naked, you can suddenly see shaved legs and scrawny arms. In the shop window, Tobi and I are sitting side by side, about the same height, both with curly hair under our caps, his blond, mine black. Tobi is broad, though — broad shoulders, narrow hips, and so on — and the whole of me is just narrow, skinnier than the skinniest girl, and surely no one could like that. But when I look around me, I don't actually want one of these H&M girls with their floral skirts and homemade handbags to like me. When I look at Tobi and me in the shop window, the thought occurs to me that we're just two arseholes, two layabouts living off our fathers and state education grants, and occasionally also studying. Except I think no one seeing us like this would think we're arseholes. Two aimless geography students, like you'd see on every street corner in every university town. We probably look like nice people, actually. I don't know if we are nice people.

I wouldn't introduce Tobi to my mother, that's for sure, even if she did learn to make dürüm one day and then came to visit. I can't imagine her standing on the threadbare carpet among the deposit bottles and the glass for recycling, chatting to Tobi. On the phone, she always asks about the girl, and how the girl copes, living with us, and whether the girl makes us clean the flat. I don't tell her that although Kristin may be a girl, she doesn't even wash her hands when she's been to the toilet, and that I scrub off her skid marks. Instead, I mutter something about a cleaning rota and hope she doesn't probe any further and never comes to visit. And what is your Tobi up to? she asks then, because she finds it funny when I tell her about Tobi. I don't even tell her the obvious things, about his chaos and all the bloody money that flows into his account from his father and out again into tobacco and music and films; I just sometimes tell her that he's on campus right now, or has to study, or has failed some module or other. And what about you, what have you eaten today? she asks then, and I don't tell her that I sometimes survive on nothing but muesli for days at a time, or that I eat frozen pizza three times a week; I say something about potatoes, which she approves of, and then she asks, Have you got any other news? I say no, and then we hang up, like every day. But at least she leaves me in peace apart from that.

She isn't like she was with Laleh, who lit a firework of maternal concern when she moved out. Mama called her several times a day and asked and asked, until she knew every detail of Laleh's life and could fall asleep reassured. I did things differently from the off. I never talked much on the phone, never asked a single question, and actually never gave a proper answer. Just yes and no. So she gave up on the detail questions. Maybe the reason she never comes to visit is that secretly, she knows she wouldn't be satisfied with how my life is here. Like it's her job, to ensure things go well in my life.

One night, when Laleh had just moved out, I heard her

talking to my father about it. They were sitting in front of the TV, the news had finished, and I snuck out for a cigarette, though I wasn't even a proper smoker at that point. I just found it kind of exciting to act like I really needed to have one before going to bed, and if the pair of them had known, it would have triggered a lot of rational, intellectual conversations about the dangers of smoking. My parents were speaking quietly, because for some reason they never talked about us in front of us, like too much transparency would harm our good upbringing.

They're kids, my father said in a low voice, they have to make their own mistakes and learn from them, we can't protect them from that, and when they move out we have to let them go. My mother whispered, I do know that, but it still hurts to let them go. Then my father chuckled and said, Think of all the things we did that hurt our parents, Nahid, and we were actually risking our lives. Because we didn't really understand anything either, my mother said. We were in danger and we just didn't see it. We thought we were doing the only thing that was right, my father said, and that shields you from the reality. Then I went to bed, because I had the sense they were talking about an intimate subject that had nothing to do with me. And because it felt like my father, who is always infallible, was confessing to errors.

The last few days have made me think about that conversation more often, and I keep toying with the idea of asking him what he really thinks of the Green Movement. I can already hear him sighing down the line, can hear him saying, Just taking to the streets isn't enough, they need to know who their leaders are, they need to have learned from the mistakes of the past. And I can hear myself saying, But they've got nothing to lose, it's not like they could end up with something worse than that so-called government. In my mind, I hear my father saying, That's just what everyone thinks when they try to start a revolution, Morad, but history has shown that it isn't enough, and that things can always get worse. And I know that's the point at which I'd switch off, because my father would keep talking and talking until he'd mentioned every side, every perspective, not just once, but at least three times. I'd sit there on the phone, hoping he was finally winding down, and still thinking: Everything *can* change. And when everything has changed, he'll be the one most touched, most moved, most relieved by it.

Tobi is talking about Maryam. I look at him, sitting opposite me with his mouth full. Shovelling in dürüm and enjoying every bite. Totally content to be sitting here with me, feeding his face. Hey man, is everything okay with you? he asks, fixing his small eyes on me. Nothing is okay, I think. Nothing. Maryam doesn't want you, I say, and then instantly feel bad about it. It isn't really fair not to let someone who has no problems talk about his one problem. Maryam wants someone in her wholesome, pretty world who isn't going to get on her nerves and isn't going to take the reins out of her dainty little hands. Tobi says, Yeah, that's true. I nod.

The first few bites of greasy meat have given me an urge to vomit. The man behind the counter is looking at us. The döner man. A man in his late forties, with greying temples and sagging cheeks. Who doesn't talk much when people like us come in and order what he must have spotted we're going to order a mile off. Kristin used to work in McDonald's. You always know who's going to order what, she said. Iranians always have a Filet-O-Fish. And then I felt caught out, because my parents did always used to order a Filet-O-Fish. But I still said, And who else do you see ordering what? and was pleased that she couldn't think of any other examples; the Filet-O-Fish thing might just have been a lucky coincidence.

The man is now looking just at me, like there's something I need to explain, like I have to justify Tobi, like there are questions to answer. The TV is showing images of people playing snooker. Tobi and I are the only people in here in this heat. We aren't looking at the screen; the man isn't looking at the screen. Why is the snooker on? I wonder. Are there people who come here wanting to watch snooker? I don't know anyone who sits at home watching the snooker. What must have been going through the man's head when he opened up this morning, wiped down the counter, chopped some vegetables, and then put the snooker on with the sound muted?

I push my food to one side. Aren't you going to eat that? asks Tobi, and I slide it over to him automatically. We could go to uni, he says. What for? I ask. I am not being nice to him; sometimes I *am* an arsehole. It's the student strike, says Tobi, and I laugh. Being on strike means you don't go in, I say. That's the whole point of it. Yes, I hear Tobi say with his mouth full, but the student strike means you go to campus.

You don't even go to campus normally, I say. With every bite, Tobi loses a bit of herby salad onto his paper plate. Yes, but the student strike means you go to campus, he repeats, looking earnestly at me. They're holding these protests and things, he says. Who are? I ask. The hippies, says Tobi. Oh, then I'm definitely out, I say. The last thing I need is rich people's kids getting angry about tuition fees and dancing to drum music. You're against tuition fees, too, though, says Tobi, like he has a clue about anything. Yeah, man, because they mean I have to work.

Tobi says nothing. My argument wasn't good, but because my arguments usually are good he doesn't respond. I'm allowed to do that, just talk about crappy situations without people then asking me what the solution is. Actually, I never have an answer to that. The man has stopped looking at us now and turned his gaze to the street outside. He's looking through the plate-glass window, his arms folded; in the mirror image, his face is quite blurred, and you can't see the eyes and nose properly. All I can distinguish is his moustache, which droops mournfully.

Outside, Tobi is still in a surprisingly good mood, almost getting silly with it. Like today is already a success just because it's still early and we've got a hot meal inside us. And so we get on the bus to campus, though my head is spinning hard and I am definitely not yet in a fit state to be on a bus. The minute you get on a bus or a lift or a tram, everything you did to yourself the night before catches up with you.

There's a band playing on campus. Latin music for blonde girls in brightly coloured, baggy Indian trousers. Everywhere, students are sitting in circles on the grass, talking. Someone presses a flyer into my hand, with the program for the week on it. Lectures and clever discussion groups and always *Education wants to be free — solidarity and free education.* I watch them from a distance, sitting there, trying to look pretty. This is your solidarity, then. How angry you are. How determined.

At my side, Tobi picks up the pace, looking left and right. He stops behind the baggy-trousered women. Tobi, come on, I say, you can't be serious. Tobi's head is turned away from me; he's looking across the lawn towards the canteen. You idiot, you're looking for Maryam, I say. Tobi lets out a bark of laughter, sits down on the ground, and rolls a cigarette. No, he says, I genuinely just wanted to see all the things we can do, when we're already paying tuition fees and then striking about it. We're not even striking, this isn't a strike, I say, sitting down on the still-damp grass with him, with a view of the small stage. What's up with you, bro? he asks, turning sleep-deprived eyes on me. Why are you being so pissy?

I can't say anything, can't open my mouth and tell him about taxi drivers and Russian ska-punk, can't use words like cudgel and news ticker when Tobi is there; I don't say that my heart sinks when I see men my father's age, in the kebab shop or wherever else, looking out of the window and saying nothing. I don't say that I wake in the night and put the TV on because something might have happened, because something could suddenly have changed, after the twenty-three years I've spent watching my parents wait for change.

After nothing, nothing notable, has changed in twenty-three years, but we still always have to watch the news and keep quiet while it's on.

But in the last few days, all of a sudden, other twenty-three-year-olds have been showing us how fucked up things are. A few days ago, there was nothing to separate Tobi and me, neither of us had any clue which exams we had to take when, we drank beer in the park and played PlayStation when it rained, and our only problem was the fruit flies in the kitchen of our student flat. Now these other twenty-three-year-olds are suddenly everywhere, on the streets of Tehran, on the news websites, even on RTL here in Germany. And in my head. Huge numbers of them on the streets, drawn out of their houses and their silence, and suddenly there, fighting back. They're sending us their pictures and shaky mobile-phone footage, and they aren't just telling us the presidential election was fraudulent, but also that something has to change, that everything is wrong, that they can't go on like this. Only, I don't know exactly what we're supposed to do about it here in sunny Germany, and so I can't give Tobi an answer, either.

I watch Tobi smoking: good-hearted, loyal Tobi. And I take a deep breath. Ah, man, all of this just gets to me — the fact that people can't simply be glad they've got parents and money and a university, and you have to label a protest a 'student strike' because otherwise no one will join in, and even when that label exists, the only people here are the ones who are always sitting on the grass playing the guitar anyway — I expect everyone else thinks it's stupid, and you know what, they're probably right.

Tobi's expression changes. A group of people walks past — one of those clever lectures must have just finished, and a few of them sit down with us: girls, bottles of Club-Mate, Maryam. Tobi grins at her and tries to draw rakishly on his cigarette. There are moments with Tobi when I feel like he's never got past the age of fifteen. Last night, for instance, when he got his bong out and was trying to convince Jolle and me to be fifteen again as well. Jolle is older than us and has been at uni for about a hundred semesters by this point, but it still doesn't take much to convince him to be fifteen again. And two fifteen-year-olds are more bearable if you fall into line with them, and so yesterday we just didn't know when to stop.

Maryam doesn't pay Tobi any attention; instead, she looks at me and asks, because she probably overheard what I said about this strike: Alright then, what do we need to do better? And I could throw up right there and then. Tobi's Maryam is not only too much like Tobi's girlfriends always are, she's political as well. Or thinks she is. Whatever — I can already predict how this will play out: no matter what I say now, she'll manage to invalidate it with her over-inflated alternative-leftist rhetoric copied off the TV, in a way that will force me into pretending to agree rather than arguing back, so I might as well not bother and just sit drooling beside Tobi, saying *Education wants to be free.*

Don't know, don't care either, I tell her. She's not that pretty; a face as dogged as that can't be pretty, plus she has bags under her eyes bigger than mine and Tobi's and Jolle's put together. She bites her too-thin lower lip, turns her head to Tobi, her ponytail swinging, and says: You're smoking again. It's totally obvious that she would say this, that she would think a smoking Tobi is a bad thing, and naturally Tobi has never tried to give up. Tobi says, Yeah, giving up is really hard, and blushes as he says it, and I stand up and say, Just going to the loo. My whole body feels heavy, the food lies heavy in my stomach, my belly is heavy. I want to get away from the Latin music and lean my head against a cool wall for a minute.

I head for the toilets, not looking at anyone so I won't have to say hello to them. Until I realise that someone is walking beside me, someone skinny and annoying. The other thing I wanted to ask you, she says, forming the words with her thin lips as I look into her dark-circled eyes. Are you in touch with anyone in Tehran right now? And I wish I'd just got into a student-strike conversation with her, listened to her left-wing rhetoric, and then gone home.

Not at the moment, I say, feeling immensely stupid. I mean, my parents are in touch with people, obviously, but I'm not. Actually, though, I'm annoyed with myself for responding to her at all, because it's really none of her business.

I saw the images online, she says, It's really kicking off there, isn't it? And she waits, and I say, Yes. So how do you see the whole situation? she asks. I don't see much, I think, I don't see much because sometimes I look at the floor when the TV is on, because sometimes I close my eyes, because I'm here and not there. I don't see much right now; I can't see much. Maryam looks at me.

It's a young country, I say, and an educated one. Maryam nods. I wait for her to say that no country is educated, just the people in it, or for her to throw something else at me that will shine a critical light on my answer.

Are you coming to the demo on Wednesday? she asks. Her eyes are blinking continually beneath her meticulously plucked eyebrows. Everything about her is somehow small and dainty and delicate and eerie. What demo? I ask. You know, the student strike demo, she says, It's going to be pretty big, in every city, right across Germany. Sure, I say, and then I turn around and look for a cool wall.

Laleh stresses me out on the phone. The ringing wakes me and she says, Mo, did you watch the news, did you see it? It's another morning after a short night, it's half past ten and she didn't think I could still be asleep, although she knows very well that even as a child I slept till midday. And it isn't all that long since Laleh was a student herself; she must know that I can sleep as long as I want and there's really no reason to change the habit.

Sure, I say, because when Laleh asks a question she wants an answer, at any price. When she says something, you have to say something back or she won't go on talking, and going on talking is important to Laleh. I called Amme Simin and she says the streets are green, completely green — they were already green before the elections, and people went to vote feeling hopeful for the first time again, Mo, did you see the news?

I try to imagine Amme Simin saying this, in her maternal way, in her calm Persian, which she addresses to us slowly, always slowly, because she knows we won't understand her otherwise and that as soon as she has uttered a sentence, she'll have to repeat it using different words to be sure we don't get the wrong end of the stick. Laleh's sentences don't sound like Amme Simin to me; Laleh's sentences sound like Claus Kleber, who I listened to last night. Claus Kleber said almost the same thing, and I looked at his face and it made me want to vomit, because Claus Kleber always acts like he's above everyone. Everything that happens in the world has been relayed to us by Claus Kleber, and why, for fuck's sake, does Claus Kleber have that much power over what I take to bed with me at night? I find Claus Kleber unsettling, because he looks into my room, at my floorboards, at my ashtray, at my laundry basket, which is overflowing, at my *Pulp Fiction* poster, at my unmade bed and my unwashed face, and says: The streets of Tehran are green.

Are Nima and Yashar on the streets as well? I ask, and Laleh says, Don't be silly, it's much too dangerous, didn't you see what's going on there? And I think, how could I not see that, but then who *are* the people out there, on the streets? When Laleh calls me I am sometimes easily riled, and she can't help that — she really doesn't call that often. It would never occur to me to call her. And nor would I ever think this is the situation, this is the moment when I need to talk to her.

Mo, they were saying on TV these are the biggest protests since 1979. Laleh sounds excited, really and truly excited. She talks so naturally about 1979, like she was there. What would she say if she knew that just the day before yesterday I googled exactly when the Islamic Revolution was. Everything could change! she goes on. Actually, she's probably feeling like I am. Actually, she's probably sitting in front of the TV like me, watching these images, these crazy, fast images, these shaky images that make me feel like they're happening right here, outside my window, outside my front door. And yet they also keep reminding me that I'm *not* there, that I'm not in the middle of things, that I'm not being any help to anyone.

Despite this, I might get something out of it in the end, if their demands are listened to, who knows, who knows what the next few weeks will bring, what the next few days will be like? Who knows what might happen even in the next few hours? Maybe something so explosive and exciting that it will bring the change straight to us here, and our parents might finally find peace, because somehow that was always what was missing from their happiness: a victory, after so long, against all odds, over what sent them here. How must it feel to have parents who are suddenly released from their waiting? Parents who have won, for once?

Yes, let's see what happens next, I say to her, because I know I have to say something. Everything alright with you? she asks. Yeah, sure, I say, it's just I was still out for the count when you called. Still? she asks, and then she sends a warm laugh down the line and says, Right, okay, living student life to the full, then. I have a little laugh as well and think, But, Laleh, you were never really a proper student, not like other people, not like me. You left school with top marks, you graduated with top marks, and now you're on this textbook career path in architecture. Laleh has had a savings account since she was sixteen.

After a while we hang up. I switch on the TV without even thinking.

I persuade myself that the newsreaders are still pretty excited: not just the foreign correspondents who report from their rooms at night, but the Claus Klebers who have stayed at home; I can see they're horny for a sensational story, like it was thanks to them that elections were held, decisive elections, against Ahmadinejad, for this man called Mousavi. And then the accusation that the election was rigged, it was impossible for Ahmadinejad to really have won, and then the people, so many people, in the streets. Crowds of people, flowing, moving, green and — this is a very important thing to mention — peaceful.

Then they show the attacks by police and say: worrying images. People yelling, men about my own age, with curly black hair and ironed jeans, holding hands, green ribbons around their wrists, holding up pictures, calling out slogans that awaken something in some corner of my brain, telling me this is directed at me. These are the things I'd be doing if I was there. These are the things that have to be done because people like my parents aren't there any longer. But it is my parents' fight they're continuing, and my father is the one who should be there, to see: Your fight never failed, it just had to be put on hold.

The footage shows crowds of people, from above and from

a distance; the picture quality is so bad and the light so grey that you can't make out individuals, and I wonder, Are there really so many, is it really possible that so many are daring to go out onto the streets, where people don't usually dare do anything? Then shots are fired, the crowds are forced apart by police motorbikes, they shout their slogans louder, move aside but don't run away. A little later, you see burning motorbikes, burning tyres. Then shots of a man being dragged along the ground, police officers beating him with their batons, then he's dragged a few metres further, where he gets another round of blows from the next lot of policemen. In the background, you can make out the water cannon, loaded with boiling hot water.

I sit there, wanting more of these images. Somehow, I always want these images — they hurt, they bring blood, but in the end they finally send everything off the rails.

And then I switch back on, punctually on the hour. It's the first item, and they say: Street battles.

I fire my laptop up. Yesterday on TV, they suddenly started talking about Iran's internet boom, saying everything was happening online, and that's hard to imagine when I think about the stone-age computers they have over there. It's also a weird thought that we have the same internet everywhere, and as the thing is starting up, it's Maryam of all people I think of, and her I-saw-images-online. I type *Iran* into YouTube. And get 363,000 hits.

We are all walking together, side by side. We haven't linked arms, but it feels a bit like we have, we're walking so close together, in such a straight line. Beside me are Jolle and Kristin and whatever else people from uni are called; they arrived in dribs and drabs, quite naturally. They thought it was natural I should be here, and that they're here themselves, too. We never actually talk about things that bother us, and certainly not when we're sitting in the lecture theatre. It never occurs to anyone to wonder aloud for a minute why we're in a lecture theatre and other people aren't, and whether that isn't all a bit unfair. But everyone has still turned up, quite naturally, because it's Wednesday, and this is the big demo — though they're still talking about the things they always talk about.

Kristin says she's finally found out who has the answers to last year's exam, and how we can get hold of them, and because so far none of us has revised for the exam and none of us wants to start now, this information instantly puts us in a better mood. And so Jolle immediately starts talking about the party they're having in his flat soon, and says we should club together to buy his flatmate a birthday present, but Tobi says the flatmate has recently stopped smoking weed, so now no one knows what to get him. The usual conversations, then; everything is as it always is. And yet they suddenly look different, in the sunshine, away from uni, away from their student flats and the student bars. In daylight, Jolle looks even more knackered than usual, and Kristin more relaxed. I should see her outside our flat more often, when she's not faffing and talking about her projects and making phone calls and chain-smoking and rolling her eyes about Tobi. Here, all of a sudden, her face looks almost childlike and content. Maybe she should go on demos more often.

I used to go on demos more often, in my final years of living at home. Mostly with Merle. Unlike everyone else at our school, Merle always did quite a lot, not just collecting signatures for the rainforest when she was twelve like we all did; she was still doing it at eighteen, and she's probably chaining herself to a railway line somewhere right this minute, to save us all. I was always a bit glad that people like Merle exist, trying to stop things going to the dogs, but somehow I imagined her life being really stressful as well — although Merle herself was anything but stressful.

She was one of the girls in our class who wasn't a complete airhead, but didn't act super-smart either, and I think she was madly in love with me all the way through school. I don't know why exactly; maybe because we were the only people in the class who had a black badge with a red star on it, and it might have impressed her in some way that I sometimes knew things in politics classes. But Merle never made any romantic advances, though she did ask me at regular intervals if I wanted to go to demos with her, and most of the time I said yes. Because not that many people are in love with you so perpetually, and I kind of wanted that not to stop. Merle knew that some Nazis were planning to demonstrate nearby, and then the people around us sat down in the street, and we did the same and didn't let the Nazis through.

Merle never shouted slogans, and she never had those sew-on patches with know-all left-wing quotes on her rucksack, either. And actually, in retrospect, I always really liked being around her, no matter whether we were sitting on the asphalt because of Nazis or sitting on railway lines because of nuclear waste. At her side, I always felt a bit more justified in being there and having an opinion, and her calmness always surrounded me. Merle was always very observant and probably thought things over afterwards, when she got home. She even thought about my parents. She was the only person who ever asked me exactly why my parents fled. The only person who gave me the sense that my parents might be impressive people, revolutionaries in our midst, so to speak. I was proud of that, though later I realised I hadn't mentioned that they aren't very revolutionary these days — apart from that on the first of May my father rings his mate Amu Ghader and wishes him well for International Workers' Day. But Merle didn't need to know that just yet; the demos were our shared thing in any case, and I enjoyed it, enjoyed thinking that what she was doing was important, and that's why I was doing it with her.

I can hear whistles and a drum group and some rattles. All these people; so many have come that there are hardly any gaps in the crowd. Right and left, in front of me and behind, there are mops of hair in all colours, flimsy fabric, sandals on the ground and suncream on skin. Around us, rows of apartment buildings — the large, beautiful prewar ones where the poor students live, until the buildings are renovated and the rich former students move in — and the group begins to shout: We're here, we're gonna fight, 'cause education is a right. They shout it close to my ear, and I yell with them, and at my side Jolle starts to laugh, and I can't help laughing a bit, too, and then we yell even louder. Other words cross my mind: Natarsid. Natarsid, ma hame ba ham hastim. My mind shouts them, shouts them loud, yells them, but in my mind is where they remain: Natarsid, natarsid, ma hame ba ham hastim. Have no fear. We are all together here.

I'm standing under a tree, alone, having lost Kristin and the others. Having said I was going to get a beer and then decided not to find them again, though I'm pretty sure I can see Kristin's peroxide-blonde hair in the distance. The lawn is full of people, a hell of a lot of people have come this time, the business students, the lawyers; there is live music, and the beer costs one euro. Maybe later, on the local TV news, they'll say how many students took part in the demo, but they won't compare it with how many came to the afterparty. At the front, some people on stage are bouncing around and dancing and running into each other. Here at the back, the guitar and the bass and the drums are mingling with warm air and conversations. Dusk is starting to fall, and the lovely thing is that dusk lasts a long time.

For a second, I imagine going home to bed. I'd have changed the sheets, I'd own some pyjamas, and I'd get into bed freshly showered. That's the only reason I'm not going home now: my bed has had the same sheets on it for three months, I sleep in boxer shorts since I stopped living with my parents, and I turn the TV on before going to bed anyway.

So I stay standing here and breathe in and breathe out and try to imagine the whole scene with no sound, with no music. Without the accordion and the violin and the annoying male voice. The band shouts out, We want free education! And the guy says, Down with Nazis! And people make noises that probably signify agreement, and people keep dancing, and the guy shouts, Legalise marijuanaaaa, and the music gets louder and speeds up, everyone shrieks and dances faster, and then in all seriousness a clarinet appears; the guy playing it goes up to the front, to the edge of the stage, and plays to the audience, flirting with them. I'd like to switch the voices off, the confusion of voices, the cloud of voices. Isolated parts of speech forcing their way into my ears, men's voices becoming women's voices, artificial laughter, familiar laughter, familiar voices. Hello, Mo.

At first I don't even recognise her, because she's standing beside me, not in front of me, and I look sideways and down at her. Maryam has her arms folded and is facing forwards, looking at the stage. Hey, I say. Do you know the band? she asks, still not looking at me, jutting her chin towards the stage. Nope, I say, why? Maryam shakes her head, very slowly. But she doesn't say anything, just watches the clarinettist dancing as he plays. Wiggling his hips and being squealed at. Until she does turn to face me after all. Funny, isn't it? she says. What is? I ask. Her voice is quiet — though I don't think she means to speak quietly at all — but I can still hear her perfectly. She isn't looking at the stage now, but at me, as she says, A Roma band entirely made up of white people. I take another look at the boys in the band. The one with the clarinet has finished his solo and is getting his applause, taking a bow. It's about as funny as a white person with dreadlocks, I say, because the clarinet guy is whirling his blond, felty hair around, and everyone is still cheering. I have a real urge to go up the front, grab the mic, and ask him: So, are you a student? Who's paying your tuition fees? Who paid for your clarinet lessons?

And suddenly I've said that out loud, and Maryam is grinning. Then she says, I'd follow that up with: So, what did your grandparents do in the Nazi period? Did they dance to Roma music, too? I laugh, and she laughs with me, and I don't know if I'm laughing because I find her funny, or because I'm slightly shocked, and it's only then that I notice I'm laughing longer than she is, and I stop, and she says, Or do you feel attacked by that kind of thing? I say, Huh, why would I? They're not my grandparents. She says, Well, you've got to be careful, everyone's always so sensitive, and I say, Yes, and I guess they have a right to be, sensitive topic and that. Maryam says, Yeah, I know, but Roma music is a sensitive topic, too, and the guys up there don't seem to be giving that any thought. Then she looks at me, closes her small eyes for a second, and says, Don't get me wrong. I have German grandparents, too. But that doesn't mean I have to stop making jokes. In fact, that's exactly why I *should* be making jokes. I nod and all at once it feels stressful again to have her standing beside me.

I wonder if I shouldn't take the opportunity to go home to my unwashed bed after all. And then it occurs to me that I decided to watch YouTube videos because Maryam had watched YouTube videos, and for some reason that makes me angry with her. Are you on Twitter and Facebook, too? I ask abruptly, and it sounds like an accusation. And it's funny how the words Twitter and Facebook move from my head into my mouth and then out into the world, the words they're always saying on TV. Maryam doesn't pull a face. Yes, she says drily, but only because of my relatives; sometimes they post really relevant things. We look at one another for a moment, saying nothing.

Laleh's boyfriend is on Facebook. Because of all the open-minded people he met on his work-and-travel thing in Australia. Now he can look at their millions of photos, and they write mindless stuff to one another and call that being networked. I was on studiVZ for about two weeks — that was enough for me. Long enough to realise that along with everyone else, I was spending too much time thinking about what unique photo and what witty bio and what intellectual side of my personality I wanted to present to the world. Then I deleted the account, only to realise two days later that there's a VZ network for school students and Tara is on it. But I can't connect any of that to street battles and Maryam's relatives.

What relatives are these? I ask, and she says, The ones in Egypt. I say, Hang on, don't you have German grandparents? And now for the first time, Maryam is hostile; for the first time, she knits her brows together, juts her lower jaw out weirdly as she speaks, and her tone grows sharper as she says, You can have German grandparents *and* Egyptian grandparents, you know, it isn't technically impossible, is it? And I feel stupid and like I've been caught out. Your relatives must be on Facebook as well, though, right? she says. As I understand it, in Iran they're much, much further ahead than they are in Egypt. And I say, Yes. And because I have no idea, I say, Quite possibly.

My relatives could be on Facebook for all I know. My relatives could also be famous rockstars or corrupt bankers. I don't know a lot about my relatives. I know what I saw when I was there, years ago, just for a few weeks. I know the little that my parents and Laleh have told me. I can't say if they're on Facebook. And even if I was on Facebook, I wouldn't get in touch. Because Facebook isn't a substitute for a real relationship. Maybe Facebook small talk would be worth something if it reminded you of a connection and a level of intimacy that you'd already built up with one another. But connection and intimacy are things I don't have, though Laleh does, I reckon. She has them because she really missed all our aunts and cousins and uncles, throughout her whole childhood, and when she was a teenager. That's the only reason she can phone Amme Simin or Khale Azar and write letters to her cousins and not feel totally stupid doing it.

For all I know, Maryam probably thinks I'm heartless and don't care, but that isn't true, I'm just pragmatic. If my heart was attached to them, it would be in permanent pain, like Laleh's is. I would miss them all the time, like my mother does. Suddenly I have an image of them in my mind, the aunts and uncles and their children, when they threw their arms around me and showed me they'd been waiting for me all those years. When they told me stories from my father's childhood, about him skipping school and breaking windows. I feel a bit sorry that they've fallen victim to my pragmatism. But that won't be on their minds right now anyway; they're currently falling victim to cudgels and water cannons.

Do you pick up a lot from the blogosphere, then? Maryam

asks now. How do people use these words with a straight face: blogosphere? No, I say, do you pick stuff up from the blogosphere? I don't actually know why I'm asking this; I just want to ask something and hear her say no, for once. Maryam falters for a moment and then says, Yes — like, in Egypt — is that what you meant? I nod as if this was obvious, and Maryam says quickly, Sure, a lot of people are blogging, a lot's happening in the virtual realm. And I think, virtual realm, those words could have come out of Claus Kleber's mouth. But Mo, it's incredible what they're doing in Iran right now, it's so important!

And then she looks past me; Jolle and Kristin and some other people have turned up, and they all go He-e-ey and hug Maryam. And they say, So, Mo, we did find you in the end.

It's the ajans, maybe — a car in any case, a rusty one, and I'm at the wheel with my foot on the gas. There are people in the car, and I say, Where do you want to go? and they say, It doesn't matter, just drive faster before they come. I put my foot to the floor and drive faster, pressing the pedal down, pressing my foot so deep into the footwell that now I'm leaning sideways, looking up at the steering wheel from underneath, and there's a woman sitting behind me wearing a black headscarf, who says, Do look where you're going, boy, and I tell her I can't see the road anymore. Suddenly the people open the doors and get out, and I scream that the car hasn't stopped, in fact it's going faster, the landscape is whizzing past, I can't see anything now, and I'm alone in the car and then I get out, too, I leap out — Natarsid, natarsid, ma hame ba ham hastim, people call out to me, and a pleasant warmth envelops me, and then I'm flying, natarsid, and I have no fear, I call out ma hame ba ham hastim along with them, and there is no ground, there is only falling.

I can smell my own armpits before I'm properly awake. It reminds me of yesterday morning and the morning before; this smell is always the first thing — though it doesn't smell like me at all, it's much too strong to be coming from me. Then the taste on my tongue, which this time is metal and dirty air and stale, heavy alcohol, far too much alcohol, and I turn on my side. That was quite a session yesterday, with the others, after the gig, in a cramped room, Tobi dancing with Maryam, me not dancing. Me standing on the sidelines and drinking and not wanting to talk to anyone. I just didn't want to go home and be by myself. And a guy going on and on to me about his uncle, who is currently travelling through Iran with a tour group.

Early sunbeams pierce my window, far too bright, poison for my eyes; I turn my head, start to feel dizzy, and only now notice the slim rope of black hair beside me and get that leaden feeling again because I don't know how this has happened. Maryam's back is turned to me, her bony shoulder blades pointing at me like weapons. She is wearing clothes, luckily, and the longer I think about it, the clearer is the relief of knowing that I've done nothing wrong, that my relationship with Maryam is still as minimal as it was a few days ago. That she's still wearing her bra, for fuck's sake, and lying under her own duvet. And that she came in when I was already in my room, sitting here cursing myself because every time I breathed in it felt like suffocating, and so I was breathing more rapidly to avoid suffocating, and feeling like a little boy again buying cigarettes for the first time, and then not being able to breathe that evening.

Then Maryam came in and said, Tobi is taking up the whole bed, there's no room for me. I looked at her, standing there skinny and drunk in my bedroom and not looking at all like a stranger any longer, and then we sat in front of my computer and shared the one bottle of beer I had left, and Maryam set up a Facebook account for me. Then we went to bed without even saying goodnight to one another, we were so tired. Now I'm the one with a woman in his bed, not Tobi, plus it's the woman Tobi would really like to have in his bed, only he started being Tobi again too soon. It's a long time since I was in bed with another person. Maryam's breathing is deep and quiet. I actually couldn't have imagined her sleeping any other way. A person who does everything right and is always right and thinks everything through properly in advance is also going to sleep properly. They'll still look clean and unsweaty even when they're asleep, and they'll use the time to rest and not for something as absurd as snoring or thrashing about or sweating.

Last night, I hugged her. Not when she was asleep. Earlier, when we were all still being loud and drunk. Before I danced, even though I think dancing is ridiculous. When I'm dancing, I always get the feeling someone's watching me. But if I switch off the person watching me, then I wonder what the point of dancing is. Anyway, Jolle arrived with tequila, and I wondered why I was feeling anxious about us all eventually going home, and had already clocked that Maryam was drunk and being nice to Tobi again, and maybe Tobi wouldn't get the night bus with me, but disappear off with her back to her high-ceilings-stucco-Ikea-flowery-bedsheets home. Then there was the guy with the uncle. One of those guys whose scarred face reveals that he went through puberty and, unlike most people, couldn't resist popping his pimples rather than just buying Clearasil. But that isn't a justification for anything, it can't be a reason to get annoyed with someone, but he did annoy me, if only because he walked over to Jolle and me uninvited and started talking bullshit to Jolle. But Jolle never does anything he hasn't chosen to do himself, and when someone comes up and starts talking bullshit to him, then Jolle walks away, and I was left standing there with the pimple-popper.

Just then, Maryam came over, red-cheeked and out of breath, stood next to me, and ordered a small beer, and the guy asked me, So, where are you from? I said, What do you mean, where? And he said, What country. Maryam rolled her eyes. Just as Jolle doesn't like stupid people, Maryam doesn't like stupid questions, and she picked up her small beer with her small hand and said, Hey, Mo, you really don't need to answer that, and the guy said, Why not? And Maryam said, Because it's none of your business, and the guy asked, So why is it your business? Then I stood aside and watched Maryam, who really went off at that point. I thought she went off

227

because she was drunk, or maybe because even Maryam sometimes has a bad day.

I ordered a large beer, although by this point it was Jolle's turn to buy the next round of tequilas, and was vaguely pleased that Maryam was there and drunk and going off. Because I had no desire to give him the answer I've given so many bloody times, which has never yet cleared things up for anyone, given them any kind of useful information, any real feeling for me, my life, the questions I have for the world. All the same, I've always answered like a good boy. I don't know how often I get asked and how often I think to myself that I really don't want to answer, and then always do, with a few awkward words, just to keep the peace and keep the conversation moving so it will eventually end. But never before had a Maryam come up and said, You don't need to answer that.

I watched her and her still-perfect ponytail; she was raising her voice and saying, That's discrimination, telling the acne guy that he was placing his interest above other people's privacy, above their feelings — and then I'd had enough. Then I thought, Actually, I can fight my own battles, and she doesn't have any info about my feelings, even if she might be right. So I said, Maryam, it's fine. Then Maryam gave me the horrified look that had previously belonged to the acne guy, and she was red in the face as she told me I only thought that because I was socialised here. She genuinely used the word *socialised*.

And now she's lying in my room and breathing. I wonder what someone who uses the word *socialised* in public smells like. Cautiously, I bring my face closer to her hair. It tickles and feels weird because I'm way too close, and I'm slightly disappointed that her head just smells of scalp and her hair just smells of air and a hint of grease and a lot of smoke.

The acne guy didn't hear her out; eventually, he just turned back to me, and I turned away from him slightly. I felt sorry that Maryam was so angry and that once again I didn't care about any of it. But even if she was right: what good does it do when the world is full of acne people? And then I told Maryam I was envious of her anger. And she asked, Aren't you angry, then? And I said, No, not about that. She just looked at me with solemn eyes and said, I think you *are* really angry, too, and I just said, No, just sad. I wasn't even embarrassed to have said that.

I turn away from Maryam and scooch over a bit because I'm annoyed that I talked to her so much, and I can smell my armpits again instead of her scalp. At some point in the evening, I hugged her. And then Tobi appeared and the three of us talked for a minute, before Tobi hugged Maryam and I turned back to the acne guy, because I thought I needed to rebuild some bridges. So we clinked glasses, and I said, Iran. I'm from Iran — but unfortunately that was his cue to start doing my head in with this story about his uncle, who was in this tour group on this bus, and it was the most boring story there has ever been.

And then I did get kind of angry after all — not Maryam-level angry, but angry enough. Because of the question and because the answer to it sounded so simple. But it's bound up with blood and pain. Because of the people fighting and hitting back on the streets, when I have two fists as well that I only use once a week for kickboxing. But there's enough power in them to hit back alongside those people, and to draw blood for all I know, but instead someone is here talking about the bus and the embassy and the travel-cancellation insurance and the warning from the foreign office. So I interrupted the acne guy and said that despite the effort he was making, his story was still boring me, and he said, Oh, so you're as aggro as the girl now, are you? Then I went off to dance, with the beer and with the others. I was thinking, the next time someone asks, and I decide to answer just to keep the peace, I'll say I'm from Spain. Or Argentina. Or Uzbekistan. From some place that isn't going to tempt any clubber into asking more questions, just into having another beer.

Then Maryam and I watched the news, I remember. I don't even know her, and already we're doing something that intimate together. And Tobi came in as well — he was there for a bit, that's right, that's a relief. We were sitting in front of the laptop, and I said I needed to watch the most recent eight-o'clock news, and Maryam nodded without me having to explain that to her, and I was incredibly grateful, and then Tobi came and joined us, just like that. The three of us sat on my bed, and it felt weirdly wholesome. Because suddenly we were all hearing everything that was said.

When they said in the media centre that there were hundreds of thousands of people again, on the streets of Tehran, and that they were silent at the demonstrations, they just walked in silence, and it was only at night, on the roofs, that they were sending their cries of Allahu Akbar up into the sky, because there are no cudgels on the roofs, and in the gentle soundscape of the streets, those cries can't be pinpointed to anyone. I said, Yes, that's right! and got goosepimples. Maryam and Tobi watched the screen quietly, and I explained they were wearing surgical masks to show they're not shouting, and felt a little like it had been my idea, the face-covering thing. And then was instantly ashamed, because they must have thought I was being self-important.

Then there was an image of the footballers who wore green wristbands, and I clapped my hands and said, That's so good, that's so good, everyone there watches football. Maryam asked, Won't they face really harsh punishment for that? Surely there are going to be consequences. Tobi asked, Have you guys got any beer left? And I said, No, we drank it on Facebook.

When the images of Ahmadinejad came on, Tobi said, He looks like George Bush, but in Iranian, and Maryam went *shh* like my mother used to when the news was on. Then it was about the Ayatollahs not having congratulated Ahmadinejad on his re-election, and Tobi said, Wait, Bush didn't get re-elected, everyone knows that, and I laughed for Tobi's sake. Obama is the most powerful man in the world now, Tobi told us quite seriously, and Obama is a superhero who's going to save the world.

Right now, I'm finding it a bit odd that Tobi was talking like that yesterday. He was being sarcastic, and he doesn't usually do that, but it didn't seem like it was going to impress Maryam. I think Maryam was ignoring it anyway; she wanted to talk about Obama, who had given this speech where he praised the president of Egypt, which according to Maryam was a completely idiotic and inappropriate thing to do, and then I went off to the toilet and found another beer that belonged to Kristin, and I'll have to replace that, because Kristin doesn't like to share. When I got back, Maryam was saying that in any case, there was no way Obama could change something that serious with a speech. And I don't know why, but it made me quite sad.

When I was in Iran, that one time, there was some graffiti on the wall, just for one day, on a wall in Tehran, and it said, *Mr Bush, don't forget: we're here too!* That was after the Afghanistan war, after the Iraq war, and I wouldn't have expected anyone there to write that, because, you know, Merle and I had been to protests against all these wars, and I thought, Surely people in Iran can't want the same to happen to them. But a friend of my cousin who saw it, who was clever, who was older, said, That's utter garbage, democracy has to come from within, it doesn't work when another country imposes it on you from outside. I told Merle about that when I got home, and I think Merle was pretty pleased with me.

What's written on the walls of Tehran now, I wonder; is it directed at Obama? When Obama was elected, the whole world was ecstatic. I thought, This Obama isn't one for imposing things on people. I thought, Obama will support the people to change things from within, but of course I didn't say that to Maryam. Because clearly we both know that in the grown-up world there are no more superheroes, although when it comes to Obama everyone does act kind of like he might be one all the same. Maryam is the first person

I've spoken to who actually has something against him, and weirdly I believed her straightaway. Suddenly I am down one potential hero — when I have much greater need of them than I did as a kid, because right now all I can do is hope, and if I could just skip forward two weeks, then everything would be good news and revolution, and all the young people would be coming back from all the countries where they're studying to build a nation from within, and my father will book a flight, and it'll be him booking it, not my mother, and for the first time in all these years he'll pack a suitcase. Not an overnight bag for two days at Laleh's place, but a big suitcase, and then we'll drive to the airport, where he'll be nervous, and he'll show his Iranian passport, and no one will detain him, and he'll fly in, and they'll pick him up, they'll welcome him, he'll see his mother, I'll see everyone, we'll be free, we won't be scared to go to the part of town where he grew up, and the whole neighbourhood will be there, because Behzad is back, Daei Behzad, Amu Behzad, and he'll sit there with them and drink tea and talk to them in that slow, considered way of his, and for the first time I'll see him surrounded by people who are like him, and together they will come to the conclusion that there is nothing to regret. I'll be there, and everything will be different, everything will change, change, change. With Obama or without him, and — for all I know — with the chaos and everything else that comes with a revolution, according to what we learned at school. But no one will be scared anymore. And everything will be okay. If only I could get a quick glimpse of the world two weeks from now and stop just waiting for everything to be okay.

I take a deep breath, but I can't get enough oxygen. I don't think there's enough oxygen in this whole room for me. Yesterday, Tobi slapped me on the back and said, Stop breathing so fast, bro. I shouldn't have been chain-smoking, I thought, but I didn't say that. Because then Maryam would have said, Yes, that is correct, and because Tobi would have laughed at me. But right now, I have no desire to keep thinking about what I did when I was drunk. I've spent too long thinking about it already, and anyway everyone was drunk, so everyone else should be embarrassed, too, and it's only now that I realise I'm feeling really good. That I'm feeling really good beside a sleeping Maryam, who is a little more likeable than a waking Maryam, though I think I no longer find Maryam all that unbearable even when she's awake. And Tobi is in the next room, which feels good too.

I get up and switch the laptop on. When Maryam showed me her Facebook account, I was still thinking it was silly for people to post private, incredibly boring details about their lives there, photos of their dinner, photos of their cats, photos of their cocktails — but it isn't all stupid, because they do actually post very different stuff as well. I realise it's a useful arrangement to have other people seeking out cartoons and funny YouTube videos for you. I don't have a single Facebook friend, just a friend request from Maryam, who is currently in my bed, still sleeping. Maryam's friends have sent her an invite to a demonstration, and that's what I'm looking for now, so I accept Maryam's friend request, because otherwise I can't see her bloody page, and when I become her friend it says: *Mo is now friends with Maryam.*

Maryam doesn't have a photo of herself on her profile; she has a picture of a fist coming out of the earth. Without friends, it's a silent space, this Facebook, a cold, silent space, and I only hesitate for a moment before typing in the names of all my cousins, uncles, and aunts, and am shocked to see their laughing profile faces on my screen. And don't dare to send them friend requests.

Maryam moves in the bed. The way you do when you're asleep, and fighting against waking up. But she will wake up; you always do when you move like that. It's something Tara used to do when she was very little. She always murmured certain words as she fell asleep, and moved a certain way as she was waking up. I remember Tara lying in bed, and Laleh and I waiting for her to wake up. Standing by the bed, having to go to school and kindergarten when it was still dark outside, and Mama was in bed, tired from the pregnancy, and Papa had to take us, which was always weird, a bit like we were worried he was going to mess it up. And then Tara opened her little black eyes for a moment, and I think Laleh and I loved her like nothing else in the world. It was a different feeling, coming home in the afternoon knowing that Tara was there, waiting; somehow, we were complete then. And sometimes, when the five of us had supper together in the evening, and I talked and Mama and Laleh laughed loudly or told me off for my choice of words by turns, and Papa said nothing and neither did Tara, I always felt like: we're all here; who else are we waiting for?

Maryam rubs her eyes. I'm slightly nervous. It might be better if I'm not here when she's gathering her memories,

I think, and so I take the laptop and go into the kitchen, though not quietly, because Maryam does actually need to wake up now. This is still my room, after all; I open the door and close it again with a bang.

Tobi is sitting in the kitchen. Tobi is drinking coffee and eating muesli, and for a second the sight of him makes me laugh. Tobi doesn't laugh; Tobi looks back at me and says, Has she left already? I say, No, she's sleeping and snoring and farting, and next time you bring people back here, don't store them in my room, okay? And Tobi says, She snores? And I say, Not really — I actually have no idea what she's doing and I don't care, either. I thought you liked her a little bit, Tobi mutters, and I reply, Yeah, she's alright, but that doesn't mean I want her sleeping in my room, so find some other solution next time, okay? And Tobi says, I think I'm in love.

I would like to tell him I have no interest in this, but it's pretty rare for Tobi to try and talk to me about his feelings, so I just don't say anything. We watched the news yesterday, bro, says Tobi. His lower lip is drooping. I've never got drunk and watched the news before. And I say, Have you ever watched the news full stop? And Tobi says, Why did your people even re-elect this guy? It's, like, properly weird, isn't it?

I sweep the crumbs off the table into my palm and look at them. Tobi is Tobi, but when there's something going on with me, he picks up on it, and in his own way he tries to figure out what's wrong. And because he doesn't really know how to help me, he supports me in his Tobi way. If I wanted to drunk-watch the news with him every night, he'd go with it. He'd get that it was important to me.

I say, Why did *your* people vote for that fat chancellor for sixteen whole years, it's like, properly weird, isn't it? And Tobi says, Hey, it's too stressful to talk politics this early in the morning, and spoons up his muesli with a serious look on his face. Eventually, he mumbles that he wants to start DJing; that music last night was unbearable, they really need to sort it out. And who the hell was that guy trying to talk to everyone? I say, the one with the acne? And Tobi says, What, he was spotty as well? And I say, No, but he used to have spots and he squeezed them, and Tobi says, Oh, what, so you knew him? And just then, the phone rings.

Your mum called yesterday, says Tobi, twice, you know you should answer your mobile when she calls you. So I pick up the landline and take the handset into Tobi's room. Hello, I say, and she says, Hello, Moradjan, salam, how are you? I say, Fine. And she asks, What news have you got? I say, None. And she asks, Where were you yesterday, you weren't at home, were you? I say, I was out, there was a demo here. And she says, Yes, I saw it on the news, what's this strike all about?

I imagine her sitting at home with my father on the dark leather sofa, looking at their big, old Sony TV that we've had since I was a kid, waiting for what the German media say about the things they've been watching all day on the Iranian exile channels, to hear as many different viewpoints as possible, to compare how things are being reported. And then the German media have these student protests as their top story. My parents are there trying to understand what's behind it, and wondering whether they should think this is a good thing or take a more critical view, and silently agreeing that it isn't their problem. Because my parents silently register everything they see on the German news as not their problem. At least, that's what I say. It might not be true, because if it wasn't their problem, they wouldn't be watching the news.

Still, it drives me insane when they go on about how great it is that we have Angela Merkel here. When they say they'd never vote for the CDU themselves, but Angela Merkel, she's special, she gets things done. And then they say, the business with the dragnet searches after 9/11, that was necessary, it was for our own safety. When the authorities regularly filmed our neighbour in his little flat and saved his data because he could be a potential terrorist, when they continually stopped and searched me at the station, and when Laleh stopped wanting to go to clubs because she was the only one of her friends whose handbag was always emptied out — my parents basically thought that was okay, too. Because it's for our own safety.

I reckon you can only decide all of this is okay if you think it isn't your problem. It's like my parents are already set for life when it comes to problems, like they've already gone way over their allocation of things to be upset about. And like they wish with all their hearts that their children will never fill their own allocation and actually, best-case scenario, never even start getting angry about things. Only that might not work, when you used to tell these same children bedtime stories about revolutionary killer fish, and when these same children help you set out the haft-sin table at Eid Nowruz and you put *The Communist Manifesto* on it in place of the Qur'an.

I imagine them watching the images of the massed German students and my mother making a mental note: Ask Morad what that's all about. It's against tuition fees, I say, hoping that will be enough of an answer for her, because really everyone has some objection to tuition fees.

We're travelling to Brussels tomorrow, she says. She never usually says things like that. At this point, she usually just asks what I've eaten and then we hang up. Why Brussels? I ask; no one they know lives in Brussels. There are protests going on there, and Amu Ghader is there, outside the EU parliament, she says. I say, Ah. I don't know if she was expecting some other reaction from me. Or if I'm expecting a reaction from her. Amu Ghader has always just been the guy we go to stay with in Sweden, for holidays. It makes me think of Merle. What Merle was to me, Amu Ghader is to my parents. Though maybe the dimensions involved here are too different to compare. While simply leaving school was enough to drive Merle and me apart, a revolution, a war, exile, and a second passport haven't caused my parents and Amu Ghader to part ways.

It gives me mild goosebumps to think about them fighting for justice in Brussels, and perhaps feeling like they did in the old days. And I'm a little relieved. Like the responsibility for everything that's happening right now, and what isn't happening, and what might happen if a revolution happens, no longer lies with me but in the familiar, reliable, and much more appropriate hands of my parents. My little parents, who have somehow grown more and more alike over the years. I imagine them standing side by side in Brussels, silent, their hands clasped in front of their bellies, looking at what they are supporting through the lenses of their glasses. Drawing attention, the way they somehow always do by just standing there, being unflappable observers. Although maybe they can't take on responsibility for any of this, I think suddenly, feeling an odd twinge in my stomach.

Have you phoned anyone? I ask. Who? she says, sounding surprised. I seldom ask her anything. Unless it's about paperwork for the Education Support Office or something. Relatives, I say. She hesitates, falls silent. Then she says, Yes, yes, we talk on the phone a lot, yes, but not now, no, the lines are full. What do you mean, full? I ask. Well, you can't get through, you can't phone. But you just said you talk on the phone a lot? I say. And she says, Yes, sometimes it works, and then I ask, Has something happened?

When my grandfather died, they didn't tell me. It was a Monday, one of the few days when my mother didn't call, and I registered the fact and ignored it. And when she called on Tuesday, everything was normal. And when she called on Thursday, she said I should come home, my grandfather wasn't well. When Laleh, Tara, and I went home on Friday, they told us Grandfather had died on Monday.

Has something happened? I ask again. She says, No, everything's fine, it's just that Amme Simin's son Nima hasn't come home. Since when? I ask. The day before yesterday, she says, but don't worry, it happens, his friends haven't come home before as well. So where are they looking? I ask. She says, Goodness me, same as in Germany, you go to the police. We both know this is a lie. She and I know the images we've seen, and that you don't just go to the police and get your children back.

So, what have you eaten today? she asks then. I think about Tobi finishing off the muesli and the fact that it's lunchtime already and I haven't eaten anything, and I say, Pasta, with bolognese sauce, and she's satisfied with that, and we hang up.

I think about Nima. When I went to Iran and met the relatives who had never been to Germany, I thought he was one of the many cousins whose names I was constantly mixing up. Until I realised he isn't actually part of the family at all; he isn't a blood relative, he just hangs around at my family's house a lot and seems to be important to everyone. I think about him saying democracy has to come from within, and remember that I couldn't find him on Facebook, like he didn't even exist. I would really like to get into bed and watch YouTube videos now, but my bed has a sleeping Maryam in it.

I am lying in Tobi's bed. He wasn't in the kitchen, and because he wasn't in the bathroom, either, I suspect he's with Maryam. In my room. Which is totally fine with me, and maybe if I just lie here in Tobi's bed, then I'll become a Tobi, too.

I pull the covers over me, despite the summer, despite the heat.

Nima is a few years older than me. When I was there, the last time, the only time, he came over on those evenings when we went out for picnics. He was in and out of my grandmother's house like it was completely natural, like he was the family's big brother. My uncle and older cousins always played cards, and I didn't want to, and they probably thought I was strangely effeminate, never wanting to play and always just sitting around, and then Nima turned up and although he was older than me, he was there for me.

He drove the car, I sat beside him, and he asked me if it was true that the police in Germany were one of authorities that safeguarded democracy. I was seventeen, and Merle had told me pretty often that Germany wasn't a true democracy, and explained it to me quite convincingly. But unfortunately, I'd forgotten the reasons why and I couldn't have made them sound plausible to Nima in Persian anyway. But I did tell him that the police were often unnecessarily brutal, and that I'd been pepper-sprayed a time or two, and that you saw *ACAB* written on the streets and it stood for *All Cops Are Bastards*. I don't know, I kind of liked that slogan at the time, and I wrote it on a couple of desks at school. But Nima didn't laugh; he seemed taken aback and asked if there were many bastards in Germany, and if society made things difficult for them. I thought that was weird, because I got the sense our conversation was suddenly about sex, which was a topic I desperately wanted to avoid, and so I hastily said I didn't know.

Now I'm lying here, and he is lying somewhere else.

Nima was in prison, four years ago, and after that he wasn't allowed to go back to university, because he was in a student organisation and politically active. Politically active. My brain automatically creates a link from those two words first to adrenaline and then to stories about torture chambers and prisons. What must he have been doing, back then? What must he have not stopped doing, this time? Politically active at university. The Stasi and the Gestapo float around my head, just waiting for Nima to say something anti-government in the student canteen, and then throwing him in jail. Though when I visited, people were cursing the government all over the place. In parks, in taxis, everywhere. No one took any notice. My uncle told me that the government used to encourage kids to tell tales on their own parents at school, and maybe today they know this would be a hopeless strategy because absolutely everyone is cursing them. The cursing was somehow okay. It's the activism they go after.

What did my cousin do? Why does Claus Kleber never say what's actually going on? Why do they show images and say, This is what it looks like, and then say, No reliable figures, and then show Peter Mezger live from Tehran, who says, We're under house arrest as well now? And no one says that totally normal people are disappearing. That parents are noticing their children haven't come home. No one says how often this happens. Why doesn't Peter Mezger just go into Evin Prison and check? Does no one there know that he's Peter Mezger live from Tehran?

Nima's hair has got a bit thinner in the last few years, I thought, the last time I saw photos of him. And he looked tired. It would be nice if Google knew everything. About everyone. I'd google Nima, and in his Wikipedia entry it would give his last known whereabouts and what he was doing when he was possibly arrested. Then there might be a picture of him being taken away. Or YouTube videos would pop up of him walking into a hospital with some other injured people, and then there'd be a link to the location of the hospital on Google Maps, and its phone number. And I would just call my parents and say I'd got the number, and calmly dictate the digits to them over the phone. Just as I dictate other things over the phone that I've found online for them, when Laleh doesn't have the time and my parents otherwise stumble aimlessly around the web when they're searching for something. But that isn't how the internet works. There isn't a search engine for Nima; there's no one to help the people looking for him. There is no solution. And why would there be a solution, when everything is shit? Everything is shit.

My insides clench, my fists bore into the mattress, my fingers claw the sheets, and I have a strong urge to scream really loudly, just once. I want to start screaming because I find these one-dimensional surfaces like the TV and the Google home page disgusting — everything is one-dimensional, and I really want to grasp things, to claw my fingers into them, to reach out and touch other people. Shout with them and throw myself at policemen when they come. And who needs footballers wearing wristbands? They're just green wristbands, for fuck's sake; I take hold of my wrist and grip it tight, and it's only then that I realise I'm pressing my face hard into the pillow, Tobi's bedding is in my mouth, and I'm tired and am getting tired and I close my eyes and think, Maybe when I wake up I'll be done with all this stuff, and the YouTube video playing in my head will have ended. And then as usual, you get the choice of whether to watch it again or click on the other suggested videos.

Tara has never come to visit me. She keeps talking about it, and I keep fobbing her off. Because I've always thought she's too little to witness my shambolic life. And even now that she's got her own place and is studying clever things, no doubt putting blood, sweat, and tears into it, I still keep trying to fob her off.

She's here now, though — not in my city, but two hundred kilometres away, at Hamburg's main station, with me, beside me, as arranged. Germany's largest community of Iranians in exile, as Maryam's Facebook friends posted. It's the largest, and I don't know anything about them. What a contrast, after being in the station just now, walking past McDonald's and Starbucks and people in white hotpants creating a soundscape impossible to grasp and decipher, but which was simply there, suggesting normality. Outside, in front of the station, at the rally, the whistling hits me, voices like at the swimming pool, confusion and cries, and I hear odd snatches of conversation, people on the phone, people meeting and kissing each other on the cheek, elongating the Persian words, singing out the stock phrases of greeting with concerned looks on their faces.

Tara, beside me, is stared at — when did people start staring at her like that? Her head is shaved and she's also wearing hotpants, albeit old, frayed ones. Tara looks cross, and that gives me a warm feeling. Because Tara can look so cross it frightens people. Two large black eyes gaze out from beneath her bushy eyebrows, looking like they could emit laser beams. And Tara talks and talks.

It's so long since I've talked to her. I used to wind her up, when I was playing outside with my friends, and then inside it was like nothing had happened, and we'd spend hours playing Uno together and talking and laughing in bed at night, until our mother came in and told us off because we had school the next day and it was already late. That was always kind of exciting, because at night we hurled the rude words at each other that we weren't allowed to say in the daytime, and when our mother had closed the door behind her and we just carried on, it made us feel very superior. And all at once I realise that I miss it, that I've never had that with anyone else, only with Tara when we were kids, and I'm at a loss to know why we barely ever see one another now.

At some point, I just stopped taking an interest in Tara. She was there, but I'd be in the next room doing other things, playing computer games, listening to music, and suddenly we had nothing in common. Though I'm assuming that overall, her life wasn't and isn't all that different to mine. That she did the same things as me, without telling anyone at home. Getting wasted at parties, hanging around in the town centre after school. Copying her homework instead of doing it herself, stealing chewing gum instead of paying for it.

Tara is carrying a bag from an army surplus store, with a large green cardboard placard attached to it that reads, *Where is my vote?* A man was giving them out at the station exit. A little old man with glasses, his head slightly bowed, holding the strings that all these green signs were dangling from. He was giving out the signs like they were balloons, slowly and carefully, and Tara went straight up to him and is now asking me if I'm sure I don't want one as well. And I say, No, why would I be asking about my vote, I didn't vote.

But you can carry a sign in solidarity, Tara says, and then she laughs and adds, Papa said the same thing. And I say, What? And Tara says, Well, Papa said he protested by not voting, so why should he protest now and act like he voted. He said he'd prefer a sign saying, Where is my brother's vote? And Tara laughs loudly. Everything about her is loud.

I think about Papa's brothers. They all look a bit like him, but also a bit different. One is taller, one is fatter, one is young. One's in Denmark. And the others he hasn't seen for more than twenty years.

Wow, all these girls with their sunglasses, says Tara, nodding towards some young women who are perhaps Tara's age, perhaps my age, but they look so put-together and grown-up, and they're all wearing these gigantic sunglasses, though it's cloudy today, humid and overcast, such a weird summer this year, either too hot or too humid. The bimbos don't want to be recognised, Tara says, shaking her head. They come here wanting to show solidarity, but they won't even show their faces. I look at them and it makes me think of all the images I've looked at online, always with the mad idea that I might spot Nima in the crowd and rescue him. Instead, there were a whole lot of pictures of beautiful, clean, made-up people, wearing narrow green bands in place of a hijab, and always with these gigantic sunglasses on. These women here aren't wearing hijabs. Tara takes off her thick hoodie. She's got a tight, strappy top on underneath, like she wants to show everyone she's not afraid.

Yeah, well, I say, maybe they want to protect their relatives, not just themselves. Tara spits on the ground, no really, she spits a large, well-aimed wad of phlegm to one side and says, Fuck's sake, Mo, they've got better things to do right now than track down relatives of Iranians in exile. Since when has Tara been right about things? I wonder; she's still little. Nothing will ever happen if everyone keeps finding some reason to be scared, she says, shaking her head. Her body is so small and her head is so big, she has something of the wicked goblin about her. Though as a child, she looked like an angel. But I'm pretty sure that if she had the choice of how she looked as an adult, she definitely wouldn't choose the angel face.

There's that woman, she whispers, tilting her stubbly head towards a placard that someone is holding up. Placards everywhere displaying pixelated, enlarged photos from the internet, all of which I've seen before. The woman is from a video they showed on the news. First, the whole video: shots being fired at her, people running towards her, the woman lying on the ground. Someone telling her not to be afraid, Neda, natars, natars, and Neda twitching and the blood flowing from her nose, from her mouth, and dying as she looks into the camera, or at the man with the camera. Later, they stopped showing the video on TV; they showed a brief image of Neda's face and said, People look for martyrs, in every revolution. Her blood-covered face looks at us, at Tara and me. It's insane, isn't it? she says. And shakes her head without looking away. I don't reply. I think it's insane to print pictures of dying people on placards. To film dying people as they die. To turn people into symbols, which is a contradiction in itself.

I guess you heard about Nima? Tara asks me, having taken a theatrically long look at the photo. I nod. There's no more news, is there? I ask. Because Tara is always better informed, because Tara talks to our parents more openly and at greater length on the phone. Tara shakes her head. They searched the hospitals, she says, but he probably isn't there. And you don't get any info from the prison.

Then there's a sudden burst of music, a blare of trumpets from the band, fanfare-like, full of feeling and so loud it drowns out everything else. It settles into the usual rhythm, familiar to me since childhood, settles into that upbeat, beautiful music and the melody I now realise I am so glad to hear, and then the verses begin and the singing, and people sing along. I don't like or dislike national anthems, I'm indifferent to them, but this one sounds like a song from childhood that everyone is fond of. I can't sing the words, don't know them, have never properly understood them. Tara and I stand side by side, looking at the people. So many of them are a similar age to my parents, and it's so long since I've seen my parents. My parents never sang the national anthem; they sang revolutionary songs, in the car when we were going on holiday, years ago, sad songs full of pathos and struggle, but never the old anthem. I could hum along — I have the feeling my body is humming it as the sounds line up in this logical order, and the middle-aged women in front of me pump their fists into the air in time.

Tara laughs. She laughs a little scornfully, like she thinks it's silly, but her eyes are shining all the same. And I, in turn, think that's silly; crying is the strangest reaction you can have to an anthem. But all I say is, Aren't you going to raise your fist?

And Tara says, Oh, I meant to tell you: I went to a demo with Mama and Papa. In Brussels? I ask, and she nods, and then lets out another loud laugh, and the people in front of us, still singing, turn to look at her. Tara says, Mama and Papa kept doing this — and then she yells, Long! Live! International solidarity! And with every word she raises her left fist and then strikes it with her right. She does it over and over, and I can't tell if the look in her eyes is ironic or serious; then suddenly, the people around us start joining in. Fat women with hair dyed dark blonde and eyebrows tattooed on shout with her: Long! Live! International solidarity! They shout it a few times, the polyphonic cry has an accent like my parents', the same throaty sounds, the same R, the same emphasis on the vowels.

And then Tara looks at me and says, Mama and Papa really went for it. That's a million miles from my image of these two small bespectacled people, standing there with folded arms.

When the anthem ends, the crowd starts moving, and Tara and I walk with them. They walk slowly, we walk slowly, and it reminds me of when Merle and I demonstrated against George W. Bush's visit, the two of us walking in the cold and all these little snowflakes settling on Merle's red hair. I suddenly remember the group of angry Iranians in exile, who were the only people at the demo shouting out slogans at the tops of their voices. It made Merle and me laugh, the way they kept shouting, Out, out, out! Terrorists out! I was kind of embarrassed that they were shouting these meaningless words with such feeling. They're noisy here, too, and shouting with feeling. And once again, I am watching them. We're walking behind a car which is blaring out revolutionary songs and megaphone demands by turns, and I'm strangely relieved.

And I can breathe, breathe deeply, though in the last few days I've been feeling like breathing was going to suffocate me, and Maryam said it can't just be the smoking, and then she knitted her brows and gave me a long look and then very quickly batted her eyelashes at me. We were having breakfast together, Tobi, Maryam, and I, and that felt like soap-opera kitsch and family at the same time. Maryam said, Everyone in Egypt is on tenterhooks, waiting to see what happens in Iran, and it's the same everywhere else, I'm sure, Saudi Arabia, Tunisia, it's important for all those countries. I thought it was odd she'd said that, when we had just been talking about my breathing problems, and I hurriedly asked what we were doing next week, when the student strike was over, were we going to start skipping lectures again? Maryam took a deep breath and Tobi asked if the tuition fees had been abolished yet or not; he'd got another letter from the university wanting eight hundred euros off him despite the student strike. Maryam just didn't say anything, and we laughed.

Tara is silent, looking around. The cloud has thickened, the sky is grey, and we're walking without speaking, not shouting any slogans. Tara plants her feet firmly on the ground with every step she takes, and sometimes she gets her crappy old analog camera out of her bag and takes photos of the banners and cardboard placards, which are followed by the hum of the film, reminding me of children's birthday parties and my father. Sit down around the coffee table again and pretend you're blowing out the candles. And there are endless photos of us sitting behind the same old table on the same worn-out sofa, bowing our childish faces over the cake. So that we can send photos to Iran with the next New Year's cards.

Everywhere people are holding their phones aloft; it looks like they're filming, and I imagine these images going up on YouTube this evening, and people in Iran seeing that demonstrations are being held in flawless Germany with its eternally victorious football team and its great electronic devices. I imagine them seeing images that look like their own, just with no cudgels.

Suddenly everyone comes to a halt, and one by one they sit down on the ground. Tara and I do the same, and for a moment I think of neo-Nazis, in whose path you sit. The music is off, and the megaphone is off, and people lift two fingers in a peace sign, and no one says anything. Tara raises her index and middle finger and turns her eyes up to the cloudy sky, which looks grey and malevolent. We sit and wait. It's uncomfortable; Tara lowers her hands again and lights a cigarette. I could say something, tell her off, play the big brother. From further towards the front, a man appears with a camera, quickly squats down and aims his lens at Tara. Tara senses it and knows it and leaves the cigarette in the corner of her mouth and raises her hands again and looks at the sky. I turn away so I won't have to watch. And yet I can't help but imagine the photo of Tara ending up on Iranian blogs.

Laleh used to bathe Tara, sometimes. Tara thought baths were stupid, and Laleh thought children were good. They made a huge game out of it; first they thought up code names for towel and wash cloth, then they sang songs to them, while Tara sank into the soap and bubbles without a fight. I always thought it was silly that Laleh acted like Tara was a tiny baby, and that Tara adores Laleh, like she's somehow achingly cool. Looking back, I think it was a relief for my mother. I decided very early on always to like baths, and to have one without anyone having to force me or talk me into it. For a little while, Laleh wanted to be a kindergarten teacher, and Tara probably still thinks bathing is overrated.

The baby is due in six months, Laleh says on the phone, sounding as pleased as if someone's just awarded her a prize. Laleh is going to get a big belly and the children she's always wanted. They'll go horse-riding and play piano and flute. They'll do ballet and later they'll sit around the fire listening to classical music. Congratulations, I say. You're going to be an uncle, says Laleh, you'll be Daei Mo, and that makes me laugh. Daei Mo. It sounds nice. It's nice that you can be a daei, even when you're in the land of the victorious football team and the great electronic devices.

I heard Tara was there? she asks then. I say, Yes, she was. And she sighs and says she would have come, too, but nothing is as easy when you're pregnant. I say, Have you got a bump already? No, she says, that's still to come. Then she adds, But it's good that the two of you went, really good. I don't say anything. Did it all go off peacefully? she asks. I think she would like it if it hadn't been peaceful. I think she would

253

like it if I told her some dramatic stories now so she could be concerned and fearful, and I think she'd find it exciting to be concerned and fearful and pregnant on top of that.

Well, there was this one aggro woman, I say. A what? she asks. An aggro woman. She had an umbrella, it was enormous, in the colours of the Iranian flag, with a gold lion in the white section, and people told her to put the umbrella away, but she got really aggro and was jumping around with this umbrella and stamping her feet. Laleh is quiet for a moment and then says, And people tried to forbid her from having the umbrella. I say, Well, the event was neutral, it was to protest the violence and call for new elections, and it wasn't really the place for symbols, not even a Shah lion. Laleh says, Only national flags, I'd have thought. I say, There's never any place for national flags, anywhere at all. And instantly feel ashamed. It's such a Maryam thing to say. But you can wave a flag without hurting anyone, Laleh says. It just means you're proud of your own culture.

I don't say anything, because I have no idea what you're supposed to say to that. I think Maryam would have an answer, though, so trenchant and so true that Laleh wouldn't be able to respond. I think Tara would have an answer now full of expletives, at which Laleh would be so taken aback she wouldn't be able to respond. I think Merle, with her provocative questions, could bring Laleh herself round to the opinion that she has no right to say such things. And I think that I've been thinking about Merle too often recently, almost as much as I did when we were at school. Surely I must be able to find Merle on Facebook as well.

Laleh says goodbye. And I know she's going to call more often in future, every time they get some new information about the baby, and that makes me think of Tara's little baby eyes, and it's nice that Laleh is having a baby of her own. Her very own Tara, with clear citizenship status and a German passport and a nursery place applied for well in advance.

I am sitting beside the driver; he drives slowly, cautiously, snaking his way through the traffic. For the first time, I wonder who he might be, and then I recognise him: it's the man who usually chops the vegetables, saws off the meat for Tobi, looks out of the window, and waits for us to leave. In the cars alongside us, women sit behind the wheel, bleached hair under hijabs. On the walls of buildings, they have painted what the tower blocks are missing: decorative carved stone, green window shutters, geraniums in pots. The next car along honks its horn, and they call out an address to the driver. Follow us, he says, and they follow us. Not so long ago, they didn't wear hijabs in cars, he says, nodding at the people behind. We listen to the song that my parents never sang, a song called 'My School Friend' that was sung at the demos. The man hums along, and I hum along, too.

I wake up next to Maryam. We are wearing clothes, of course, and there is as much distance between us as there always is when she stays in my bed. As there always is when she's supposed to be staying in Tobi's bed and Tobi either takes up too much room or says something so idiotic that she can't stand being there any longer and comes to my room and shows me YouTube videos. Though I'm starting to get bored of them now. Anyway, she keeps wanting to rewatch Obama in Egypt, talking about his childhood in Indonesia, and then she laughs at him, and sometimes I simply don't listen; I just close my eyes and enjoy not being alone.

Maryam is already awake. She looks at me without saying good morning, without explaining why she came here in the night again; she looks at me with her morning eyes, which are even smaller than usual, and says, I've got 'Beat It' as an earworm. We all constantly have 'Beat It' as an earworm. Ever since Michael Jackson died, the whole world has been singing 'Beat It'. I was the first one of us to hear about his death; Maryam and Tobi and Kristin were playing cards in the kitchen, and I wanted to watch the news. Although it's increasingly slim pickings now. Although the news from Tehran is the second story now, not the first. Although they barely ask Peter Mezger to comment now, because he has nothing new to say, or maybe because he's had too much airtime, and no one wants more Peter Mezger with no tales of revolution to tell us. And then the top story was that Michael Jackson had died, and I went into the kitchen and it reminded me of when Princess Diana died and my mother wept and bought the Elton John CD single. Michael Jackson's dead, I said, and Tobi clutched his heart and then they carried on playing cards.

I switch the laptop on while Maryam sits up, stretches, gets out of bed, and marches off to the toilet barefoot. When I open YouTube, it gives me the latest images uploaded in Iran. I've stopped looking at them. They're always the same.

Yesterday, I called my father. By chance. I called the home phone, and he never usually picks up, but suddenly he was there. He spoke softly and slowly. He'd probably just woken up, I thought. He was probably tired from work. But then he started telling me things, and I realised he wasn't tired at all, he was emotional; he'd just been talking to Amme Simin. Nima had shown up again, had come home; he'd been in custody and then in hospital, after everyone had stopped enquiring at the hospital. Some friends picked him up from there, and his mother opened the door and threw her arms around him. That was all Amme Simin had said, calm and composed, wanting simply to transmit information and facts to us in Germany and not to touch on her emotional state or what was going on in her head. My father knew that; he's known Amme Simin for such a long time, and he just asked which of her children were there currently and would they like to talk to him, and she said, Nima is here, and my father spoke to him and asked him how he was. He didn't ask if Nima was alright, just how he was. And Nima replied in a firm, cheerful voice and asked after us.

My father told me this, and then he fell silent, and so did I, and I didn't ask him if he read the blogs sometimes, too. Because he'd understand the Persian, whereas I never learned the script, and he could read and find out much more than I could. I didn't ask him, because in the blogs I read, the English ones and the ones translated into German, the bloggers talk about all the things that are happening in the prisons. All the things that have happened to the bloggers themselves.

My father hasn't seen a single one of the images and videos. He hasn't watched Neda die or heard the shots from the student halls of residence. He's put the news on and looked out of the window. They're still out on the streets, everywhere, he said. Their numbers haven't gone down, and they're still a long way from getting violent. Yes, that's the problem, I wanted to say, but didn't, for his sake. Say hi to Nima from me next time, I said. I didn't ask if Nima is allowed to go back to university now. If he wants to leave the country. Then my father asked if I'd like to talk to my mother, and I couldn't for the life of me remember why I'd called, but it was nice to hear her voice then, just as gentle and comforting as it was in my childhood.

Maryam comes back from the toilet, lies down beside me, looks at the screen, and doesn't want to see any more of these pictures, either. Always the same, she says. Then she says, Look: 'Beat It'. Under one of the videos that has a still of Ahmadinejad as its thumbnail, a caption really does say *Beat it, Ahmadinejad*, and we put it on and lean back. There are video montages set to music everywhere — people must have got bored of watching the shaky mobile-phone footage of street battles. Instead, the street battles are recut with dramatic music playing over them. And in this case it isn't street battles, but Ahmadinejad, Khomeini, Rafsanjani. The faces change in time with the music, confronting us, as Michael Jackson cries out, Beat it! Beat it! Beat it! Ahmadinejad with a broad smile, giving a thumbs-up. Beat it. We laugh and then both stop laughing at the same time. Watch the remaining two minutes thirty in silence, as the video carries on with more of the same.

When it's finished, the room seems very large and very empty, and we look at the next set of suggestions. There's Neda's death, underscored with Celine Dion. I close YouTube and open Facebook.

Did she write? Maryam asks in the same tone Laleh and her friends used to use when they talked about boys, and this actually makes me slightly nervous. I say, Well I don't know yet. Checking in the morning to see if someone has sent a message when they hadn't the previous night is ridiculous. Is she a night owl? Maryam asks. I don't know, I say. Merle hasn't responded, although I know she likes to; over the past few days, we've messaged back and forth a lot, telling each other what we've been doing, generally in life to begin with: what we're studying, where we live, what we eat, where we go out, what we've read. She's doing law, and studies round the clock, and doesn't live very far away. I was pleased to hear that, and now I want to see her again all the more. Maryam looked at Merle's Facebook page and said it was good, and I don't know if the two of them would get on or not.

Play this, says Maryam, her eyes on my profile, like that's completely normal. Because she set it up for me, of course, and did all the privacy settings, and so my Facebook profile is actually her Facebook profile, too. She points to a video that the youngest of my uncles, Amu Mehrdad, uploaded, and we watch it, the images again, the same images as in the folder on my computer, as on the placards at the demo with Tara, and he's rapping in the background. I don't understand all of it; he's rapping too quickly, and I don't know all the words. It's about Hugo Chavez and Assad. Maryam says that's the guy in Syria, who's every bit as bad as Ahmadinejad. And then that video ends as well, I close the open tabs, close the laptop, lean back, and close my eyes.

Maryam says, Hey, don't worry. It will happen. It's just the fucking media, acting like nothing else of any importance is going on in the world right now just because some paedophile pop star died. But it's still happening. She looks at me and nods. You'll see. As soon as Ahmadinejad is gone, it'll kick off in Egypt, too. Then Mubarak will be gone, and Assad will be next, and eventually all the dictators will be out. And I say, Out out out, terrorists out, and she laughs with me, because I've told her about the demo.

Epilogue
Tara

I'm going to be the aunt all the kids love, I used to think. When Laleh doesn't let them do anything, they'll come to me and we'll drink whisky and Coke. When they get a boyfriend, they'll just happen to be staying over at mine. And if someone has to forge signatures, I'll do it, and then there'll be a high five and a little kiss. But they never took me up on any of that.

Parastou doesn't overtake cars, just trucks. Parastou, we'll never get there at this rate, I say. We've been on the road for hours already. Parastou pulls in at the next petrol station. Cigarette break? I ask, rolling one for myself. Time to switch drivers? Guess I need to man up, says Parastou. She's too vain to smoke; it makes your teeth yellow, she says. Could you woman up instead? I mutter, with the filter tucked in the corner of my mouth. She laughs. So that was what all my years of queer feminist activism were for, I sometimes think. So that later, my own niece thinks it's a joke.

Coffee? she asks, and we get out of the car, because she

already knows my answer, and head for the shop. She goes in, while I stand outside. I look over at the glass door, my reflection blurred in the dirty pane; I hardly recognise myself. Work has made me thin, they say, all that travelling. Tara, it isn't a competition for how many crisis zones you can visit, Mo sometimes tells me. *You're looking thin* is another way of saying you look like shit, I think. All the same, I promised Mo and the others to cut back.

Well, now I've had a holiday for the first time in forever, and that at least is something. Ten days in the middle of nowhere, in the middle of Sweden, with nothing to remind me of the world and my work. Just Parastou, the mountains, hiking and fishing, and me. A period of self-imposed exile for us both, an experiment, and in a few hours real life will be expecting us back.

An enormous man with a white beard and sunglasses is filling his car up and scratching his balls. I throw the cigarette butt on the ground and go into the shop. It's nice and cool inside, soft music from the radio, and there's a faint smell of cold smoke and cleaning products. I can't see Parastou; she isn't at the till or by the chocolate bars. Parastou! I call, but not too loudly, because this bloody world hasn't progressed far enough that a name like that wouldn't attract attention in a Brandenburg petrol station. For a minute, I'm frightened that someone has done something to her in here, dragged her behind the counter — before we left, there were rumours about a third generation of the neo-Nazi NSU — and then I see her thick curls over by the magazines.

What's up, Parasite? I ask. She doesn't look up. Her

skinny, shaved little legs are kneeling on the floor, her tender hands trembling. Tara, she says, not looking up from the newspaper, Tara. I bend down to her, a little amused, a little annoyed; she gets her love of drama from her mother. And her grandmother. Besides which, she's holding a Springer publication. My little Parasite, don't tell me ... I say. And then I catch sight of the picture. The headline. The faces. Bearded men, white turbans, fire, blood.

I kneel down beside her. Fuck Brandenburg. We only spent ten days without the internet. No emails, no phones, no newspapers. She looks up at me, her blue eyes shining, and I let out a laugh. It sounds throaty and dirty in my ears; I slap my thighs and can't stop. Khale Tara, she says, horrified. It just had to be now, didn't it, I think, it had to be now. There were nearly two thousand people killed, she whispers. I skim the start of the article. No one spotted the signs. A theocracy for decades, and now an anti-terrorist beacon in the region. So say Israel and America and Syria.

Parastou and I stand up. With the Springer paper. And all the other newspapers we can find. It had to happen now, I think as we take them to the checkout. It had to happen now, Parastou says, shaking her head as we walk to the car.

Can we switch our phones back on? she asks, taking her seat beside me. I took her phone off her because when you're heartbroken that just makes everything worse. And I switched mine off because the rules have to apply to me, too. And because I decided to take my therapist's words seriously for a change.

We switch our devices on, and they vibrate and hum and

beep. Friends sending euphoric congratulations, my siblings, Parastou's siblings, my colleagues who are there on the ground, everyone, everyone is writing to us and sending us pictures of flowers and peace signs. A euphoria that is already a few days old and has just been sitting here, waiting for us.

We are entirely silent. Taking deep breaths. I put the air conditioning on the highest setting and we let it blow through us. The sun shines wearily between the car-park trees. Outside, the enormous man gets into his car.

I'll call Grandma and Grandpa, says Parastou, and I start the engine and think, You do that, Parastou. If the pair of them are still at home. If they aren't already on their way to the airport.